Praise for *Unfair Advantage* by Qwillia Rain

"Be prepared to be utterly titillated, cry at times, and experience a wonderful sense of completeness as you read this story. Don't miss Qwillia Rain's *Unfair Advantage*, a true BDSM masterpiece."

– Victoria, *Two Lips Reviews*

"Qwillia Rain has written a highly erotic and extremely life-like tale of two lovers finding their way to each other's hearts."

– Natasha Smith, *Romance Junkies*

"Awesome! That is the best word to describe *Unfair Advantage*. This story has so much going for it with suspense, love, conflict, and past issues to be resolved. The sex was so freaking hot, I needed relief in the worse way."

– LT Blue, *Just Erotic Romance Reviews*

"Not exactly your typical marriage-of-convenience story, *Unfair Advantage* places two interesting characters into a scenario that will test them both and is a tale that is sure to please."

– Jennifer Bishop, *Romance Reviews Today*

LooseId®

ISBN 13: 978-1-59632-941-6
UNFAIR ADVANTAGE: DIABLO BLANCO CLUB
Copyright © August 2009 by Qwillia Rain
Originally released in e-book format in January 2009
Cover Art by April Martinez
Cover Design and Layout by April Martinez

All rights reserved. Except for use of brief quotations in any review or critical article, the reproduction or utilization of this work in whole or in part in any form by any electronic, mechanical or other means, now known or hereafter invented, including xerography, photocopying and recording, or in any information storage or retrieval is forbidden without the prior written permission of Loose Id LLC, 870 Market St, Suite 1201, San Francisco CA 94102-2907. http://www.loose-id.com

DISCLAIMER: Many of the acts described in our BDSM/fetish titles can be dangerous. Please do not try any new sexual practice, whether it be fire, rope, or whip play, without the guidance of an experienced practitioner. Neither Loose Id nor its authors will be responsible for any loss, harm, injury or death resulting from use of the information contained in any of its titles.

This book is an original publication of Loose Id. Each individual story herein was previously published in e-book format only by Loose Id and is a work of fiction. Any similarity to actual persons, events or existing locations is entirely coincidental.

Printed in the U.S.A. by
Lightning Source, Inc.
1246 Heil Quaker Blvd
La Vergne TN 37086
www.lightningsource.com

UNFAIR ADVANTAGE
DIABLO BLANCO CLUB 1

Chapter One

"Bryce. My office."

The ring of Jacob Halsey's voice greeted Bryce as he exited the elevator. Despite the irritation and disgust riding him, he deferred to his father's tone and position as the CEO of Halsey Unlimited, Incorporated. He might be the oldest son and next in line to run the company, but in the office he was still just an employee. The headache that had started with the incident at the restaurant intensified behind his left eye. When he had the time, he'd deal with it.

Catching a glimpse of himself in the glass doors leading into the reception area of his father's office, Bryce paused to straighten the maroon silk tie he'd loosened in the elevator. The emotions nagging at him were not visible in his green eyes or on his face. He grimaced at the length of his white blond hair. Having missed the appointments to have it trimmed, it now curled over his collar onto his shoulders and brought to mind the shaggy style he'd sported the summer before his stepmother died, when he was teaching her and Michael how to surf. Shaking off the memories, he nodded at his father's admin, and then stepped through the open door and into his office.

Once inside, Bryce knew the situation was worse than he'd suspected. Besides his father, four other chairs around the small conference table were occupied. Victor Prommer, one of the company lawyers, relaxed in his seat next to Bryce's personal attorney, Dixon Jeffers. The company's head financial analyst, Becka Swinfield, tapped perfectly manicured nails against the beige file folder in front of her. She met his gaze for a moment, then looked away. Richard Bennett, Halsey's director of mergers and acquisitions, who, as vice president, shared joint authority with Bryce in running the company, leaned back in his chair, his gray eyes devoid of emotion.

Definitely not a good thing if Richard was shutting down. With his father at the head of the table, it left Bryce to fill the chair directly across from Jacob. Feeling like the fattened calf being led to slaughter, he took his time settling into his seat and nodded an acknowledgment to each of the others.

"We have a problem," Jacob began.

A casual toss dropped a magazine in front of Bryce's fingertips. He didn't bother looking at it. He'd shoved a prerelease copy into the garbage can at his home two weeks earlier. Knowing that his image was plastered across the cover with the ridiculous headline BILLIONS? YES. MARRIED? NO! in bold red letters above it, he addressed the problems related to the article. "I'm aware of the issues IT is having with voice and e-mails due to the increased traffic the article created from women trying to get my attention."

"And the problems with security?" Jacob asked.

Bryce didn't allow his frustration to show; he nodded. "I've spoken with the head of security. Extra men have been placed on all shifts to reduce the number of non-business-related visitors into the building." The throbbing behind his left eye increased.

"It goes beyond the minor inconveniences, Bryce."

"It'll blow over." He shrugged, leaning back in his chair. "It has before."

"It isn't just the magazine," Richard added. "With the recent cuts in government spending, one of our military contracts has been eliminated, and two other contracts have been suspended pending Department of Defense budget negotiations."

"Frieda and Lionel Makepeace, Frans Heilbeck, and Jonathan Reynolds have voiced some concerns." Jacob rose from his seat. Pushing back his suit coat, he tucked his hands in his trouser pockets. His gaze turned to Becka.

After flipping open the folder, she read off a series of figures. The faces around the table grew grim as she concluded, "If our losses continue, cuts will have to be made in a minimum of two departments. Manufacturing and services are the divisions that would bear the brunt of the staff reductions."

Bryce watched his father's face before scanning the others around the table. This was serious and not just rooted in a silly magazine article. "What can we do about it?"

"We're working every angle possible," Richard assured him.

"Fortunately, the Conlin merger is still progressing." Victor smiled.

Becka nodded. "And the investment in King Enterprises of Australia should see some ship construction and cargo contracts come our way."

"But the most important thing we need to address is the situation with you, Bryce." Jacob gripped the back of his chair.

Bryce leaned forward and pushed the magazine back to the center of the table. "Beyond this article, I don't see how I can be held responsible for problems with the company. Most are a result of downturns in the economy and reduced defense spending."

"It's been suggested I delay my retirement." The knuckles of his father's hands went white with the force of his grip.

"Why?"

"In order to find a suitable replacement."

It took everything in him to keep from protesting. Holding his father's gaze, Bryce kept his tone flat, emotionless. "I'm sensing there's more."

His father nodded. "Frieda and some of the other board members have requested that you tender your resignation once a candidate has been selected."

Bryce's gaze turned to Richard, but the slight shake of his friend's head could have meant not to say anything or that he wasn't in the running for the position. Turning his gaze back to his father, Bryce held himself still as he asked, "And when do I have to make my decision?"

Jacob ignored his question. Instead he turned to the others. "Thank you for your information."

Although Dixon remained in his seat, Victor, Becka, and Richard rose and exited the office.

When only the three of them remained, Bryce shoved back his chair and stood. Thrusting his hands into his trouser pockets, he glared at his father. "Hell of a way to ambush me, Dad. Thanks."

"This is your only wake-up call, Bryce," Jacob snapped back. He was still an imposing figure. Standing just two inches shorter than Bryce's own six feet four, his body reflected the care he'd taken with exercise and diet in the last three years since a heart attack had almost killed him. Very little gray showed in his dark brown hair and his brown eyes were as sharp as a man twenty years his junior.

"What do you mean 'wake-up call'?"

Dixon's ebony eyes held Bryce's for the longest time. "He's right, Bryce. More than just the four board members he mentioned have been bitching about you and your lifestyle for the last five years."

"My lifestyle? If you're talking about the Diablo Blanco Club, how is my membership any different than yours?"

"They really don't care about your sexual practices, son," Jacob scoffed. "If they had, my own membership would have been discussed years ago. What they object to is the number of women you've escorted and the image it represents."

"For God's sake, didn't that attitude go out with the nineteenth century?"

"Apparently not, or I wouldn't be asked to suspend my retirement five weeks before I'm supposed to hand the reins over to you." Shaking his head, Jacob settled into his chair and motioned Bryce to take a seat again.

From the expression on Dixon's face and the tension visible in the fingers interlaced and resting on the file in front of the attorney, Bryce began to grow concerned. The older man was the epitome of a cautious lawyer, with his close-cropped, wiry hair sprinkled liberally with gray and his dark skin that contrasted with the white silk shirt he wore beneath his charcoal suit. If Dixon was uneasy, Bryce knew he had serious problems.

"You have to understand, Bryce, that when Jacob suffered his heart attack, the board was understandably shaken." Dixon's voice carried the barest hint of disquiet, further worrying Bryce. "Even the company stock took a bit of a hit. Although the board members were reassured when you and Richard stepping in to run the company while your father recovered, they weren't completely at ease until Jacob's prognosis included a full recovery"

"How does this figure into my resignation?" Bryce fought the urge to press his fingers to his eyes. The throbbing had increased. Every sound was like a hammer blow against his skull, forcing him to concentrate on what was being said.

"They're running scared," Jacob admitted.

Dixon agreed. "They see the drop in values, the reduced income from the lost or stalled contracts, and worry what other disaster is waiting." He tapped the magazine. "Then something like this comes out and disrupts the smooth running of the company, and they panic even more."

"The incident during the contract negotiations with Conlin didn't help," Jacob snapped.

"Right, Dad. Like I enjoy having desperate single women throwing themselves at me?" His mind reran the incident at the Stone House just an hour earlier. "Was it Heilbeck or Reynolds who came whining to you?"

"Reynolds came to me," Jacob admitted. "Heilbeck probably ran to the Makepeaces."

"Either way," Dixon interrupted, "your sudden celebrity bachelor status is counting against you in the estimation of the board."

"What?"

Jacob continued where Dixon left off. "Simply put, they see you as some rich playboy who's more into revolving-door girlfriends and kinky sex. Every minute of negative publicity is just one more bit of ammunition Frieda and Lionel can use against you with the board."

"That's bullshit," Bryce snarled. "I spend most of my free time working with the different interests in this company, Dad, and you know it." He forced himself to stand still and not pace the carpet like a caged lion in a zoo.

"Hell, most of the board knows that, but with Frieda and Lionel stirring the pot, son, you haven't a snowball's chance in Hawaii of ever replacing me." He nodded at Dixon.

Dixon pulled a paper from the manila folder he'd left on the table. "Each of the board members has mentioned receiving the same letter from Frieda and Lionel."

Bryce read the letter, his lips twisting as he realized how the woman was ruining everything around her to gain revenge. "So how do I fix this? What do I have to do to convince the board that the Makepeaces are wrong?"

"Get married." As if rehearsed, Dixon and Jacob spoke at the same time.

"Get married?" Bryce nearly laughed.

"Yes." Jacob nodded. "Get married."

Dixon added, "She has to be someone the board, the company, and the world are going to view as dependable, solid, and loyal."

"Not one of your typical women."

"And if I choose not to take your advice?"

Jacob's brown eyes held his for the longest moment. "If you can't find it in yourself to marry a woman and stay married to her long enough to gain the board's confidence, then you need to prepare yourself to walk away."

"This company has built ships and transported cargoes around the world for nearly two hundred years, son. I can't see you, the namesake of the man who started it all, blithely handing it over to a complete stranger."

"What about Richard? He's more than capable—"

Dixon shook his head. "Also single and known to frequent the DBC, as well as share partners with you. The board wants stability, Bryce."

"This is blackmail."

Jacob laughed for the first time, the humor in his voice dark. "No, son, this is business." Standing up, he concluded the discussion. "Think about it, Bryce. Think about someone whom you've built a relationship with. Who understands the business and its priority in your life and who can withstand the scrutiny of the board members without losing her cool."

"How long do I have?"

"No more than five weeks. Be engaged or married by the time I'm supposed to retire, or I'll have to demand your resignation."

* * *

Leaning back in his desk chair, Victor Prommer pressed a button on his cell phone and waited.

"Yes?" The southern drawl was pronounced and aggressive, just like the woman herself.

"It looks like he's on his way out."

"Looks like or is?"

"His father delivered the news not forty minutes ago. I doubt even Bryce Halsey could dig up a suitable bride in five weeks," Victor assured her.

"I don't pay you for your opinions, Mr. Prommer. I pay you for results."

Stifling the urge to hang up on her, Victor tempered his tone. "And I've provided them, Mrs. Makepeace."

"Not enough. When Bryce Halsey hands me his resignation and we install our man in the CEO's chair, then you will have delivered on your promises."

"You'll have it."

"I had better, Mr. Prommer." The abrupt disconnection of the call was as familiar as her condescending attitude.

"Cold fucking bitch," Victor muttered, stuffing his phone back in his pocket. He'd paid good money to have specific, critical meetings disrupted by women "desperate" to gain Halsey's attention. She'd get the damned results she wanted, but he'd get his as well.

Double-clicking to open the file on his computer desktop, he skimmed the document for the key terms he'd included. Frieda and Lionel Makepeace may have hired him to destroy Halsey Unlimited, but he wasn't going to put his neck on the line without providing himself a little compensation.

* * *

"What the hell is she doing here with him?"

Richard's question had Bryce glancing over his shoulder toward the front of the restaurant. It had taken most of the afternoon, six pain relievers, and two glasses of single malt to reduce the throb behind his left eye to a dull pain. The sight of Mattie Lawrence, his administrative assistant, and Victor Prommer making their way across the floor toward a table nearby had the pounding increasing all over again.

"They just came from work." Bryce sipped his drink. He followed the sway of Lawrence's hips as she crossed the room and debated the decision he'd come to following the meeting with his father.

"I don't care where they came from; I want to know why she's here with him." Annoyance increased the soft drawl in Richard's voice. Gray eyes narrowed on the couple as the maître d' seated them.

If Bryce hadn't know Richard as well as he did, he would suspect there was more to his friend's interest in Lawrence's dating habits. He assessed the couple seated four tables away before looking at his friend. "Is there something wrong with Lawrence going out with Victor?" Until he came to a definite decision, Bryce couldn't stake his claim on Lawrence. Bryce took a deep breath and attempted to relax when he realized his own ire was rising at the thought of Victor making advances toward her.

"She should know better," Richard growled before stabbing a chunk of steak and carefully chewing on it.

A master controls no one if he cannot control himself. The saying floated through Bryce's mind in the interval following Richard's comment. He split his attention between Richard's grumblings and the couple across the room while he consumed the delicious prime rib dinner before him. He was working on an after-dinner coffee the waiter had poured when he spotted the first touch.

It had been subtle, just the slide of Victor's hand over hers, but Lawrence's body stiffened, and she eased away from the man the tiniest bit. Hackles rising, Bryce leaned back in the booth, his focus on the pair across the room. "Well, what have you heard wrong about him?"

"He's the perfect gentleman until he feels it's time he doesn't have to be anymore." Richard cursed beneath his breath as Victor tried to stroke his hand down his date's arm.

Again she stiffened and moved away, her chair lurching slightly as she nudged it farther right.

"You're not going to do anything about this?" Richard met his gaze. His gray eyes were disbelieving, almost accusatory.

"Why should I?"

"You've spent the last eight years waiting, Bryce. Are you going to let another man take what you've been preparing?" He shook his head, the tight brown curls barely moving. "Hell, I haven't been able to figure out why you just didn't claim her when she first showed up."

"She wasn't ready." The tension in his neck eased as Bryce recalled the anger and defiance dancing in Lawrence's brown gaze. In many ways, she'd been wise beyond her twenty-two years, but in the most important ones, she'd been far too young for what he wanted.

"How? She was interested. I watched her trying to get your attention."

Bryce watched her rebuff another of Victor's touches. From the stiffening of the other man's body, the grip he had on his fork, and the short, quick stabs he used to spear his food, Bryce suspected he'd become more aggressive in his next attempt. "She didn't trust."

"Excuse me?"

His attention stayed on Lawrence and Victor, although he could see Richard shift his attention between him and the other pair from the corner of his eye. "When she came to me, Lawrence was incapable of trusting any man."

"How do you know?"

"Didn't you ever notice she never allowed any one, especially a man, to get behind her or between her and an exit?" Bryce glanced at his friend, surprised he'd missed such an obvious clue. It had frustrated the hell out of him eight years ago when he'd occasionally look up to see the heat of attraction in her eyes. The moment he smiled or started to approach, the fires were banked, and the shield snapped back into place.

Richard cursed beneath his breath. "You think she was raped?"

Bryce gave a quick nod. "It was my original conclusion. I had Henderson run a background check for me."

"And?"

"No rape. There were allegations of abuse, physical not sexual, when she was eleven, just before her parents died." He didn't reveal the details, but he did have to concentrate to keep from crushing the cup in his hand. "She and her sister were taken in by Gino Laguardi and his wife and brought here to San Diablo." Bryce sipped his coffee, remembering the lecture he'd received from Gino about treating Lawrence like the lady she was. If the man had detected even a hint of what Bryce had imagined sharing with his precious foster daughter, Gino would have never signed the contract to merge his ship-building business with Halsey's. "Getting her to this point has been a battle."

"A fruitless one if you're going to allow that snake charmer to poach on your grounds," Richard warned.

"It took nine months to get her to the point where she would stay in my office to discuss the shipping schedules and the delivery contracts without double-checking to make sure her path to the door was free." Bryce's fingers ticked off each of the points as he mentioned them. "Another two years to get her to come out to my home in order to help organize a dinner party and hostess it for me. And another six months after that to get her to voice her opinion without being afraid I'd retaliate in some way. I just about came the first time she argued with me over a comment I'd made about Mike and his career and didn't run when I yelled back."

Richard's chuckle and nod reminded Bryce his friend had been present at the heated discussion over Mike's career path. "She did have a point, though. Mike is a hell of a photojournalist."

"That goes without argument." Bryce nodded when the waiter approached offering to refill his cup and cleared the finished meals from the table. Waiting until the server had left, he kept his gaze on Victor and his assistant. The set of her shoulders and the way she watched Victor were familiar to Bryce. She could trust a few people only so far before she froze up. Pushing her beyond those boundaries would prove a challenge, but one he looked forward to meeting.

"Have you thought about what Jacob discussed?"

Since that had been the original purpose of their dinner meeting, Bryce asked, "Did he tell you what my alternative to resigning is?"

"No, but I have an idea"—he paused to sip his coffee—"and a suggestion if I'm right."

Turning away from the couple across the room, Bryce waited. Having grown up with Richard, Bryce didn't doubt that the plans he'd been carefully devising since his father's ultimatum had also been weighed and measured by his friend. "A solution to my problem?"

"Mattie."

"Lawrence?" His attention turned back to the table in time to see Victor slide his hand over her thigh. The flare of anger and possessive indignation surprised Bryce, but the urge to stride over and grab Victor by the throat was eased when Lawrence slapped Victor's hand away and stood up. Her words were quiet, but the expression on her face left little doubt she was furious, before she turned and strode out of the restaurant. The other man remained in his seat, finishing the last of his meal and ignoring the pointed stares of the diners around him.

Richard chuckled as he watched the exchange across the room. Leaning back in the booth, he nodded. "Yes, her. If Jacob is pushing you to get married in order to placate some of the board members, then she's the perfect candidate for your wife."

"How?" He'd rationalized his own arguments, but wondered if his eight-year-long attraction to the woman was clouding his judgment.

"She's familiar to the board, knows the way the company works, and is a loyal employee."

"You sound like you're creating an argument for giving her a raise." Bryce shook his head.

"She's cool under pressure. Makes decisions based on a balance of gut instinct and logical research. And can plan a dinner party for six to six hundred guests with little to nothing going wrong. You need her, Bryce. Her reputation alone will gain you points with the board."

"Reputation?" He acknowledged all the assets Richard listed with a nod.

"Mattie isn't a party animal, Bryce. You and I both know the primary concern Frieda and Lionel are using to turn the board against you is the playboy persona *Upscale's* article hyped." Richard shrugged. "Considering the tidbit your last playdate helped circulate in *The National Recorder* last year about the things you and she did at the Club, someone with a wholesome reputation is just what you need to get back in their good graces."

"And what if I don't want to be blackmailed into marriage?"

Richard watched him carefully. "If memory serves me correctly, you never intended to marry. At least that was your decision just after Miss Helen died."

"I said a lot of things when I was sixteen, Richard." Bryce shrugged.

"True."

"And it isn't like I haven't tried to get married. Am I the only one who remembers I've been engaged? Twice."

"No, most of the country has been reminded of those facts. That may be part of the problem with that blasted article, my friend. Third time's a charm, and every woman with her eye on the easy life is hoping she'll make you change your tune." Richard smiled. "But you never would have married Sybelle or Carolyn, even if they hadn't broken the engagements. You've spent the last twenty-four years of your life working to make Halsey Unlimited the first name off anyone's lips when it comes to the construction of ships, from tugs to cruise ships to aircraft carriers. Neither of those women understood what was necessary to keep the company growing."

"I could do other things."

"What are you going to do with the rest of your life, Bryce, if you don't have Halsey Unlimited to run?" Ticking off each item on his fingers, Richard continued. "You're not needed for the day-to-day stuff at DBC. You haven't assisted in the training of any new Doms or Dommes—let alone submissives—in nearly three years. And you have a talented manager and staff handling the stables, orchard, and gardens of your home."

Pushing his empty coffee cup away, Bryce held Richard's gaze. "There's always travel."

"You haven't taken a vacation from the company in five years, my friend." Richard signaled the waiter for the bill before turning back to face him. "You'll never convince me you'd be happy as some jet-setting playboy. You were never meant to be some high-society, feckless celebrity."

"And what if I don't want a 'wholesome' bride?" Bryce offered, his mind conjuring images of his assistant that were the complete opposite of "wholesome." Hell, if she'd even suspected some of the things he'd contemplated introducing her to, Mattie Lawrence would have never lasted eight years in his office.

"I never said the reputation had to remain that way, my friend." Richard finished his coffee. "In fact, I've been just as anxious for you to stake your claim, so I can assist you in tarnishing her reputation just the slightest bit."

A flash of irritation ignited at his friend's words but was quickly stifled. In the years they'd known each other, it hadn't been unusual for them to share a lover, so it disturbed Bryce that he'd react poorly to Richard's anticipation of a similar act. Keeping his expression calm, he shrugged. "I'll think about it."

Chapter Two

"We have a problem."

Mattie Lawrence clenched her thighs and fought the shiver that zipped down her spine. The sound of Bryce's voice was always a turn-on for her. Add to it six feet four inches of lean muscle, broad shoulders, and smooth Southern charm, and it was no wonder she found it nearly impossible to keep from creaming her panties at least once a day around the man. Since he'd decided to lean over the back of her chair and make his statement close to her left ear, Mattie was treated to not only the sound of his Southern drawl, but the crisp citrus smell of his aftershave, the brush of his hair against her ear, and the heat of his breath over her cheek. *Yup, there goes another pair.*

She waited until he'd returned to his desk before looking up. "What kind of problem?"

From his forefinger dangled a white lace thong. Though his face showed little emotion, anger glittered in his pale green eyes. Panic had Mattie's heart slamming against her ribs as she considered the panties could have come from the stash she kept in her desk. Before she could stutter out an excuse for their presence, Bryce continued and eased her worries.

"These were tucked into my pocket in the middle of my meeting with Heilsbeck and Reynolds, along with a very X-rated proposition." With a disgusted look, he dropped the item in the trash. Legs crossed at the ankles, Bryce leaned against the polished mahogany desk and gripped the edge with his hands. "They weren't very happy about it."

"Is that why you canceled your afternoon meeting?" Mattie tilted her head to hold his gaze.

"Among other things." He took a deep breath, his knuckles going white from his hold on the desk before he continued. "The board approached my father about rethinking his retirement."

"But—"

Bryce lifted his left hand and motioned her to stop. "They want him to continue running the company until a suitable replacement can be found."

Mattie could tell there was more. Long fingers raked through his hair, mussing the white blond waves. The gold hoop in his left ear flashed in the sunlight before his fingers tugged at it. A sign she'd learned years ago meant he was working through a problem in his head before discussing it.

"Suitable replacement? How can you not be a suitable replacement?" Mattie finally asked when he remained quiet.

"That's where the problem comes in." His arms folded over his chest and his gaze held hers. "The board is reluctant to have me replace my father. Factoring in the recent downturn in the economy, two stalled contracts, and one outright canceled, along with the mess created by the article in *Upscale*, some on the board feel I no longer have the right image to represent Halsey Unlimited, Inc."

"But that's crazy." Mattie rose from her seat and began pacing the wheat-colored Berber carpet beside his desk. "You ran this company for Jacob while he was recovering from his heart attack. You and Richard worked hard to reverse the losses on the stock and even increased the profits. How can you not be the right image?"

Bryce seemed to choose his words carefully. "Some of the board members feel there are aspects of my personal life that reflect poorly on the company."

Mattie understood just what he was saying. His partial ownership of the Diablo Blanco Club and his reputation as a Dominant were undisputed facts in San Diablo. The board, especially Frieda Makepeace and her husband, Lionel, had tried to demand his resignation over a year ago, when one of Bryce's former lovers had given details to a reporter with one of the less-reputable gossip magazines. "The Makepeaces are leading the charge, right?"

"They have some of the others concerned with the direction the company would go if I were in charge."

"Frieda Makepeace is a conniving, backstabbing bitch," Mattie snapped, dropping onto the arm of the leather sofa. "Everyone knows she's resented your position in the company for years. She's fought every attempt you've made to diversify the interests of Halsey's."

"This time she may actually get what she wants."

"You aren't really going to resign?" Mattie shook her head. Rising, she moved closer, her hand gripping the back of one of the chairs facing his desk. "You can't let her win, Bryce."

"Then marry me."

She couldn't have heard him correctly. "Excuse me?"

Bryce grinned, his white teeth a sharp contrast to his sun-darkened features. "I'm not crazy, Lawrence. Both my dad and Dixon feel that if I present the board with a wife, I have a chance to regain some of the support I've lost. Most of the members are only wavering. Makepeace has convinced only a few to side with her, but the others are on the fence."

"But why me?"

The warm clasp of his hand around her wrist had Mattie's heart picking up its pace. When he tugged her around the chair to stand directly in front of him, it grew worse. The muscles in her belly clenched, the slick heat between her thighs pulsed, and her breasts ached. Against the lace of her bra, she could feel her nipples harden. She swallowed and focused on steadying her breathing.

"I need a wife that the board can respect and who knows that the interests of the company are paramount." He watched her face, seeming to read every thought that spun through her head. "She has to be able to face down any objections and possibly take on Frieda and Lionel when it comes to convincing everyone that the marriage is real."

Mattie shook her head. "I'm not sure—"

"I am." He gripped her hands in his. "You're smart, Lawrence. Most of the board likes and respects your hard work and dedication to the company. Hell, some of them keep complaining about your refusal to be promoted since you finished your MBA. It's a win-win situation."

Needing to be able to think, Mattie pulled her hands from his and moved back behind the chair, putting distance between her and the man who did such intense damage to her self-control. "How is it a win-win situation?"

"It's pretty likely that if I'm forced to resign, you'll lose your job. Anyone replacing me would be an idiot not to keep you, but business doesn't usually work that way. I doubt whoever takes over would allow your promotion to one of the other management positions for fear of you carrying out some of the policies I implemented." He shrugged. "Your reputation has never been called into question, and the board would likely see our marriage as a settling influence on me."

A snort of laughter escaped before Mattie could stop it. Meeting Bryce's gaze, she smiled and apologized. "Sorry, I just can't see you 'settling.'"

Bryce pushed his hands into his pockets and paced away from his desk. Stopping at the liquor cabinet, he poured a measure of his favorite single malt. "That's the problem, Lawrence. The board doesn't believe it either." Watching her, he sipped his drink. "I'm not talking about a quick-fix type of solution here. The marriage would have to be real in every sense. As long as the Makepeaces have any power in the company, we will have to present a united front. No divorce. No separations. No infidelities. We stay together for as long as it takes."

"How long do you think that will be?" Unsure her legs would continue to hold her upright, Mattie settled into the chair, her hands clenched together in her lap.

"At the very least, five years." He grimaced, and then shrugged. "At most, until the old harridan and her husband croak and quit manipulating the board with their horror stories."

Mattie couldn't hold back the laughter at his comment. "That's a heck of a long time to pretend to be married, Bryce, just to keep my job."

"Who said anything about pretending?" Bryce moved back to his desk and set his drink on the clear vinyl protector covering the polished wood.

"Well...I...I assumed..." Mattie wasn't sure what she was going to say, but all thought exited her mind when Bryce leaned forward and braced both hands on the arms of her chair.

"We would arrive and leave work together, live in the same house, share the same bed. It would be a real marriage, Lawrence."

Mattie sank farther into her chair. She could feel the heat in her face, and her fingers tangled together to keep from latching on to the man and kissing him silly. Inside, she wavered between euphoria and dread. True, she'd fantasized about being with him for years—hell, since the first day she saw him—but marriage? "I...I'm not..." She shook her head and eyed him carefully as he moved back to lean against the desk.

"Too much?"

"I've just never..." Mattie waited, then tried again. "I'm going to need time to think this over."

"How much?" After finishing his drink, Bryce returned it to the bar and leaned against the built-in cabinet to await her answer.

"A week?" she offered.

He shook his head. "That's too long. I want to make the arrangements so everything is in place before my father's retirement party in five weeks. I need an answer before you leave tonight."

"That's less than an hour." It was Mattie's turn to shake her head. She was used to this type of negotiation with the man. His determination to come out on top was apparent, but she was equally resolute about gaining time to seriously think about her decision. "You're talking about a serious commitment, Bryce. If you aren't going to give me a week, I need at least the weekend to make a decision."

"Forty-eight hours is too long. I want to get the ball rolling on this before the weekend is over." Glancing at the grandfather clock across the room, he countered. "It's just past four now. Think about it and give me a call by ten tonight."

"Five hours?" She rose and moved to pace the area between his desk and the seating area. "Still not enough time, Halsey. You're asking me to make a decision that could affect the next five years of my life. If not more. No"—she shook her head and sat on the rolled arm of a hunter green leather chair—"I need at least thirty-six hours to seriously think this through."

"Too much time." He seemed to be thinking something through as he crossed the room toward her, one hand tugging at the earring while the other rested on his hip. "You're coming out to the Folly tomorrow to go over the details for the King party, correct?"

She nodded. "Yes."

"And you're probably going to go to your sister's and talk to her about my proposal, right?"

"More than likely."

"Okay then." He settled his hands on the back of the chair. "That gives you eighteen hours to think over my offer. When you come out to the Folly tomorrow afternoon, give me your answer."

She hesitated to ask but knew it needed to be broached. "What if I decide I can't agree?"

The green of his eyes darkened. His expression grew blank, as if the amusement he'd found participating in their test of wills had been wiped away. "Then I'll have to consider tendering my resignation."

"But—"

He shook his head. "I'll have to, Lawrence." The fingers of his left hand cupped her chin, sending tremors of awareness skittering through her, tingling along her nerve endings and pooling in the heated center of her body. "I need someone who knows why my days are taken up with work and my nights as well. Someone who is just as dedicated to making this company more than it is without losing the integrity my namesake built it on. I can't recall meeting any other woman with those qualities in the last few years. Except you."

"You're taking unfair advantage," she grumbled, knowing he was attempting to manipulate her decision. The fact that her body was in favor of immediately agreeing didn't make holding off and thinking the matter through any easier.

The grin he gave her was unrepentant. "I'm a businessman, Lawrence. And there's nothing fair about business."

* * *

Mattie stared at the entrance to the Diablo Blanco Club. She'd called and canceled dinner with her sister and come here instead. In fact, for the last eight years, when she couldn't fight her curiosity, she'd drive by and occasionally stop. On those nights, she sat in this same spot, sometimes for hours, sometimes just a few minutes, wondering just how wild things could be inside the infamous Club. On Halloween it was worse, because she knew a single request could produce one of the exclusive invitations to the Midnight Masquerade.

Now chances were she'd never see the inside of the Club. If she accepted Bryce's proposal, she doubted he'd escort her inside. She didn't know what frustrated her more, knowing that her own insecurities had kept her trapped from exploring a sexuality that drew her, or the fact that Bryce didn't feel she was capable of meeting the needs of his Dominant side. His proposal had been direct and clear: a marriage that included sex, but nothing that would create a negative image to the board of directors. Translated, that meant no bondage play, discipline, or trips through the doors she'd dreamed about entering for years.

The tap at the passenger side window had Mattie turning her attention and thoughts from the man connected to the edifice in front of her to the woman shaking her head at her from outside the truck. Pressing the button, she unlocked the door and waited for her older sister to scramble into the seat.

"I thought I'd find you here." Lyssa twisted sideways in her seat and leaned against the closed door.

"What's up?"

"You tell me; you were the one to cancel dinner. I was hoping to hear about the date you had last night." Curling one leg under her, Lyssa pushed the strands of blonde hair that had come loose from her ponytail behind her ears.

"I had some thinking to do." Mattie grimaced. "And as for the date, don't remind me."

"Didn't go well?" Concern lit her sister's blue eyes as she waited for an answer.

"Let's just say his idea of dessert and mine differed."

"Bastard." Lyssa turned to glance at the building. "I'll bet it isn't as scary as you imagine."

"Probably not." Mattie shrugged. Arm propped on the door frame and head resting in her palm, she watched as a couple approached the broad double doors. "But I doubt I'll ever see it."

"Why? From what I've heard it's relatively tame in comparison to some of the meat markets in San Diablo and farther north."

"Because, Lys, I know me. I talk a damn fine game, but when it comes to actually playing, the only person I trust to play with isn't interested." She glanced back at the Club. "At least not with me."

"How do you know?" Lyssa's fingernails, trimmed short to accommodate her sewing and design work, plucked at the frayed inseam on the leg of her jeans.

"He proposed." Mattie didn't turn her attention from the DBC. "It would be strictly business, but there's little likelihood of divorce."

Lyssa's fingers stopped for a moment and then returned to playing with the frayed fabric. "Bryce Halsey really proposed?"

Mattie nodded. "There's a lot more to it, but essentially we would present an appropriate image to the board of directors so Bryce can take over Jacob's position when he retires."

"But I thought he was already going to take over?" Her brow wrinkled in confusion.

"He was until Frieda and her little toads decided they didn't like the idea. There are other factors involved, but suffice to say, Bryce's image isn't the rosy one the board of directors wants presented to the public." Mattie turned to face her sister. "His father thinks if Bryce marries before the retirement party, we can convince the board to let him assume control."

"So, you'll marry him until he gets to take over, get a quiet annulment—"

Mattie shook her head. "No. No annulment, no separation, no divorce. At least not for a few years."

"A few years? That's crazy. He can't actually expect you to put your life on hold for years."

"He'll be doing the same, Lys." Her head dropped back to rest against the window. "That and more."

"What are you talking about? What more could he possibly be…?" Lyssa glanced from her sister to the building, then back. "You're not suggesting?"

Mattie didn't need to hear the rest of her sister's question before she nodded. "Yup. He said he's trying to gain favor with the board. I interpret that to mean he'll have to curtail his association with the DBC until the board had been suitably won over."

Lyssa whistled beneath her breath. "That's hard to believe, Mat. I mean, the man is…" She seemed at a loss for words.

Mattie wasn't. "He's a Dominant, Lys. The control practically oozes from every pore, and when he stands a certain way or gets a look in his eye or uses a specific tone, there's no way you can doubt who's in charge."

"And you find dominance sexy?"

"Sexy doesn't even come close. I told you I've had to keep extra panties in my desk because of the times I end up having to change them when he's around." Mattie groaned. Sitting up, she shook her head. "It'll only get worse if I marry him."

"How so?" Lyssa's brow furrowed in confusion. "I mean, if he wants it to be a real marriage, like you said he did, then I'm sure he'll be giving you all the kinky lessons you've been dying to learn from him. If he isn't here at the Club, all his attention will be on you." She laughed. "You might even be able to talk him into buying some of those toys you're always ogling in the catalogs you steal from his house."

"That's the problem, Lyssa. There won't be any kinky lessons," Mattie snapped. "He says my steady reputation is what the board likes, and they think I'll have a 'settling' effect on him."

"How does that translate to no kink?"

"Do you really see me inspiring him to play master?" Mattie shook her head. "No, if I agree to marry him, all I'll ever get is vanilla sex."

"Vanilla sex?" Lyssa hooted.

Mattie glared at her sister. "You do realize part of this is your fault, right?"

Lyssa choked on her laughter. "What? How is any of this my fault?"

"You're the one who gave me that book on S and M." She sat up in her seat. "I mean, sheez, Lys, I'd barely started working for Bryce when you dropped that in my lap."

"I was keeping you informed, little sister." Lyssa leaned forward as well. "You come home mooning over your new boss and sighing over the rumors you'd heard about him from one of the other administrative assistants. What was I supposed to do?"

"I don't know, but learning about the lifestyle certainly didn't help."

"How was I to know you'd get all hot and bothered over the idea of Halsey tying you up or spanking you?" Lyssa shook her head. "You were supposed to remember the shit Dad pulled."

Mattie looked at her sister, confused but curious. "Did you ever read the book? Or do an online search about BDSM?"

Lyssa shrugged. "Not when I first gave it to you, but when you started bringing over those catalogs, I…"

"Got curious?"

Her sister nodded.

"When you learned more about it, did you think of Dad?" Mattie wondered if she was the only one who could see the difference between the abuse meted out by their father and the controlled direction of a Dominant.

"No."

"Neither did I." She looked back at the Club. "And now I'll probably never know what it's like."

"Are you seriously thinking about accepting his proposal?" Lyssa seemed worried, her blue eyes uncertain.

Mattie nodded. "I am." She met her sister's gaze and tried to explain. "I'm thirty years old, Lyssa. I've never had a steady boyfriend. Hell, I've never been interested in a man enough to overcome my issues and have sex. With Bryce, I know where I stand. He doesn't love me, and I don't love h—"

"Liar."

"I'm not—"

"Don't even try to convince me you haven't been head over heels in love with Bryce Halsey since the first day you met him." Lyssa crossed her arms over her ample chest.

"I don't know what you mean." Mattie attempted to avoid admitting her sister's suspicions could be correct.

"Don't lie to me, Mat. And don't lie to yourself." Lyssa's tone gentled.

Mattie groaned. "I don't want to be some clichéd old maid who pines after her boss like those women in the romance novels."

"So don't be."

"But—"

"If you'd told me about this proposal eight years ago, or even five years ago, I'd have been doing everything in my power to talk you out of it." She shrugged. "But I've watched how you've changed, Mat. You aren't my scared little sister anymore." Reaching out, Lyssa pushed a loose strand of Mattie's curly brown hair off her cheek. "Yes, you're thirty and you've never had a lover, but you have a solid relationship with Bryce."

"As an employee."

Lyssa shook her head. "No. As a friend. It may have started out as just business, but you've developed an understanding with him. You push him to do what you think is the right thing when others would be afraid to."

"But that isn't enough." Mattie motioned back to the building. "That's the part of himself he'll be ignoring while he's married to me."

"Would you be satisfied if the only sex you have is 'vanilla'?"

"I think so." But she wasn't sure. The fantasies she'd indulged in, the books she read, her dreams all carried the element of submitting to Bryce. The sex life he'd alluded to in his proposal was devoid of that aspect, and she doubted she'd stay happy with it for very long.

Her sister's head tilted to the side and an assessing expression filled her face. "But you don't think he will? Be satisfied, I mean."

Mattie nodded. "No, I don't think he'll be satisfied." She sighed just as heavily as she had when Bryce proposed to her. Her head dropped back to the hand she'd leaned on the door frame. "He's a Dominant by nature and training. If he stifles that part of himself, he'll never be happy. He'll never be himself. Our entire marriage would be a sham, and I'm positive the board will see right through it. And it'll all be for nothing."

"So make him change his mind."

"About marrying me?" A sharp pain arrowed through her chest, surprising Mattie and stealing her breath. It dissipated immediately, but she couldn't deny its meaning. "If I don't marry him, he'll resign, and I'll likely lose my job."

"Is that the reason you're thinking about marrying him? To keep your job?"

"No." Mattie didn't hesitate in her answer.

"Because, with your MBA, you could have quit years ago." Lyssa had voiced this opinion often.

"Or taken one of the management positions Bryce offered me," Mattie agreed.

"Exactly. But what I mean is, make him see you as a submissive."

She balked, worrying her bottom lip with her teeth as she contemplated her sister's suggestion. "I'm not sure."

"You haven't agreed to marry him yet, right?"

"I'm supposed to give him my decision tomorrow."

"So tell him what you just told me. That you're worried he won't be able to maintain a marriage while ignoring his own personality."

"And then what? Throw myself at his feet?" Mattie shook her head. "I don't know. Heck, I don't even know if I could play the role of a submissive."

"True. In the last few years you've gotten so pushy with him, it's a wonder he hasn't paddled your butt."

She had to laugh since her sister's prediction had actually been a threat voiced by Bryce on a few occasions. "He's mentioned doing just that."

Lyssa's eyebrows bobbed up and down in an amused expression. "Turned you on, didn't it?"

"Oh yeah." Mattie chuckled, remembering the scene. Just as it had happened when Bryce made the threat, Mattie's body reacted, dampening her panties and making her groan with embarrassment and arousal.

Lyssa laughed. "Okay, so we know spanking turns you on. And the toys you've shown me in those catalogs definitely have an effect on you, if you're telling me the truth." She grinned. "So, that just leaves the actual practice with a Dom."

"Which I doubt he'd be interested in providing."

Lyssa watched her and seemed to think over what she'd said. "Did he come right out and tell you that he would no longer be coming here?"

"No, but—"

Her sister held up her hand and continued, "Did he tell you directly that he wasn't interested in engaging in any Dominant/submissive play with you? Ever?"

Mattie thought back over the conversation before she'd left the office. "No. He never used those specific words."

"What did he say?"

She couldn't stop the grimace that twisted her lips. "That my reputation would give the board the impression that I would have a 'settling' effect on him and his wild ways."

"That doesn't mean you can't convince him to change his mind."

"What do you mean?"

Instead of explaining, Lyssa popped the door open. "Follow me to my house." Once out of the car and on the ground, she smiled at her sister. "In fact, why don't you go grab us some Szechuan takeout, and I'll tell you my plan when you get there."

Mattie had no time to argue. Lyssa pushed the door closed and moved to her own sedan parked a few cars away.

* * *

The chime security had rigged went off, but Bryce had already heard the hum of the elevator and cursed. "Not another one." A flashing green light on the black box beside his phone signaled the use of the bypass key card, which had him relaxing back into his chair. Only four people besides himself and the head of his security department had a bypass card for the elevator leading up to his penthouse.

He was pretty sure his father and Mattie were safely in bed at this time of night. Richard had headed out of town immediately following their dinner, and since his friend was diligent about locking his card away in his home safe, Bryce figured that only left his brother.

As the doors slid open, the weary look on Mike's face made him look years older than thirty. As he stepped off the elevator, the slump of his shoulders had Bryce rising from his seat. He watched as Mike schooled his expression into a cheerful mien the moment he became aware of Bryce's presence.

"Hey, Bryce, I didn't realize you were here." He shifted the duffel bag on his shoulder and gestured behind him at the closed doors. "I'll just head down to the—"

"No. There's plenty of room. Unless you'd like to stay at the Folly?" Bryce approached him.

Mike set his duffel bag and camera case on the floor. "Thanks. Here is fine." He pushed his fingers through his rumpled brown hair and gave a halfhearted grin.

The moment he was in front of him, Bryce gripped the other man's shoulders and pulled him close. "You need to stick close to home for a while, kid."

Mike returned the hug, pulling back when Bryce did. "Yeah. I intend to."

"Do you want to talk about it?"

The way he eased onto the sofa had Bryce stifling a curse. Even their dad didn't move in that down-to-the-bone-tired way. "It should have been me."

Settling onto the sofa opposite Mike, he waited for his younger brother to continue.

"I was supposed to cover the skirmish, but I passed it off to Simon."

"Simon Dunstan?"

Mike nodded, dropping his head against the back cushions and closing his eyes.

Bryce waited, then asked, "Where were you? Dad and I tried your cell as soon as we heard."

His brother chuckled, the lines of his face looking younger for just a few moments. "It's probably at the bottom of the Aegean."

"You went sailing?"

"Yes and no. I was doing some photo editing and enhancement work for a friend. They happened to have a boat, and I went out to get some shots and lost my phone over the side."

"Okay, so you were helping a friend." Bryce kept his skepticism quiet regarding the work Mike was doing. He'd broach that subject later. "How did you find out about Simon?"

"The friend I was helping told me about the story. They knew I'd passed the job to Simon when I agreed to help them."

"How's he doing?"

Mike shrugged. "Doctors say he'll make a full recovery."

Bryce could read the doubt and concern in his brother's face. "You don't think he will?"

"Physically, yeah, he'll be fine. There was no permanent damage done to him. It's what they made him do and what he saw that're tearing him up inside."

Bryce didn't ask any questions, he simply waited for his brother to continue if he was going to.

"I keep thinking it would have been me. I would have been forced to take pictures of..." Mike shook his head. "When I found out Vance was the soldier who led the unit to rescue Simon, I felt even worse."

"Vance? Justiss?"

Mike nodded. "I stopped by the hospital on the way into town to see if Vance's friend, Ben Murphy, was on duty, but they said he'd just left."

"Will he make it?" Bryce made a mental note to contact the hospital in Germany. Make sure Simon and Vance were getting the best care available.

"He'll survive, but the doctors were whispering about secondary infections and shrapnel when I had to leave to catch my plane home." Mike leaned forward, one hand rubbing at the back of his neck. "I'll go by Ben's house in the morning. They told me he was working second shift."

"Since she lives on the same street as Ben, try to be nice if you run into Lawrence's sister," Bryce cautioned.

"I'm always nice."

"No, you're always propositioning her."

Mike held his hands, palms up in front of him. "Can I help it if my artistic nature demands I get her on film?"

Bryce laughed. Resting his arms along the back of the sofa, he warned, "Rein in that artistic nature, little brother. By the end of next month, Lyssa may be your sister-in-law."

His brother surprised him when he lunged out of his seat and glared down at him. "You proposed marriage?"

Baffled by his sudden anger, Bryce rose to face Mike and nodded. "Yes."

"Why her when you've already got Mattie?" Mike demanded. "Okay, hell, I admit Lyssa is beautiful and smart and amazingly talented. What man wouldn't want her?"

Bryce held up his hand. "Whoa. Stop right there. I think you're a bit confused, Mike."

"You just said you proposed—"

"To *my* Lawrence," Bryce clarified, chuckling at the chagrined look on his brother's face. As he watched the information register in his brother's exhausted brain, Bryce wondered if perhaps Mike's interest in Lyssa went beyond art.

"Oh." Mike dropped down onto the sofa with a low snort of laughter. "Well, that's embarrassing."

"Not to mention enlightening."

"Wait." Mike looked at Bryce carefully. "You're serious? You really proposed marriage to Mattie? When?"

"Today."

"What did she say?"

Bryce returned to his seat facing Mike. "She'll give me her answer tomorrow. She wanted some time to think it over."

"Why?" Mike asked.

"Why did she want some time to think it over?"

"No. Why propose to her?"

Bryce could feel his brother's scrutiny. "It was time."

"There's more to it than that. You've been circling her like a great white with a sweet yellowfin tuna for eight years. Proposing sex I can see, but marriage? No. There's something else going on here."

"I didn't think I'd been that obvious."

"You weren't, but I know you better than most people." Mike fought a yawn.

"Why don't you go get some sleep?" Bryce suggested. "We can discuss this in the morning before I head out to the Folly."

Dragging his hands down his face, Mike agreed. "Yeah, I'm beat." Groaning, he pulled himself off the sofa and picked up his bags. Before he turned toward the bedrooms, he met Bryce's gaze. "Is Dad okay?"

Having risen from his seat, Bryce nodded. "Yes. He's fine." Settling his hand along his brother's back, he squeezed Mike's shoulder. "We were both nervous when we first heard about the kidnapping, but once we confirmed it wasn't you, and that the journalist had survived, we both calmed down."

Mike grimaced. "Sorry about that."

"Just don't let it happen, again, Mike." Bryce met his younger brother's brown eyes. "I don't want to think what losing you would do to the family."

Chapter Three

Hovering beside her SUV, Mattie hesitated. The drive out of San Diablo to Bryce's home had taken her past the Club and toward the cliffs overlooking the Pacific. The challenge she was about to issue reminded her of the first time she'd stood at the western edge of the land surrounding Pirate's Folly. The sheer drop at some spots was easily eighty feet or more and had made her stomach roll at the thought of tumbling over. A well-maintained fence kept guests from nearing the edge of the precipice, while hidden near two wild rosebushes, one with white blooms and one with red, was a set of steps carved into the rock face that led to an expanse of beach and a finger of land jutting out into the water. The combination of safety and danger had stirred the need she'd developed to test the boundaries of propriety. Ironic that Bryce should choose to marry her for the very thing from which she struggled to break free.

Shaking away the thoughts, she smoothed the skirt of her dress and crossed the cobblestone drive to the three broad steps leading onto the wraparound porch. Ionic columns supported a similar covered porch above it around the second level of the Greek Revival mansion, before ending where the angled roof became a widow's walk around the four turreted corners of the third floor. Near the eastern corner of the veranda, a wide porch swing sported white and green gingham cushions. Similar pillows rested on the seats of two rocking chairs on the western side of the door. Refusing to lose herself in imagining the sunset from either comfortable spot, Mattie pressed the doorbell and waited, fighting the urge to tap the toe of her low-heeled slide.

"Miss Mattie." The smile on the older woman's face was welcoming as she pulled open the door.

Mattie smiled back. "Hello, Etta." She followed Bryce's housekeeper into the foyer.

"Bryce is upstairs, but he should be down any moment."

"He told me he'd purchased another horse and it was supposed to arrive today." Mattie was surprised that, as nervous as she was, she could recall the comment Bryce had made the previous week.

The older woman glanced over her shoulder as she led Mattie into a sitting room. "That's why he's upstairs. He just couldn't let Deacon handle it. Had to see to the horse himself." Hovering near the door, she asked, "Would you like a glass of sweet tea?"

"That would be nice, thank you."

Left alone, Mattie didn't bother sitting down. Having visited Bryce's home in the past to help with various parties and events, she was familiar with the different downstairs rooms.

Antiques mixed with modern furniture in many of the rooms. Mattie had always been impressed by how comfortable the house felt. Although the polished wood floors and tiled entry and hallways were showroom quality, the Folly, as Bryce liked to call it, was a home. Etta had been housekeeper on the property for nearly twenty years while her husband, Deacon, managed the stables for Bryce.

"Here you go." Etta set a tray with two filled glasses and a pitcher of sweetened iced tea on the coffee table before moving toward Mattie as she stood beside one set of French doors leading onto the porch.

"Thank you." Mattie accepted the glass the older woman held out to her and sipped.

"That's a lovely dress," Etta commented. "One of your sister's?"

"Yes." Mattie nodded, smoothing the purple silk and smiling at the sensual feel of the fabric.

"If I hadn't known your voice, Lawrence, I would have never recognized you." Bryce's comment from the open door of the sitting room had both women turning.

He was always so sexy in his business suits, with ties and perfectly pressed shirts, that Mattie forgot how much more devastating a pair of faded jeans, boots, and a T-shirt looked on him. His gaze skimmed over the knee-length halter-style dress she wore, as well as the simple braid she'd twisted her waist-length brown curls into. Her pulse skyrocketed. Something in his pale green eyes had her body on alert, but she held her ground and fought the urge to stammer out an explanation for her appearance.

Bryce took his time collecting a glass of sweet tea from the tray. His attention remained on Mattie, taking in the flush on her cheeks and the way she gulped her drink. He'd known there was a figure beneath the boxy coats and loose trousers she wore at the office. The sedate gowns she'd worn during the dinner parties she'd helped him with had hinted at the full breasts and curving hips, but this dress did nothing to hide them. The deep V of the halter and the fitted light purple band of material highlighted her hourglass shape and had his imagination substituting something black or even red and made of leather to show off her body.

"You know," he began as he walked around her, his eyes taking in every fold of fabric and the curves it revealed. "I have to say, the investment I made into your sister's design business has been profitable, but I've never seen the real benefits until now."

"I'm sure Lyssa would be surprised at your comments," Mattie returned with a hint of annoyance. "Her designs are becoming very popular, and your returns have reflected that."

He could see her pulling her composure together and tallied another mark in the plus column for reasons to marry her. Not that he needed any more proof to support his decision. "True, but I could have a valid argument in my favor if she could see what you normally wear at work."

She laughed, propped a hand on her hip, and smirked. "Who do you think designed the clothes I wear at work?"

She was definitely going to be a handful, but the taming would be as stimulating as her training. More than just the dress was making his cock hard. The flirty look in her eyes, the smile, all of it was producing an effect he hadn't lost control of in twenty years. "I'll have to talk to her about that."

"You can try, but my sister is very independent."

"Like you?" He stepped closer, watching for any signs of discomfort.

Mattie shrugged, sipped her tea, and waited.

It would take her time to adjust to his play, but she'd get there. The spark of challenge in her eyes, the determination in her expression, all pointed to a strong will. And it was just that kind of will that would make her the perfect sub for him. He'd known that when he first met her. As Richard had said, he'd put years of work into getting Mattie to this point, and he would be able to reap the benefits soon.

"You've made your decision?" he asked, finishing his tea and setting the glass back on the tray.

"Shouldn't we discuss the party?" she offered, gulping down more of her tea. "That was the original reason I was coming out here."

Bryce waved off the idea of discussing the dinner for the Australian businessman. "I trust you have everything under control, Lawrence. You always do." Crossing his arms over his chest, he repeated his question. "You've made your decision?"

"With reservations." The hand came off her hip, and she set her glass down beside his.

"Reservations?"

Mattie nodded. She could hear the curiosity in Bryce's voice and hoped it wouldn't become something else once she explained her request. After talking it over with Lyssa the night before, it made sense. "Yes."

"Yes, what? Yes, you'll marry me, or yes, you have reservations?"

"Both. I'll marry you, but I wanted to discuss something with you first." Moving toward the French doors, she chose her words carefully. Hell, she'd spent half the night trying to figure out just how to broach the subject. "You said my reputation would make the board believe I'd have a settling effect on you."

"Yes."

She glanced over her shoulder. He was still standing where she'd left him, beside the coffee table, thumbs tucked into the waistband of his jeans. "Would that also mean the board would expect you to end your visits to the Diablo Blanco Club?" Her gaze returned to the expanse of grass leading to a small gazebo. "A-and your other…interests?"

"If it's necessary to gain the support of the board, then perhaps I might. But according to my father, the primary concern the board has isn't with the type of sex I indulge in, but the variety of partners I've had."

"And their tendency to blab secrets to reporters?" Mattie offered as she turned to face him.

Bryce nodded. "And that." He seemed to gauge what she might be thinking before suggesting, "Is there something you want to know about my interest in dominance and bondage?"

His expression didn't change nor did his voice, but there was something about how he held himself that had Mattie hesitating. Still, she wanted an answer to the doubts plaguing her. "As your wife would you expect me to do…that?"

"By 'that,' do you mean submit?"

Mattie held his gaze and nodded. "Yes. I would like to know what role you see me assuming in our marriage."

"Partner." His response was cool and immediate. "I'll expect you to give as much as I do to the relationship. Compromises will have to be made on both sides, and I don't intend either of us to deceive each other about the goals we set for ourselves and the company."

Glass-fronted bookcases were built into the walls beside the French doors while between them was a black marble fireplace. Leaning against the lower, cabinet-style portions of one of the bookcases, Mattie shook her head in disbelief. "That doesn't sound like the expected arrangements in a master/slave relationship."

"How much do you know about the lifestyle, Lawrence?" Bryce settled into one of the wing chairs near her.

"Only what I've read online and in different books." Moving closer, Mattie eased onto the settee, facing him, and leaned forward to refill her glass with tea. Lifting his glass, she filled it after he nodded in answer to her silent question.

"What kind of books?" He accepted the glass and waited for her answer.

"Some fiction, some nonfiction."

"Depending on the authors of the nonfiction, you'll run across the various philosophies associated with the scene. As for the fiction, ninety to ninety-five percent of that stuff is garbage, made-up ideas and fantasies from an overactive imagination." His reasonable tone had her relaxing.

"Still, an equal partnership doesn't give me the impression you expect me to participate in a…" She wasn't sure how to complete her thought.

Bryce finished for her. "A Dominant/submissive relationship."

She nodded and sipped at her tea.

"Why would you be concerned about a D/s arrangement?"

Mattie set her glass down and rose to begin pacing again. "Because I can't see you maintaining a regular marriage if you deny your sexual interests."

"I told you we would have a normal marriage, Lawrence. If I need sex, I'll be coming to you."

She looked so agitated and out of sorts pacing the floor in front of the French doors. Bryce hid the smile tugging at his lips behind his glass. Perhaps her introduction to his lifestyle wouldn't be as far off as he'd planned. Though he'd intended to gradually introduce her to the D/s scene, her preoccupation with his past Dominance boded well for him.

She seemed to come to a decision and turned to face him, her hands on her hips. "Yes, but you're a Dominant, Bryce. I can't see you staying satisfied with nightly servings of the missionary position."

"So, what are you offering?" He leaned forward, keeping his head down and hiding his smile from her as he set his empty glass back on the tray. Schooling his expression before he turned to her, he added, "That as long as I keep it discreet,

I can indulge my need for spankings and anal sex with other women?"

"You said infidelity wasn't an option." Her tone was curt and the heat of anger darkened her brown eyes.

Bryce nodded and rose. "True, keeping it secret from the board would be difficult since a few of them, as well as my father, are members of the Diablo Blanco Club."

Mattie nodded. "You'd lose whatever gains you'd made if you decided to stray." Her arms folded over her chest. "Not to mention the speed at which I'd be slapping you with divorce papers."

"Don't like to share, huh?" Bryce moved closer. He had to admit, it excited him when this woman stood toe-to-toe with him in verbal battle. Nothing got him harder faster than Lawrence in a snit and ready to chew him out over some perceived infraction. Hell, he could practically name every time he'd intentionally ticked her off just to get a rise out of her.

"Never have. Never will." Her expression was stern.

Leaning close, he held her gaze and whispered, "How do you feel about being shared?"

He watched the motions in her throat as she swallowed. Her arms dropped, and she started to step away from him. Time to test his theory. "Freeze, Lawrence." Every inch the Dom, he held her eyes and let the master inside take over.

She stilled, arousal warring with unease in her wide brown eyes. The arousal won.

"I know you've listened to the rumors." He waited until she nodded. "What have you heard?"

"Th-that you like to tie up your partners and use…things on them."

"Toys." Again, she nodded. He waited for her to continue. When she didn't, he prompted, "Was that all?"

She shook her head. "No. I…someone said you like to include another man sometimes. That you like to watch him have sex."

Holding her gaze, he trailed the fingers of his left hand down her arm. Unlike her reaction in the restaurant the evening before, she didn't pull away or protest his touch. He could feel her body tremble beneath the stroke of his hand. "I must admit, I enjoy the feel of a woman's soft curves sandwiched between me and Richard." His smile grew at the feel of her shivering. "Are you really concerned that I might miss the life?"

"If we marry—"

"If?" He shook his head. "You've already said you'd marry me, Lawrence. There's no going back on that."

"Yes, I'm concerned you might become frustrated or dissatisfied with the restrictions our marriage would put on you," Mattie admitted.

"And if I tell you I won't?"

"Don't make promises you can't keep."

Her face as well as her voice was devoid of emotion, the very nature of her response reminding him why he'd spent so many years building her trust in him. "How do you think we can resolve this, then?"

Bryce wanted to hear her decision. Despite the maneuvering he'd done to get her to agree to marry him, there were no guarantees she would be comfortable taking on the role of a submissive. All his training and every instinct he had identified her as a true sexual submissive. Now it was just getting her to recognize that part of her nature.

"I need to know." Her fingers curled into her palms.

"Know what?" She had to be the one to ask. The one to make the first overture. No matter how he ached to begin her training, Bryce knew she had to be the one to seek the pleasure her submission to him could give.

She felt like a specimen under a microscope, he watched her so closely. With no expression on his face and despite the years of knowing practically his every mood, Mattie couldn't figure out what he was thinking. A part of her wanted to drop her gaze from his, to show deference she didn't normally show. She fought the feeling and forged on with the suggestions Lyssa had made last night. "I need to know what is required of the role."

"You would arrive and leave work with me. On days either or both of us feel we don't want to deal with the traffic out to Pirate's Folly, we'll stay upstairs in the penthouse." He continued his list as he moved to step around her.

When Mattie attempted to turn as well, his voice stopped her. "Don't move, Lawrence." The callused tips of his fingers skated along the skin of her back, teasing the tendrils of hair that had escaped the braid earlier.

"But there's more to being a sub than that." Forcing herself to disobey him, she turned to face him. "In the books

I've read, there are names used—" She cringed at the thought of the names and the memories they conjured. Memories she'd kept locked away and didn't like revisiting.

"Depending upon the school or philosophy the Dom has adopted, the use of names can be part of the play." Bryce stepped back and crossed his arms over his chest.

"Humiliation and degradation isn't something I can..." She shook her head.

"Nor is it part of what I find arousing." He stepped closer, his body nearly touching hers as he held her gaze. "Let me make this clear, Lawrence. I like to be in charge when it comes to sex. I don't need to humiliate and degrade my partner. I find nothing arousing about tearing another down until there's nothing left of the person she was."

The heat of his body warmed her from forehead to toes. The rasp of denim and cotton against silk could barely be heard over the stuttering breaths she drew in. His gaze held hers, drawing her into the vivid green pools as they darkened from peridot to forest.

"My focus is on seeing how far a submissive is willing to go to achieve climax. Not some simpering, juvenile shudder that lasts all of two seconds." His voice caressed her ears as his fingers coasted over her jaw and down her throat. "No, I want your mind and body to explode, then reassemble and come back begging for more."

His nose nuzzled hers before settling at the crook of her neck. Leaning her head to the side, she gave him more access as his hands skimmed over her shoulders and explored the flesh on her back. Against her cheek, the gold hoop in his ear was a warm weight conducting the heat from his body to hers.

"I want my sub to understand the pleasure in pain," he whispered against her throat. "Surely, having read what you have, you've learned that."

"Yes." Mattie fought to stifle her protest when his hands slipped away and he moved back. Wanting to keep her eyes on him, she started to shift when he stepped past her, but the firm tone in his voice froze her in place, again.

"Don't move, Lawrence."

She could hear him stop behind her.

"I assume, in your readings, you've come across the concepts of 'safe, sane, and consensual'?"

Mattie nodded. "The idea of a safe word was one of the more appealing aspects."

"So establishing a safe word between us would be necessary, if you agreed." Bryce circled back around to face her. "But your question was more about some of the things I would ask you to do if you agreed to submit to me, wasn't it?"

Allowing the master to slip free, Bryce watched Mattie as he began describing some of the fantasies he'd kept under tight control these last eight years. "One of the first things I'd have you do is strip out of your clothes." Stepping closer, he smiled inside at the faint shiver going through her body. "I want to see every curve, confirm that your nipples are the same strawberry red as your lips."

Moving behind her again, he stepped close enough to allow his shirt to brush her bare back. "Then"—he leaned closer, dipping his head so it hovered next to her cheek, his breath stirring the curls that had escaped the braid and covered her ear—"I'd experiment with touch. Stroking over your body with my hands to find out whether you respond to a firm or light touch. Of course, in order to establish what arouses you, I'd need to slide my hand over your pussy. Tangle my fingers in your brown curls, maybe tug on them to see how the slight pain turns you on."

He shifted so his voice floated into her right ear, his eyes registering the increase in her respiration, the flutter of her pulse in the delicate flesh at the base of her throat, and the flow of color and heat from her chest, up her neck, and to her cheeks. He hadn't even begun his seduction, and she was already responding.

"Spreading those plump, wet lips, I'd next determine what kind of clit you have. Some women have obvious ones that enjoy the slide of a finger, cock, or tongue. While others have tiny little buttons that need to be coaxed out of hiding." Dropping his voice, Bryce whispered, "I'm hoping you have a small button. A very shy, sensitive nubbin."

"Wh-why?" Mattie croaked, her voice barely audible.

"Because I want to spend hours eating you, Lawrence. Days buried between your thighs. Stroking your lips open, building your arousal so the juices slide out of your body like water in a fountain. And using every kind of touch, lick, or nibble to get your clit so hot and hard, my breath blowing across it will make you come."

Stepping in front of her, Bryce watched her sway. "Spread your legs a bit, Lawrence." His grin widened at her immediate compliance. "Does that sound like something you'd be willing to do?"

She nodded.

"I need to hear the word."

"Yes."

"Shall I tell you more?"

Again a nod, but no reminder was needed when she added, "Yes."

Holding her gaze, he assured her. "Your pleasure will feed mine, Lawrence. Just as my pleasure will feed yours. I may make you wait for it, but my cock doesn't touch you, doesn't enter, until you've come at least once. Understood?"

"Understood."

He could smell her arousal. The musky scent blended with the clean smell of her skin and hair. "As for my pleasure, your mouth, hands, and body will take care of it. You asked about the Diablo Blanco before, and I'll warn you, if you agree to submit, I'm going to take you there to display you and fuck you." He nodded at her wide-eyed gasp. "Yes, in front of other men, Lawrence. I want them to see what your passion looks like. In the Club, I'll make you come, probably more than once. Then it'll be your turn. I don't care what your other lovers have taught you. I'll instruct you in the ways to give me pleasure." The bitter tone in his voice surprised Bryce.

The sexual experience of his previous partners had never bothered him before, but the very thought of another man having shown his woman how to suck him off grated on unfamiliar nerves. Shaking away the thought, Bryce continued, "You'll use your hands first."

Lifting her right hand, he settled it over his hard cock, introducing her to the feel of his flesh through his worn jeans. "You'll like having your hands over and around it. Up and down, applying the pressure I've taught you best pleases me. I haven't decided if I'll have you dressed or naked in the Club, but while the other members watch from the bar or seating areas, these sweet lips"—his right hand rose to stroke over her strawberry curves—"will swallow me down. What won't fit in your mouth, you'll hold in your hands, stroking and squeezing."

He let his grin slip free when he felt the flex of her fingers over his tumescence. "You like that idea, hmm?" Bryce asked, watching the flash of heat darken her eyes and the tip of her tongue stroke over her lips, wetting them. "Once I come and you've swallowed it, I'll still require attention, but instead of keeping your back to the room while you slide onto my lap and I press my cock deep inside your slick pussy, I'll have you face those watching. Your back will be to me, because I'll want everyone to see how much you enjoy riding me."

Again a moan slipped past her parted lips and the lids over her eyes drooped. He watched her breathing increase as the images he'd described seemed to bloom in her mind and then waited until it had slowed before continuing. "You seem to be comfortable so far with my expectations."

"Tha-that isn't what I was talking about, other than the…the audience."

Holding her gaze, he could see her working up the nerve to continue. Wanting her to voice her concerns without any input from him, Bryce stayed silent.

"What else?"

"What do you mean, what else?" He wanted her to tell him exactly what she meant. Their agreement might be based on a business arrangement, but it would be a real marriage nonetheless. If they were to proceed as he hoped they would, ambiguity could have no place in their marriage.

Mattie heaved an exasperated sigh and settled her hands on her hips. "Will you expect me to do all of the other stuff you mentioned?" She fought the urge to wince at the eager, breathless tone in her voice.

He didn't try to hide his grin. "You mean the ass fucking, the ménage, and the bondage?"

She sent him an annoyed grin. "Let's not forget the spankings."

"Definitely, let's not forget those." He chuckled.

The sound of his laughter rumbled through her belly, sending pinpricks of arousal through her body.

"Do you want the bare-bones truth, or shall I sugarcoat it for you?" Bryce asked.

That tone was back in his voice, Mattie noted. The inclination to dip her head and wait until he asked her to speak stirred, but she pushed it down, no matter how it excited her. Yes, she'd fantasized about Bryce controlling her, but now wasn't the time to give in to it. If she was going to keep her head and use this opportunity to make him accept her, she needed to keep her wits sharp. "Bare-bones, please. I'm sure I can take—handle it."

He grinned and stepped closer, so the heat from his body seeped through his clothes and wrapped around her. "Bare-bones, it is. One of the first things I intend to do is clamp these hard little peaks." Between the forefinger and thumb of each hand, Bryce pinched her nipples as they pressed against the silky fabric of her dress. "After I've gotten you used to the clamps or chains I'll use, it'll be time to bind you. First just your hands behind your back, so you won't be tempted to distract me from my investigations. From there we'll progress to tying you spread-eagle on the bed so I can see just how much you can stand to be aroused without climaxing."

Mattie swallowed, but the warmth filling her face was nothing compared to the inferno his descriptions were building in her body. She could visualize each step he described. In them, she could see the culminating events play out like images on a movie screen. Legs splayed wide, hands bound to the thick posts of his bed, Mattie could see him sliding into her wet, aching body, wrenching climax after climax from her. Even as her body heated and her pussy grew wet, he continued talking.

"After the binding comes the toys. Not just because I like using them on my lovers, but it'll be necessary." One hand slipped away from the soft stroking of her nipple to cup first one butt cheek, then the other. "Although you've read the books"—his grin was wry—"I'm not seeing you let one of your boyfriends drill your ass, so I'm sure your tight little rose will need a bit of stretching."

Involuntarily, the muscles in her backside tightened, and Bryce's chuckle grew throaty and raw as he pressed a finger into the crease, rubbing against the strap of her thong, with the soft silk of her dress the only barrier between her flesh and his hand.

"You like that idea, don't you?"

Mattie didn't know how to respond. Yes, she had to admit to liking the sting of the small plug she'd purchased for herself a few years earlier, but to actually allow him to enter her body there...her fingers became difficult to control. She clenched them into fists to keep from reaching for him.

"Then you'll enjoy the next step. After I've stretched you and spent some time enjoying your new territory, Richard will join us on occasion."

Swallowing, Mattie forced away the new images bombarding her. "You act as if I've agreed to these things already."

His hand stroked over her bottom before slipping under her skirt to slide over her wet underwear. "Your body seems to find the idea arousing."

"That I won't deny, but what my mind and my body decide are often two different things." She wasn't sure she could make herself step away from Bryce, so she was relieved when he chose to do it himself. The temptation to groan at the loss of his touch was stifled, barely.

"If you aren't interested in submission, then why bring it up?" He didn't sound annoyed or angry at her halting of his teasing—more curious than anything.

"Because I need to know if I can take on the role of a submissive." She stopped herself from adding, *and if you can accept me as one.*

Arms crossed over his chest, Bryce watched her. "I assure you, our marriage won't suffer if I don't indulge in the lifestyle."

Mattie matched his stance. "And I think it would. It's hard enough when two people love each other and they marry. We're going into this without that connection. If we have to spend the next few years together, we should at least agree that keeping each other content will go a long way toward making sure the marriage lasts." With a shrug, she added, "And it'll go a long way in convincing the board that you have settled."

"So what are you suggesting?"

"To give you two weeks to show me what it would be like to be your sub."

"And then what?" His hands settled on his hips.

"We can begin making the wedding plans."

The light of battle darkened his green eyes to emerald. Ignoring the unnerving flutters building in her lower belly, she waited for his response.

It wasn't long in coming. "Too long. Dad's retirement party is in just over a month. I want to be married by that time. Giving you two weeks would delay things, and I don't trust the board not to act, especially once the Makepeaces learn we're engaged."

"Twelve days, then."

"Three."

Again, Mattie shook her head. "You've implied that you won't have any problem doing without the BDSM lifestyle, but you've had years to understand it. Three days doesn't give me enough time to figure out what it could represent in our marriage, let alone the rest of my life. What about ten days?"

It was Bryce's turn to shake his head. "Still too long. Five days."

"Let's split the difference and make it a week," Mattie offered.

Bryce thought about it and began to nod, but Mattie continued, knowing her next words would either piss him off or amuse him. "And no sex."

Chapter Four

"Are you sure you've never dabbled in BDSM before?"

Color filled her face, but the flush seemed more from embarrassment than from guilt at getting caught in a lie. "No. Why?"

"You discuss rules of play rather skillfully, Lawrence."

A wry smile and small chuckle escaped her. "I learned it all dealing with you, Halsey."

Negotiating a scene with one of his past lovers had never been as stimulating as bartering for favors with this woman, but Bryce forced himself not to smile. Once he'd determined she was the best candidate to woo the board to his side, he'd planned on spending a week getting her well and thoroughly fucked. A test drive, so to speak, while he began introducing the idea of submission to her. Having her suggest experiencing his lifestyle struck him as rather ironic. Not to mention arousing. "Why?"

She didn't seem confused by his question. "Why no sex?"

He nodded.

Mattie shrugged. "If I decide I can't take on the role of a submissive, I don't want to associate the sex we have during our marriage to the type of sex we engaged in during this week of experimentation."

Her tone was so matter-of-fact he didn't doubt she had thought the situation through. Knowing her as he did, he should have expected her to throw a spanner in the works. "How are you supposed to understand what I'll expect from you if you refuse to have sex?"

The flash of fire in her eyes tugged at the smile he repressed. She remained in place before him, her legs nearly shoulder-width apart, bare toes curling into the silk carpet. In a typical Lawrence habit, she'd abandoned her shoes sometime after entering the room.

"If you want me to be more specific, I will."

Bryce dipped his head. "Please do."

"No penetration. I understand some types of foreplay will be required for me to determine if I think I'll be able to take on the role you want from me, but I want your promise that no intercourse will take place." Her expression was nearly defiant, stirring his need to make her see the type of satisfaction to be found in sex during submission.

"Am I still allowed to use my tongue, fingers, and any toys?"

Mattie swallowed heavily. The heat in her cheeks returned as she responded, "What kinds?"

Give-and-take—that was always the way with her, and the thought of that tenacity and fire in his bed had him fighting the urge to demand her immediate surrender. Forcing back the response, he listed a few items, taking note of her body's reaction. "Butt plugs and lube, of course." She swallowed, and her toes flexed deeper into the carpet's fibers. *Definitely a yes*, he thought. Aloud, he continued, "As I said before, clamps and chains for your nipples, cuffs and ropes for binding."

A tiny shiver trembled through her frame.

Another yes. "My hand, a paddle, and a flogger for punishment."

This time, the tension in her body hovered between fear and arousal. Remembering what he knew of her past, he assured her, "Right of refusal is still yours, Lawrence."

She cleared her throat, her eyes shadowed and hard to read. "But will using the safe word negate our agreement?"

Although he disliked the thought of holding back with her, he also knew he would have to go slowly with the part of her training that dealt with physical punishment and its use in creating arousal. The idea of pain to stimulate pleasure wasn't abhorrent to her, but as it related to anal penetration, not the application of hand or paddle to flesh. "The use of our safe word won't end the agreement, merely alter certain aspects of what I'd like to introduce you to."

She nodded, indicating her understanding, before adding, "What do you mean by punishment?"

Stepping closer, he stroked his finger along the side of her neck. "You are a stubborn woman, Lawrence." He traced the edge of her dress from throat to the deep V between her breasts. Eyes holding hers, he continued, "I don't expect this claiming to be easy for either of us."

"Claiming?"

He smiled, enjoying the throaty tone of her voice as his finger continued to slide along the silk, absorbing the heat building in her skin, and noting the subtle swelling of her flesh. "I prefer to think of it that way. You'll belong to me, Lawrence. As your master, everything you do or say when we're at the Club will reflect on my training of you."

"But..."

"No buts, Lawrence." Bryce's tone reflected his expectation of immediate compliance. "In effect, I'll own you."

He could see her fighting the need to argue. And losing.

"Only as it pertains to sex," she snapped. "You don't have any say in how I conduct myself outside the bedroom."

"I don't limit my play to the bedroom, Lawrence; you should know that." The urge to paddle her ass then fuck her was difficult to overcome, especially when she stepped away from him and rolled her eyes at his comment.

"You know what I mean," she grumbled.

He nodded. "And you understand that many of the men I conduct business with are men I've trained in the lifestyle. Even one of the board members."

In her eyes, he could see comprehension dawning. With it, trepidation slipped into her expression; he addressed it before she could backpedal out of their agreement. He had no intention of wasting the plans he'd set in motion eight years ago because of some imagined fear. "I don't need a twenty-four-seven D/s relationship. I never have. I'm not expecting you to become compliant in all areas of our relationship, Lawrence, just our sexual one." He waited for the suspicion to clear in her eyes and then continued, "But, while you're deciding if you can handle my ownership, there are rules you'll have to agree to and follow."

"Rules? What kind of rules?"

"Just like any trainee, you have to learn what is and is not acceptable during this trial period."

Her furrowed brow smoothed. "Like what I can and cannot say?"

"Not that confining, but things to keep in mind in order to keep you safe."

Keeping her arms crossed, Mattie followed his progress toward her. "And who was in charge of making up these rules?"

Bryce didn't bother responding to her question. "Rule number one, no being alone with other men."

"Don't you mean men or women?" Mattie demanded. "If you've agreed to fidelity, I think it's important that these rules apply to you, at least during the trial period."

Bryce shook his head. "Doesn't work that way, Lawrence. I'm not the one wanting a trial run, remember?"

Drawing a deep breath, Mattie reluctantly admitted he was right. "True, but…"

"No buts. Rule number one, no spending time with, or allowing past lovers or other men to touch you."

"Agreed." She knew her resentment at having to put up with such one-sided restrictions was apparent in her tone, but she wasn't about to hide it from him.

"Rule number two, no self-stimulation unless given permission."

Mattie seemed to think about it for a moment. It wasn't like she lay in bed every night masturbating. Going without self-stimulation shouldn't be that hard to deal with. With that thought in mind, she gave an absent shrug. "Okay."

"Rule number three, there are no restrictions on where or when I can give instruction to you."

Shaking her head, Mattie again objected. "I'm not sure about that one. I have to work with the different people in the various departments. If we're seen by employees…"

"I told you I don't restrict my sex to the bedroom, Lawrence, but I can see your point." Taking a moment, he seemed to debate the best way to alter the directive before voicing it. "All right, during the trial period, there are no restrictions on where or when I can give instruction as long as, while we are at work, there is no risk of another employee seeing us. Will that satisfy you?"

"Why not say no touching at work?"

His laughter was both arousing and sinister. The gleam in his eyes should have warned Mattie, but the words that followed stole her breath. "Because I have every intention of bending you over my desk and making you come at every opportunity."

Images flashed through her mind, making her sway on her feet. The heat flooding her pussy and the gush of juices soaking her panties only made matters worse. Maintaining rational thought after his comment seemed unlikely, but she shook it off. Moving to the sofa, she settled onto the arm and took a deep breath. "I... Okay. I'll agree to rule number three."

"Rule number four." He began taking the few steps necessary to close the distance between them. Bryce took a seat in the wingback armchair that sat at an angle to the sofa. "No climaxing without my permission."

"Now wait..." she began to protest.

"There's no negotiating this one, Lawrence." His tone was firm, implacable. "If I'm to be your master, I own your body and your orgasms."

"But..."

Leaning forward, his eyes darkened to jade. "Trust me on this. No coming unless I say you can, agreed?"

Despite the protests she was all set to voice, Mattie wasn't surprised to hear herself agreeing. "Yes, Bryce. Okay, no coming without your permission."

"Good. Rule number five, use the safe word whenever the situation is too much for you." He held her gaze. "This one is the most important rule. You will *not* go along with something if you don't think you can handle it. If you think you need to use our safe word, do so. We can stop, discuss what's going to happen and how you feel about it, and then you can decide if you want to continue or not."

"All right. I'll use the safe word if I feel I can't handle something."

Leaning back in the chair, Bryce watched her carefully for several seconds. The intensity of his gaze had a part of her desperate to jump off the sofa arm and run out to her car. A little voice in her head demanded to know what bit of insanity had her contemplating agreeing to his rules, but her heart overruled it.

"Those are the rules, Lawrence." Bryce watched her closely as she squirmed in her seat. "Do you agree to follow them?"

As keen as his gaze was, Mattie prayed he wouldn't be able to guess at just how arousing the thought of his punishing her for breaking one of his rules was. If she was very lucky, not to mention very naughty, maybe she'd be getting one of those spankings he'd been threatening her with for years. Shaking away that disturbing but erotic thought, Mattie took a deep breath before responding. "What kind of punishment are you talking about?"

Bryce merely looked at her. "One appropriate for the situation and the rule broken. When it happens."

"When? Are you expecting me to intentionally break one of your rules?"

"Lawrence, you've been pushing boundaries and skirting the rules since the day we met." Rising, he moved closer and tugged her to her feet.

The heat of his body almost distracted her from hearing the rest of his statement.

"Not only do I expect you to break one rule, I anticipate you breaking all five of my rules, simply because they're *my* rules." In a move too smooth and quick for her to counteract, Bryce secured both her wrists behind her back in one hand while the other cupped her cheek, holding her gaze with his. "Do we have a deal now?"

Heat flared in his eyes when she dampened her lips with the tip of her tongue. "I..." She cleared her throat and began again. "I let you show me what's expected of your sub for the next week, follow the five rules, with your promise there won't be any intercourse, and at the end of the week I decide whether or not I'll take on the role during our marriage."

"In a nutshell."

Mattie tilted her head without breaking eye contact. "Okay, it's a deal. I agree." She let a wry smile curve over her lips. "So, do we shake on it? Bec—"

The wicked smile crossing his lips barely registered before Bryce shook his head. "Oh, no, Lawrence. This type of agreement requires something a little more personal."

The feel of his lips sliding over hers stilled the breath in her lungs.

In all the times she'd contemplated what his kiss would feel like, she had assumed it would be similar to his take-charge approach to business.

And she was wrong.

Instead, Bryce's kiss was a soft caress. Coaxing a response by easing over her lips, pressing and rubbing against the sensitive tissues before she felt his mouth open just slightly to allow the tip of his tongue to trace the seam sealing her lips.

The heat of his body, the patient teasing of his mouth on hers, had her head spinning. Without thinking about it, she arched closer to him, her breasts desperate for the feel of his firm, broad chest. The grip of his hand around her wrists didn't deter her motions in the slightest. The difference in their heights forced her on her tiptoes when he began to draw away.

The hand at her cheek slipped aside to drift down to her hip before he released her hands and set her firmly away from him. His grin at her throaty groan of protest had Mattie flushing and forcing herself to slow her breathing. The soaked silk between her thighs could be ignored, just as the obvious protrusion of her hardened nipples could. If Bryce wanted to tease her with kisses, she'd let him. There was no telling, based on what she'd gleaned from rumors and overheard over the years, to what lengths he was going to go to test her suitability.

Meeting his gaze with what she hoped was a serene expression, despite the heat flooding her body, she waited.

"A safe word," he prompted, his arms folding over his chest.

She didn't stop to think, only blurted out the first word that came to mind. "Pirate."

Laughter erupted from the doorway to her left, drawing her gaze and making Mattie curse beneath her breath until she recognized the sexy figure lounging against the frame. "Michael." She grinned, pushing past Bryce as she moved to give the other man a quick hug. "I'm so glad you made it back. When did you get into town?"

"I got in last night. Did you miss me?" Mike teased, returning her hug and urging her back toward Bryce, his left arm draped around her shoulders.

"Please." Mattie groaned and shook her head. "You had us freaking out when we saw the report about the journalist held by terrorists." Leaning back, she smacked his shoulder and glared up at him. "Don't do things like that anymore. Next time leave a number or tell your brother and dad where you are."

"Ow," he teased, rubbing at his shoulder. "I've already gotten the lecture, thank you."

"Well, this time pay attention." She huffed but gave him another hug. "I'm getting tired of watching your dad worry and your brother grumble and growl about your gallivanting all over the world to take pictures."

"Hmmm." He shifted his gaze between her and his brother before raising his eyebrows in curiosity. "Do tell, darlin'."

The intentional deepening of his Southern drawl had Mattie chuckling. It still surprised her that the same dropping of the ending of a word and drawing out of the vowel sound from Mike didn't cause the breath-stealing, panty-creaming effect that Bryce's use did. Then again, she wasn't in love with Mike, whereas Bryce…

She turned her attention back to the man she'd been bartering with. The heat surged up her chest and into her neck and cheeks at the wry amusement tilting his lips and darkening Bryce's green eyes. Realizing she'd nearly broken the first rule, Mattie shifted out from beneath Mike's hold and casually stepped away from him and closer to Bryce.

"Was there something you needed, Mike?" Bryce asked.

"Yeah." Draping his arms along the back of one of the wing chairs, he nodded. "I wanted to know if you were familiar with the warehouse over on Bridgerton."

Mattie stayed quiet. Excitement stirred at the thought that Mike might actually be thinking of settling down in San Diablo. Permanently. His career had taken him all over the world, and although Bryce was proud of his younger brother's accomplishments, she knew he was also uneasy at some of the places Mike ended up. After the last scare they'd gone through two weeks earlier, she was beginning to be afraid for his safety. If he was looking at property in town, she reasoned, he was probably thinking of setting up a studio of some sort, which would mean less time on the road and in war-torn countries.

"Yes, in fact, the owner is a Club member. Would you like me to set up an introduction?"

Mike shook his head. "No, I was just wondering if you thought the area justified the price."

That had Bryce chuckling. "No, but Charles has a tendency to overinflate everything."

The grin on the younger man's face acknowledged the advice. "I'll keep that in mind when I get my agent to look over the offer."

"Do you need…?" Bryce began.

His brother waved him off. "No, I can handle it. Thanks for the help." Glancing toward Mattie as she perched on the arm of the sofa again, Mike added. "Sorry to interrupt."

"Oh, you wer—" Mattie started, but Bryce overrode her comment.

"We'll talk later."

"Of that I'm sure." Mike again chuckled as he smiled at Mattie before leaving the room.

"You didn't have to—" she protested.

"Come here, Lawrence."

There it was again, Mattie noted, even as she immediately followed his directions and moved to stand in front of him.

"You chose 'pirate' as our safe word."

"Yes."

"Then 'pirate' it is."

Chapter Five

Leaning over Dana's desk, Mattie didn't pay attention to the door opening behind her until the receptionist's expression warned her that the visitor was one neither of them welcomed. Standing up and turning to face the man smiling at her, Mattie fought the urge to move away from Victor. After the one date she'd had with him, she knew not to trust him to be a gentleman.

"Good afternoon, Miss Lawrence." His greeting was polite enough, but the way his cool blue eyes slid over her silk blouse and skirt made it seem anything but appropriate.

If it hadn't been for the heat that had filled Bryce's eyes when she walked into his office this morning, she'd have ditched the stockings and heels for her more comfortable flats. But look at her was all Bryce had done. After tossing and turning most of Saturday and Sunday night following their discussion, Mattie had assumed he would have made some kind of move or gesture to begin testing her. Instead he did nothing. Nada, zip, zero. Nearly forty hours since she'd agreed to let Bryce instruct her, and he'd left her alone.

Now she had to endure Victor's scrutiny. "Was there something you needed, Mr. Prommer?" He was a slime, but he was still an employee of the company. With Bryce out of the office and Richard in San Diego dealing with a client, she was the most logical choice for him to bring any concerns to.

"I needed to speak to you." His gaze moved from her to Dana, then back. "Alone."

Mattie forced a smile to her lips. Just what she didn't need. Motioning toward her office, she met Dana's gaze over his shoulder. When the younger woman held up her hand with three fingers spread, Mattie gave her a quick nod. Three minutes would be more than enough time for her to have to deal with the melodrama Victor had dreamed up this time.

At her door, she hesitated when he held it open for her but entered anyway. The sound of the latch clicking had her turning to face the lawyer. "I really don't think we need to close the door, Mr. Prommer—"

The smarmy grin spreading over his lips should have been warning enough, but Mattie's thoughts were still distracted by Bryce's inattention and the discussion she and Dana had been having regarding the last details of the dinner party for Ian King.

"Now, Mattilda, didn't I say you could call me Victor?" He moved closer, his hand sliding along her left shoulder to her elbow.

Pulling away, Mattie shook her head. "And I believe I told you I wasn't interested, Mr. Prommer."

"We really didn't get a chance to talk very much, Mattilda," Victor continued, seeming to ignore her very obvious disinterest. "You left so quickly."

Tugging her elbow from his grip, she stepped away from him again, but the man continued to follow. "I have absolutely no intention of discussing personal issues. Now, did you have something you wanted to talk about regarding the Conlin merger?"

This time when she moved away, Victor followed until the edge of her desk pressed into the back of her thighs. His grin spread, and both hands reached out to grip her arms. "Why would I discuss an important deal like that with you, Mattilda? Come on, you know you've been waiting for me to ask you out again."

Unable to twist free of his grip, Mattie halted his approach by pressing her hands against his chest and leaning back. "Are you insane?"

"If you weren't so determined to play hard to get we wouldn't have to go through this." He smiled at her. "Besides, who else would you slip on come-fuck-me shoes for, but me?"

Mattie blinked in surprise, speechless.

"I know it's your way to get me to pay attention to you," Victor purred, one hand reaching up to stroke her cheek. "So, here I am, paying attention."

"If you haven't any business to discuss…"

"You want me." His superior tone matched his look. "You've been begging for me to ask you out again."

Snorting in disgust, Mattie assured him, "You have got to be joking. Didn't my leaving you high and dry at the restaurant give you a clue? Or are you that hard up for attention?"

The blue of his eyes grew chillier, and the smile turned bitter. "You just need a little convincing, Mattilda."

"I don't need anything from you, Victor. Now get your hands off me." She used her firmest tone and held his gaze.

"What? Are you saving yourself for the boss? You're too blue-collar for him, Mattilda. Haven't you figured that out yet? Hell, you're not even his type." Victor sneered just before he yanked her off balance. "But I like a little struggle in my women, so let's see how much fight you've got."

His lips slammed against hers, the wet slide of them making her shudder and work harder to get out of his hold. When one of his hands slid over to grope her breast before slipping down her side and squeezing her ass, Mattie finally gained enough leverage to free herself from his hold and move away. She didn't bother trying to slap his face; she didn't want to get that close again. The nasty gleam in his eyes made her take another few steps toward the door just as it opened.

"Your four-thirty appointment—" Dana's hazel eyes grew wide, Mattie assumed at her disheveled appearance.

Taking the opportunity to move even farther away from Victor, she eased past Dana into the reception area. "Mr. Prommer was just leaving."

As he moved out of her office and toward the door leading into the hall, Victor smiled at her. "We'll talk later."

"Not if you know what's good for you," Mattie snapped, but the self-satisfied grin and casual wave he sent her as he sauntered out the door reinforced her suspicion that he wasn't taking her warnings seriously.

"Are you okay?" Dana asked, concern in her gaze as she walked with Mattie toward the reception desk

"That man is a menace," Mattie growled. Taking a tissue from the box on Dana's desk and wiping at the smeared lipstick and dampness his kiss had left behind, she watched through the broad glass doors as Victor swaggered down the hall.

"You should be careful around him," Dana warned, handing her another tissue.

Mattie looked at her, noting the concern in her gaze. "Is there something I should know?"

Dana hesitated. "I'm not sure how true it is, but Frannie in records mentioned the way he tended to corner some of the interns working in the legal department."

"Has anyone filed a complaint?"

"One of the women tried, but as soon as she mentioned going to personnel, she ended up transferred to the Charleston office."

As Mattie plucked another tissue from the container, she thought over who might have been behind the transfer, while grimacing at the distasteful moisture Victor's kiss had left behind. "I just don't get it." Mattie wiped again at her mouth. "Why do they act like such cavemen?"

* * *

The man strutting down the hall toward him had Bryce's hackles rising. There wasn't anything overtly annoying about Victor Prommer, but his instincts had warned him to be wary of the younger man. Admittedly his brilliance in the legal department had some board members singing his praises, but it was the whispers that had gotten back to him, through the office and the Club, that had Bryce contemplating shortening the man's employment with Halsey's.

"Mr. Halsey." Victor nodded, a sly grin lifting his lips.

Something in his blue eyes and the cocky swagger had Bryce paying close attention to his appearance. The smear of lipstick near the corner of his mouth, combined with the direction the lawyer was coming from, had Bryce reaching out to halt the other man. "Were you looking for me?"

"No, just had a little…matter to discuss with Mattilda." Victor smirked. Glancing at his watch, he added, "Gotta go. Have five-thirty dinner reservations. Don't want to keep my date waiting."

Pointing to his mouth, Bryce suggested, "I'd take a minute to wipe my face if I were you." The grin lifting his lips was meant to warn rather than show humor as he added, "I'd also watch the 'matters' you discuss with my assistant, Victor. Wouldn't want them getting you into any trouble."

The heat flushing the younger man's face and the narrow-eyed glare assured Bryce his warning had been interpreted correctly. Unconcerned with Victor's response, he left the man sputtering in the hall and moved toward his office.

Wiping at her smeared lipstick, he heard Mattie grumble. "Why do they act like such cavemen? It's disgusting." Tossing the used tissue in the trash, she added, "He even had the audacity to accuse me of dressing to turn him on!"

Already suspicious about the subject of the tirade, Bryce closed the door leading into the reception area from the hall and asked, "What's disgusting?"

"Nothing," Mattie snapped, glaring at him and stepping into her office. The door between the reception area and her office closed with a distinct slam.

Beside him, Dana winced and shook her head. Having been with the company five years and spending the last two manning the desk that led into his and Mattie's adjoining offices, Dana was familiar with the battle of wills he and his assistant engaged in on occasion.

Not bothering to acknowledge the slammed door, Bryce glanced at his watch. "It's almost five, Dana. Why don't you head on home?" He watched as Dana grinned, her fingers moving swiftly over the phone and powering down her computer.

"No problem." Scooping up her purse and coat, she smiled, calling out from the door, "Have a good night."

Pushing open the door to Mattie's office, he took a moment to examine her as she angrily paced the carpet between the tiny sitting area and her desk. The swish of her skirt hem skimmed the top of her knees and the black heels gave her hips a sexy sway. If he hadn't already set his plans in motion over the weekend, Bryce figured the sight of Lawrence's round ass draped in midnight blue silk and bent over the lower drawer of his filing cabinets when he came in this morning would have had him rethinking his eight years of hands-off. Just as she had on Saturday, Mattie had dressed to kill...or arouse.

Despite the anger fueling her pacing, Bryce enjoyed the sight of the black silk stockings, blue skirt, and black blouse she wore. The sensual fabrics caressed her skin, outlining every curve, and tempted him to break his promise of "no intercourse" before she made her final decision. Fighting the urge to strip her and spread her over her desk for a fast, furious fucking, Bryce focused on the subject of her continued mutterings.

"So, Lawrence, I can assume your tirade about 'disgusting cavemen' has something to do with Victor wearing some of your lipstick when he left the office?"

Rounding on him, her chocolate eyes blazed. One fist propped on her hip and the other flexing angrily at her side, she responded, "I told you he would be trouble."

"Are we going to go—"

"You wouldn't listen to me," she growled, striding closer. Spreading her arms wide, Mattie continued, "You liked his résumé and the fact that he came so highly recommended."

"Yes, we are." Bryce didn't bother to hide his amusement at her dislike of the other man. Ignoring the fact that his own opinion had changed about the attorney, he added, "If we're going to go through this again, Lawrence, let's go into my office so there are more walls between us and the rest of the company."

Leaving her to follow him or not, Bryce strode into his office. Knowing her as well as he did, he wasn't surprised when the door thudded shut.

"Hey, if you have no problem being named in a sexual harassment suit, it's no skin off my nose," she snapped, dropping onto the sofa and rubbing at her lips.

Tossing his suit coat over the back of his chair, he unbuttoned the cuffs of his shirt and rolled the sleeves up as he moved to stand over her. Crossing his arms over his chest, he demanded, "Explain."

"Just because I made the mistake of going out with him once, he thinks I'm available to scratch any itch he might have."

The swagger and cocky attitude of the younger man made more sense now, but the warning he'd given him should work to quell any future poaching efforts. "So that was what you meant by 'disgusting'?"

Meeting his eyes, she asked, "Why is it guys think they have to slobber and maul a person as some sort of mating ritual?"

"I'm assuming you're talking about Victor."

The heat filling her cheeks assured Bryce that Mattie was now remembering the encounter in the sitting room at his home on Saturday.

"Yes." She nodded. Shuddering, she added, "With Victor, it was like having an octopus grope me. Slimy lips and too many tentacles to watch out for. With you…" Mattie's voice trailed off and she shrugged.

"Stand up."

It was the tone she associated with his master personality. On Saturday, she'd gotten a brief glimpse of it when he'd outlined all the erotic things he'd planned to introduce her to. The wet pulse between her thighs reminded her of the sensual attention he'd promised to…

"Lawrence." His reminder had her getting to her feet and moving to stand in front of him. Giving in to the impulse to avert her gaze from his, she dipped her chin so her eyes focused on the third button of his shirt.

"Tell me what he did."

Remaining in place as he stepped away from her, Mattie fought the urge to follow his progress as he moved behind her. Swallowing, she recounted Victor's visit. "He came in and asked to speak with me privately."

"Did you allow that?" The wash of his breath over her shoulder warmed her. The deft treatment he gave the hook and zipper on her skirt had the garment pooling around her ankles, with her thong soon following.

"Y-yes," she stammered.

"That"—his voice was implacable—"was your first mistake." Circling around to her front, his finger beneath her chin lifted Mattie's gaze to his. "Continue."

"Wh—" She stifled her gasp as his fingers slipped the buttons through their holes on her cuffs, before he began with the row down the front of her blouse. "When he followed me in, he suggested I was trying to gain his attention so he would ask me out again."

"And you disabused him of that notion?"

Mattie nodded, her breath catching in her throat as his hands eased her silk shirt over her shoulders and off.

"Lawrence." The command was in his voice again.

"Yes, I made it clear I wasn't interested in him." Through heavy-lidded eyes, she watched him carefully fold her blouse and set it on his desk.

"Hand me your skirt and underwear, then remove your bra."

Blatantly conscious of her nudity and its contrast to his fully clothed state, Mattie stepped out of the puddle of silk, stooped to gather the fabric, and carefully folded each item before handing them to Bryce. Fingers trembling, she had to try twice before getting the front catch of her bra to release so she could hand it over to him.

Again, Bryce turned away to settle her clothing on the corner of his desk. When he returned, he held her gaze for long, heated moments. "Where did he touch you?"

Her hands rose to graze the midpoint on her upper arms. No bruises showed, but the grip Victor had used had proved to be difficult to wrestle free from.

Bryce's look was cool, remote, as he stepped closer, his gaze tracing the path of her hands. "Is that the only place?"

"No." She could feel the heat in her cheeks as his eyes followed her fingers as she traced them along her jaw, where Victor's hand had stilled her attempts to turn away from him. From there, she hastily slid her hand over her left breast and hip, before stopping with her hand cupped briefly over her left butt cheek.

"And those are the only places?" His gaze held hers, searching for any secrets she might try to hide.

At her nod, Bryce tamped down the primal urge to mark his territory. Leaving bruises on her would do nothing but create rumors throughout the building. Not that their marrying wouldn't send a wave of whispers rippling through the staff, but love bites the size of silver dollars would only increase the rumors. With the way the Makepeaces had tried to steal his position from him, he wanted to keep them in the dark about his marrying Lawrence for as long as possible.

As she stood before him, the dark curls between her legs glistening with her arousal, Bryce fought the urge to smile. His first challenge had presented itself, and now he needed to analyze how she responded to it.

Taking her wrist, he led her around the coffee table and settled onto the cushions of the sofa. When she moved to sit beside him, he shook his head. "Stand there." Releasing her hand, he presented his first question. "What were my instructions on Saturday?"

The puzzled look on her face reassured him that she was searching for the rules he'd laid down when they'd struck their bargain. "Which ones?" Mattie asked, her tone reflecting both confusion and suspicion.

"About other men."

Her gasp was all he needed to warn him. Before she could move away, he sat up and tugged her, facedown, over his knees.

"You can't possibly..." she cried, her body twisting in his hold.

The first blow stilled her wriggling. Sharp enough to sting but not truly hurt. Bryce waited. "What were my instructions?" A firm strike on the opposite cheek followed his request.

"But he isn't...owww!"

A third blow landed, stifling her protest and drawing a cry from her lips. More protests followed the fourth and fifth swats, each just a shade more solid than the last, but the safe word remained unspoken. After another strike on a rosy cheek, Bryce asked again, "What were my instructions?"

Emotion clogged her voice, but he clearly heard Mattie's response. "No contact with former lovers." Pushing off his knees, she knelt beside him, her shimmering eyes glaring at him, not with tears—his cock ached, pressing against his trousers as he realized it was arousal heating her gaze even as she finished arguing. "But he isn't—"

Lifting her onto his lap, Bryce shook his head. "No other men." Tracing his lips along the jaw Victor had held still, he continued, "You don't allow *any* other men to touch you, Lawrence." While one hand trailed over each of the spots she'd identified as where Victor had touched her, the other eased the high heels from her feet. His lips followed his fingertips, ghosting light kisses over the soft skin of her upper arms, before easing across to the slope of her left breast. The strawberry red nipple poked upward, begging for attention, as he eased Mattie onto the cushions beside him.

"You asked a question earlier." Bryce's reminder pulled Mattie's focus away from the teasing of his lips.

"Uhmmm, yeah," she muttered. Threading her fingers through his silky hair, she arched closer, hoping he would stop talking and pay attention to the nipple begging for attention.

"Something about men and kissing," Bryce continued, his lips moving downward to coast over her ribs and hip.

As he shifted away, her body settled into the soft cushions of the sofa, the smooth leather cool against her heated skin. The moment her sore bottom touched down, Mattie couldn't hold back a whimper. Planting her heels in the cushion, she lifted her hips, avoiding the pressure and the strange tingling it sent through her body.

"No, Lawrence." One broad palm covered her belly, pressing down.

Heat entered his eyes as he watched her absorb the pain as her bottom settled onto the leather. The sensations accompanying the pain confused and aroused her. Before she could figure out why her body was reacting the way it was, Bryce eased apart her thighs and settled between them.

Propping his weight on his bent elbows, he drew her gaze back to his. "You likened Victor's kiss to that of an octopus, right?"

"Y-yes, slimy and too many tentacles." She repeated her earlier analogy, her mind spinning and barely capable of registering his question.

"Cock of the Walk."

"What?"

Bryce chuckled, his fingers stroking through the curls beside her ear. "It's one of three kinds of kisses."

"There are 'kinds' of kisses?" Mattie's attention was now focused on the heat the closeness of his body engendered. Through his trousers, she could feel the firm length of his arousal against her hips, reassuring her that, though his words might seem offhand, his body was responding to hers.

"Over the years, I've discovered there are basically three types of kisses. Each one can have any number of kisses, but the styles are broken down into three distinct categories."

Needing to feel him, Mattie eased her hands up to the buttons on Bryce's shirt. Fingers hovering over the first, she waited until he nodded approval before opening it. Keeping the conversation going as she slid each button free of its hole, Mattie offered, "So the slimy, groping kind of kiss is…"

"Cock of the Walk." He pushed himself up so she could tug the tail of his shirt loose from his trousers before he settled back into place, this time allowing his hips to rest firmly over hers. "It's the type of kiss I consider the one-night stand. Lots of tongue and groping, little finesse."

Mattie grimaced at the reminder of the other man's attentions.

Bryce chuckled. "I take it Victor needs to work on his finesse?"

"And how." She nodded, her gaze transfixed by the tanned muscles roping his chest and abdomen. A T-shaped dusting of fine, white blond curls stretched between his nipples and arrowed down toward his belly.

The brush of Bryce's lips beside hers drew her attention back to his face. "Then there's the Big Brother."

"Big Brother?"

He nodded. "Um-hm." Leaning down, he pressed a light kiss to her cheek, then one to her forehead. "You know. The type a close friend or relative gives when they haven't seen you in a while."

"Oh, familial," Mattie grated out. Having him so close, his attentions focused on her, spun the coil of arousal tight in her belly. The awareness of her nude body pressed against his was playing havoc with her concentration. The heat from her spanked bottom seemed to be seeping into her pussy, warming it, drawing forth fluids. "Oh—" She cleared her throat as she tried to ignore the sensations stirring between her thighs. "Okay, so there's the Big Brother and the Cock of the Walk. What's the third type?"

"That's the kiss that takes the most time and the most patience to learn," Bryce assured her.

The wry grin lifting his lips was a subtle warning Mattie recognized, but with her senses as muddled as they were, she was unable to prepare for it. Instead, she stepped into the trap he'd set and didn't realize it until it snapped closed behind her. "It is? Why?"

"Because the 'Knock the Socks Off'-type kiss incorporates all the senses." His gaze held hers as one hand slipped beneath her hair to stroke the muscles at the back of her neck. With his weight braced on the arm beneath her, the other hand rose to stroke the fluttering pulse at the base of her neck.

The warm, callused fingers trailed over the slopes of her breasts as his words whispered against her lips. "If done correctly, the sense of touch increases the arousal." His cheek touched hers before smoothing along the firm jut of her jaw. "The feel of a lover's skin against a fingertip or cheek heightens the awareness, the knowledge of the inevitable conclusion just waiting for them."

The rasp of his evening beard seemed loud in the silence of the office. "Hearing adds to the tension building between a man and a woman. The rustling of fabric against fabric, or"—his hips pressed into hers, the feel of his hard length stilling her breath as he finished—"fabric against flesh, stirs images that stimulate and seduce."

His lips settled over hers, sipping at the curves, coaxing them open before delving inside to tangle his tongue with hers. Taking his time, he teased and taunted her with a rhythmic advance and retreat until her own lips sought his as he pulled away.

"But one of the best things"—his voice was a raspy throb as he eased his hands from beneath her and moved down her body, pressing a sucking caress on a breast, a tug on a beaded nipple, a nip from his teeth to the light swell of her stomach—"is that the 'Knock the Socks Off' isn't limited in where it can be used."

The breadth of his shoulders pressed her thighs apart as he dipped his head and settled his mouth over the damp curls hiding her sex. The first swipe of his tongue over the sensitive flesh had Mattie crying out. The second had her hips arching upward, her hands clutching at the leather beneath her.

Around her waist, Bryce used one arm to reduce her movements while the second slipped between her thighs and parted the swollen petals, exposing the wet, pink flesh to his attentions. The vibrations of a rumbling growl set off tiny explosions through her center. Heat filled her belly and worked its way up through her chest and into her cheeks as the juices of her arousal seeped out. His hold kept her from pulling away, and the long, slow swipe of his tongue over her exposed flesh pulled another cry from her lips.

Chapter Six

"Christ." His words were muffled against her skin as he feasted on the delicate flesh. "You taste so good, Lawrence. Sweet, but just a bit spicy." Again she shifted beneath him, but he stilled her movements with his words. "The urge to spread you out and feast on you was hard to override on Saturday."

Lifting his head, he captured her gaze and continued, "But we needed to focus on setting the ground rules, so I held off." Now that she'd broken one of them and taken her punishment without protest—or much of one—his reward for abstaining lay before him.

Settling his grip more firmly at her hips, he stilled their rocking while using the fingers of his left hand to tease the hidden knot of nerves from beneath its hood. The discovery that his wish regarding the size and nature of her clitoris was granted had him pressing his aching cock into the leather seat beneath him. Testing her arousal was the primary goal of this particular exercise, Bryce reminded himself. The fact that one of the benefits happened to allow him to indulge in suckling and teasing her clit had no bearing on the situation.

Stroking his tongue, and then his fingers, over the sensitive nubbin, Bryce monitored the various reactions of her body from the pulse of her hips, the increase in her respiration, to the steadily increasing production of juices. Sliding away from the knot he'd coaxed from its hiding place, Bryce slipped his fingers into the tight opening of her sheath. First one finger was introduced to the narrow channel. Stroking slowly, he carefully investigated the throbbing walls, searching out and finding the soft spots that stole her breath or caused the muscles to clutch at his digit.

With his tongue and teeth stroking and nipping at the tiny bit of flesh, Bryce coaxed her tight pussy to accept a second digit. The way her body tensed had him pausing. Despite the moisture coating his fingers, the walls surrounding them resisted deeper penetration. His thumb replaced his mouth on her clit as he lifted his gaze to her face. Slow, deliberate pressure increased the flush of arousal reddening her breasts, neck, and cheeks, but the difficulty in advancing remained.

Before he could ponder his suspicions further, the flutter of her intimate flesh and the shuddering breaths signaled her approaching climax. Needing to test her ability to hold off orgasm, he slipped his fingers free of her channel. Her protest filled the room as she released the cushions beneath her to clutch at his shoulders.

"Hush," Bryce ordered, fighting his own need to strip away his slacks and slide into her hot, wet pussy. Lifting his moist fingers to her lips, he coated the swollen, pink curves with her juices. "Taste, Lawrence," he urged, holding her stunned gaze.

Even as he watched her tongue tentatively sample her flavor, he moved his fingers to the stiff peaks of her breast, anointing each crest thoroughly. Heat flared in her eyes, and the pressure of her fingers on his shoulders would surely leave impressions from her short nails. Holding her gaze, he licked the last of her moisture from his fingertips before dipping his head toward her breasts.

Millimeters from his goal, he stopped, lifted his head just enough to regain her attention, and ordered firmly, "No climaxing." Leaving her little time to absorb his command, he fastened his lips around one nipple and concentrated on removing the residue of her passion from the hot, puckered tip.

Beneath him, Mattie squirmed. Her hips thrust against his rock-hard cock while her fingers flexed, leaving more half-moon-shaped indentations in his skin. The heated flesh of her thighs wrapped around his waist. Pleas spilled out between gasps and moans, each sound increasing his arousal and determination to extend her passion for as long as possible.

Long before he'd had enough, but not as soon as he'd expected, the first shudder of climax rippled through her body. She'd held herself still so long that he knew from her movements that she'd fought coming until gaining his permission. Returning his lips to hers, he sipped the last of her taste from her mouth, eased away and down, so her thighs once again bracketed his shoulders, and urged, "That's it, Lawrence, come for me."

Another gasp slipped between her lips as the two fingers within her began thrusting in tandem with the attentions of his tongue on her clit. Yes, she'd touched herself and masturbated before, but the orgasms she'd attained had never been anything like this. The knot twisting tighter and tighter within her belly frightened her with its intensity. Her tits felt as if they would explode; they swelled, and the nipples were so hard she didn't think they'd ever return to normal. Her eyes closed, her head tipped back, as she relinquished control and let herself drown in the sensations washing over her.

Those last three words were her undoing. Unable to hold back her cries, she lost herself in the pulsing wash of orgasm. Stronger than any she'd created on her own, she was barely aware of the way her thighs squeezed tight around his shoulders. Moisture flooded her passage and coated her thighs. The swipe of Bryce's tongue and the growl of approval rising from his chest as he lapped up her juices sent another wave of pleasure through her, surprising her at the almost-painful pulse of her body.

Spent, her body feeling boneless and tired, Mattie lay beneath his rangy frame as he licked away all evidence of her climax. Aching but sated, she remained still, awaiting Bryce's next direction. His first words were a bit of a surprise, but not unexpected considering how intense her reaction had been to his attentions.

"I take it it's been some time since you've had sex, huh?"

"Mmmm-hmm," Mattie responded, without giving away the whole truth. *Try never.* Of all the things she knew about Bryce, the one thing that worried her most was his avoidance of innocents. Having watched him over the years, and the relationships he'd drifted in and out of, Mattie concluded that a woman's virginity was the last gift Bryce would want bestowed on him.

Bryce shifted into a seated position, tugging her along so she straddled his lap, her wet pussy centered over his cock, held safely away from her flesh by the barrier of his slacks. One hand stroked the damp curls away from her cheeks and behind her ears, while the other seemed to measure the weight of her breasts, the beat of her heart, perhaps even the texture of her sweat-soaked skin as he smoothed his callused palm over her body. The lower it moved, the more ragged her breathing grew.

Even as she thought to voice a protest at the arousing stroke of his fingertips, he slipped them between her thighs and had one finger buried knuckles deep inside her. Arching upward, her hands clutched at his shoulders. "Please." She wasn't quite sure what she was begging for, she only knew the need was growing again.

His gaze held hers as he pulled her close; his free hand shifted from her cheek to the nape of her neck, and finally, to her back. "Please what, Lawrence?" Lips drifting against hers in a soft caress, he slid his hand against her back in counterpoint to the digit stroking the moist walls of her pussy.

"I…" Mattie swallowed, her thoughts lost in the tangle of feelings his touch invoked. Unbidden, her body moved in the same rhythm as his touch. Rising and falling with the advance and retreat of each stroke of his finger.

"Please what, Lawrence?" Bryce prompted again, his thumb coming into play against her sensitive clit. Circling, then applying just the lightest pressure to the nerve-rich tissue, he smiled against her lips. "Tell me."

"Uhmmmm." Her eyes squeezed shut, the better to enjoy the building tension constricting her lower belly. Words were lost to her as she indulged her body's need to ride the digit filling her.

Teeth nipped at her ear, and his breath stirred the damp curls as he whispered, "Your ass isn't the only part of you that needs stretching, huh, Lawrence?"

A startled cry left her lips as he again tried to introduce a second finger into her taut sheath. Despite her earlier orgasm and the flow of her body's own lubricating syrup, Mattie tensed at the painful stretching the new invader was creating. Even more confusing for her was the spike in arousal that bit of pain was producing.

It went against so many preconceived notions that she'd held, this correlation of pain and pleasure. At the same time she railed at herself that the pain shouldn't turn her on so much, a part of her was remembering the stirring his spanking had induced. The application of his hand against her ass followed by her sore butt against the sofa cushions had turned her on more than any other man she'd dated.

Holding still, thighs tensed to avoid lowering herself farther onto his broad fingers, Mattie met his gaze. How could eyes that were usually so cool and emotionless when conducting business be so hot, intense? She wasn't sure. But the darkening centers focused on her, as if he needed to gauge every emotion that flickered across her face.

"Do it, baby," he whispered, a blend of challenge and encouragement in his voice.

The soft pressure of his thumb on her clit teased her. His hand on her back slipped upward. A twist and pull warned her that he'd tangled his free fingers in the loose curls spilling down her back and had her mouth opening on a gasp. His next words had the breath freezing in her lungs.

"If we don't get you stretched, darlin', you'll never be able to take my cock. And much as you like me paddlin' your butt, that's how much I've been cravin' your sweet little candy box. You need to be able to take at least three fingers for me to fit, and even then, it'll be tight." His thick drawl hinted at how turned on he was.

His words had her body soaking his hand, the flow of her cream dripping over and around his touch as she unlocked her muscles and lowered herself, centimeter by centimeter, onto his probing fingers. With each advance, a moan passed her lips, the blend of pain and pleasure intertwined, stirring the heat in her abdomen into a steady blaze. His whispered words of praise were a muted jumble of sound, indistinct encouragement registering, but not clear in the chaos of her mind. Images of repeating this same slow descent with his penis rather than his fingers stretching her had Mattie swallowing heavily to wet her desert-dry mouth. *If his fingers feel this good, just how hot will his cock feel?*

She must have spoken the thought aloud because Bryce's laughter preceded his words. "Like pure, fuckin' heaven," he assured her.

* * *

Settled in the darkness of his studio, Bryce gazed at the completed painting on the easel. His latest work sat in the center of the room. In the morning and afternoon, the broad expanse of windows on the twin sets of French doors and the skylight above allowed him the luxury of natural light to work in. Now, with the pale, milky wash of moonlight drifting over the stretched canvas, Bryce admired the image.

The background was a mixture of colors: gold, amber, sienna, and walnut. Hues most complementary to the olive tone of Lawrence's skin. Each of these shades accented her riot of chocolate curls and highlighted the voluptuous curves of her small frame.

Every line, every curve his portrait revealed was taken from his imagination and eight years of careful, discreet observation. In a few days, his planning would come to fruition. She would be his. His fingers tightened on the crystal rocks glass in his hand as he visualized his woman, just as he'd painted her.

Arms bound above her head, pussy tight around his cock as he thrust in counterpoint to Richard's advance and retreat within Mattie's snug little ass. Each emotion would dance across her expressive features, heightening his arousal as her climax built. He could practically feel the wet clasp of her flesh. Hear the ragged breaths soughing in and out of her lips. Sense every subtle tightening of muscle as her body wound closer and closer to release, intensifying his own arousal until the rhythmic ride of his cock within her would escalate into a hammering frenzy of motion. Spiraling need demanding he and Richard fuck her harder, faster in order to assist her in achieving euphoric oblivion. Reaching for the single moment when every nerve in her body stretched to its very limit before snapping. Flinging her entire being into an ecstatic free fall that seemed to last forever and just the blink of an eye all at once.

Bryce released the tight grip he had on the crystal as he envisioned the hazy, dreamlike quality his possession and sharing of her would produce in Mattie's wide brown eyes. The deep chocolate color would turn black as she slipped into orgasm. Her strawberry lips would part with a gasping cry of his name, and her tight, wet cunt would squeeze his cock dry.

Lifting his gaze back to the painting, Bryce smiled. He was looking forward to enacting his eight-year fantasy. After the events of this evening in his office, his imagination now had more material to work with. The grip of her sheath was tighter than he'd thought; just as the taste of her cream left him wanting more. As for the look on her face—his free hand dropped to stroke the hard evidence of his arousal—watching her come as she fucked herself on his fingers surpassed any fantasy he could have contemplated.

With five more days to go, he knew the need to take her completely would test his control, but it would all be worth it once she married him. Introducing her to the world she'd been born to inhabit, it was his responsibility to protect her even as he pushed her boundaries. His own disquiet at the thought of sharing her would need to be harnessed, despite his never having experienced it with any of his other lovers. Once he'd shared Lawrence with Richard, everything would return to normal. He had to keep reminding himself of that. It was all falling into place.

Just as he'd planned.

By the end of the week, the oils should be dry to the touch, thanks to the alkyds he'd mixed with the paint. The leather for the frame was coiled and waiting for him to braid into a rope on the workbench against the wall. Taking a sip from the scotch he'd poured earlier, he reached for his cell phone and punched in one of the programmed numbers.

A deep male voice answered, "Henderson."

"David?"

"It's past eleven, Halsey."

"I need you to do a background check."

"Couldn't this wait…?"

"I need details."

The private investigator paused, seeming to understand the curt tone as one not to be argued with. "Who?"

"Lawrence."

"Lawrence who?"

"My Lawrence."

"Mattie?"

The surprise in David's voice made Bryce smile. "Yes."

An exasperated sigh sounded over the phone. "My father did a thorough background search when you hired her."

"Not what I want." Taking a swallow of his drink, he waited for the mellow burn to loosen the twist in his gut. The damned knot had developed the moment he'd contemplated another man teaching Mattie how to use her mouth to bring pleasure. After the time he'd spent getting her pussy to accept his fingers, the knot had only tightened further.

"I want to know every man she's ever been involved with, dated, or had coffee with in the last eight"—he caught himself—"no, ten years."

"How detailed?"

"Down to the type of condom they used."

"Staking your claim?"

He ignored the quip. "I want it before the end of the week."

David was still cursing as he hung up. Setting his drink on the arm of his chair, Bryce rose and approached the painting. He didn't attempt to touch the paint, knowing that the medium wasn't fully dry, but his eyes traced the dark chocolate curls depicted on the canvas. It was most satisfying to know that his imagination had been accurate, all the way down to the carmine red of her nipples.

* * *

"I may not survive this week, Lyssa, so I need to know what you want when I write my will." Mattie lay sprawled across the wide sofa in Lyssa's living room, her body exhausted but well satisfied.

Looking up from the drawing table behind which she was perched on a tall stool, Lyssa examined her. The rise of her blonde eyebrows and the smirk on her lips assured Mattie she probably looked as debauched as she felt.

Hell, she had to grin herself. She'd never considered debauched such a stimulating and sexy term until she'd stumbled out of Bryce's office two hours ago. A long, hot shower later, she'd pulled on her sloppy jeans and a sweatshirt and headed for her sister's house.

"I guess I don't need to ask if he agreed to your deal."

Groaning, Mattie sat up and pulled one of the jewel-colored throw pillows into her lap. "Yup. One week to show me what it would be like to be his submissive."

"And?"

"If I decide I can't handle it, we'll still get married, but he won't ask me to submit to his Dominant side."

Lyssa leaned an elbow on the table and propped her chin on her fist. "And if you can handle it?"

"While we're married, if he needs to indulge in some bondage or Dominant/submissive play, he'll come to me for it."

The look on Lyssa's face was hard to read. It seemed she had a mixture of amusement, surprise, and trepidation fighting to take over, but curiosity won when she finally asked, "So, how'd you like it?"

"It?" Mattie wasn't sure just what "it" Lyssa meant.

"Sex."

Heat filled her cheeks as she cleared her throat. "I didn't...I mean, we aren't..." Drawing a deep breath, she paused and tried again. "We didn't have sex. Well, oral sex, but not...I mean, intercourse. We didn't have intercourse."

Lyssa choked on her laughter. "Why not? If you're getting married anyway, why not indulge the need?"

Frustrated because those were the same thoughts whispering through her own head and ticked off that despite her climaxing multiple times, there was still an ache she couldn't stop, Mattie grabbed one of the other pillows from the sofa and tossed it at her sister. The soft cushion *whumped* against the wall, carefully aimed to avoid the swatches of fabric pinned in place. "Because I don't want to have to remember the sub sex."

That only made Lyssa laugh harder. Leaving the stool, she gathered the pillow from the floor and tossed it back on the couch. "That doesn't make any sense."

Mattie rolled her eyes. "If I can't handle the Dominant/submissive stuff, we won't do it. Which means we'll just be having regular sex. And if I have sex while seeing if I can handle being a submissive, then when we're having regular sex, I'll always be comparing it to the other kind of sex and wondering if Bryce is doing the same thing, and it'll drive me crazy."

Lyssa shook her head. "Sorry, sis, but you're already there."

"I know." Mattie buried her face in the pillow and groaned. "This is all crazy. I should have never even thought about trying to get him to think of me that way."

Pulling the pillow from her face, Lyssa smiled at her. "It's going to be okay. Now, just breathe. In and out." She waited for Mattie to follow her instructions and then nodded. "That's it. Just take your time. Calm down."

Relaxing back into the cushions, Mattie shook her head. "I'm not sure about it, Lys. If I'm this freaked out over a spanking and oral sex, just how bad am I going to be when he really starts with the kinky stuff?"

"Spanking?" Lyssa whistled and curled onto the couch. "Tell me more."

Mattie couldn't stifle the laughter her sister's eager look prompted. "Knock it off."

Leaning an arm on the back of the sofa, she rested her head against her propped fist and smirked. "It got your mind off freaking out, right?" Reaching out with her other hand, Lyssa patted Mattie's knee. "Listen, you're curious and scared and excited. I remember what it was like the first time I thought about having sex."

"Oh ancient one, tell me!" Mattie yelped when Lyssa pinched her leg. "Ow." Rubbing at the spot, she grimaced. "You're only six years older than me, Lys, and I'm sure there were a dozen guys trying to get you into bed."

"Maybe, but only one succeeded, and I wasn't stupid enough to try it again, thank you very much." There were very few occasions when Lyssa's voice filled with that bitter tone; most of the time it was when they discussed their parents.

"That bad?"

It was Lyssa's turn to flop back against the sofa cushions. "Let's just say, it was disappointing."

"I'm sorry."

Her sister waved off her apology. "Not your fault, Mat. But I can understand what you mean about not wanting to have to remember one type of sex while you're having another kind."

Chapter Seven

If he could videotape this image, he would. The sight of Mattie stretched across his desk, her skirt folded neatly beside her, panties on top of it, was the stuff of fantasy. Watching the wet, pink lips of her pussy swallow the last two inches of the silver vibrator he was working in and out of her had his own cock sitting up and demanding attention. The scent of her arousal filled his nostrils, assuring him that his directions and his touch had produced the slick cream coating the shiny surface of the toy.

"That's it, baby, take it all," he encouraged, his eyes rising to take in the expressions crossing her face. Gauging just how deep and how fast he could press the vibe, he noted her sharp inhalations as he fed the last few inches into her. "Been so long, we don't want you too sore…"

Lawrence, being who she was, didn't disappoint him with a lame response. Instead, between moans and gasps, she reminded him, "You're still assum…*ahhh*…assuming I'll be…*eeee* able to h-handle…*oh God, more*…submitting."

Even as she protested, her short nails flexed into the padded desk calendar on the smooth mahogany surface, and her ass lifted to help press the last bit of silver tube inside.

"You're doing so well now," he taunted. He waited, anticipating her response, and then eased the motor on.

And wasn't disappointed.

A delicate shudder racked her frame. The already-stiff nipples grew dark as the heated flush moved from her breasts upward. Dropping his gaze to the moisture glittering in the dark curls at his fingertips, he could feel the smile on his lips widen, and the throb of his erection kept time with each flutter of her labia.

Hooking her legs around his hips, Bryce eased forward, the hand between her thighs shifting to free his cock from his pants while he braced his weight on the hand he set on the desk just behind her hip.

Her eyelids slid open as his heated length pulsed against her mound. The soft curls teased the underside as he flexed his hips. Each delicate scratch pulled his balls tighter to his body, forcing him to restrain his need to climax. It taxed his control even more as images of her mound, waxed smooth and glistening with her juices, flashed across his mind.

Keeping his thumb hooked over the top of his shaft, his fingers twisted the base, increasing the hum and vibration of the toy, drawing another moan from Mattie. Her eyes dropped to take in his length and grew wide once she saw it. Leaning forward, he breathed a chuckle into her ear. "Told you three fingers would be a tight fit, darlin'."

Taking a closer look, Bryce realized it wasn't fear that widened her eyes, but interest. Settling her weight onto her left hand, Mattie cautiously reached for his member, halting when her fingertips were just brushing the crest. Wide eyes met his before she whispered her request.

"May I?"

Cupping his fingers over hers, he nodded. "Please."

Her touch was light, whisper soft, drifting over his crest, dipping into the hole to feel the texture of the silky drops of precum bubbling from it. Sliding her fingers over the glans, she investigated the ledge, tracing the ridge of flesh separating the knob from the shaft and stimulating the production of more creamy droplets of arousal.

When she wrapped her fingers around the shaft, he pressed against them, letting her know just what type of pressure needed to be exerted against his flesh. "Stroke it, babe," he encouraged, his hand hovering over hers to allow the perfect hold. Just the right force and pressure to increase the stimulation.

The taut muscles in her thighs tensed against his hips. She shifted, moaning at the press and vibration of the toy still lodged inside, her hand tightening around his shaft. Her eyes remained on the motions of her hand, watching the slide of her fingers over his flesh, noting the subtle thrust of his hips as he aided her in her caress.

Moving his hand from around hers, he gripped the silver vibrator, eased the motor to a higher level, and pulled it free of her sheath, stopping just shy of her entrance before pushing it back inside. Atop his desk, Mattie shuddered, her back arching and her hand tensing on his cock. He waited, wondering what his woman would do next.

Her chest expanded as she drew a deep breath. Holding it, she closed her eyes, released the air in a slow, soft exhale before opening her eyes and meeting his gaze. The heat simmered in her brown eyes, darkening and enlarging the pupils until only a narrow ring of chocolate remained. "Show me."

Her whisper slid over his skin. The tone challenged his Dominant nature and the need to test her response rose up. "Show you what, Lawrence?" he queried, wanting her to be clear in her demands.

"How you want to fuck me," she retorted, her hand flexing around his length, her thumb skimming the leaking tip.

With her gaze locked on his, she released his cock and lifted her dampened thumb to her lips. The slow swipe of her pink tongue over the pearly drop of his cum drew more from his body. When she wrapped her lips around her thumb and suckled it, Bryce couldn't stifle the groan that rose in his chest.

"Take off your blouse." His order was clipped, emotionless.

Shrugging off the already-open garment, Mattie shed her top, then the lacy bra that matched her panties. Bracing her hands on the desk behind her, she continued to wait for his next command.

"Lie back, Lawrence."

She did so by lowering herself to her elbows before settling her back against the padded desk cover. Arousal battled defiance in her eyes, but her need won out. It was only a matter of time, though, Bryce knew, before her will would override her need, and he'd have to punish her again. He was looking forward to that. Now, though, she needed to understand that his possession wouldn't be an easy one.

Despite his own need to touch her, he tucked his erection back into his trousers and secured it behind the zipped placket once again. His shirt and tie had been shed earlier when he'd drawn her into his office after the last of the staff had left for the day. "You want me to show you how I intend to claim you?"

"Fuck me," she corrected.

His hackles rose at the distinction she was making, but he controlled the need to shake her. To make her admit that his claiming of her was what she desired most. Hell, the way her eyes followed him when she thought he wasn't paying attention more than warned him of her interest. Why she was trying to deny it now, he wasn't sure, but he'd find out soon. "There's a difference, Lawrence, between claiming and fucking."

Before she could voice the response he could see in her eyes or hovering on her lips, he tugged her hips to the edge of his desk and wrenched the vibrator to the very entrance of her channel. Holding her gaze, he twisted the toy to its highest setting and shoved it deep inside her. Twice more he pulled it free and forced it back. One of his hands rose to grip the hair at the back of her head when she attempted to turn away from him.

Keeping her attention on him, he explained, "Fucking takes care of only one person's needs, baby. It's quick, hard, and only one gets to come." Pulling the vibrator free, he switched it off and set it on his discarded shirt. "Claiming," he assured her, leaning forward to slide his lips over hers, "satisfies both parties involved."

Releasing her hair, he smoothed his hands over her full breasts, tugging at the peaked nipples before coasting his fingertips over her belly. His lips followed, suckling the hard tips while his fingers tangled in the moist curls between her thighs. "We're going to have to see about trimming these," he murmured against her mound as he lowered himself onto his knees beside the desk. Parting her tender flesh, his tongue took one slow swipe through the drenched folds, lapping up the cream filling her pussy and glistening on her thighs.

"Trimming what?" Mattie gasped, her hips arching into his touch, fingers clutching at his shoulders.

"These." Bryce tugged again on the short, dark curls covering her pussy. His grin widened at the gasp and increased flow of her juices at the slight pain his teasing produced. "Not that I don't like your curls," he assured her. "I just like the sight of your skin more."

* * *

"There's something going on, but I haven't quite figured out what it is yet." Victor leaned back in his desk chair and waited for his caller's response.

"Well, you need to figure it out quickly." The crisp tone didn't mask the Southern drawl or the anger filling it.

Rising, he tucked his cell phone beneath his chin and set the last of the papers into his briefcase. "As soon as I have more information, I'll get word to you. For right now, you should be glad that the changes in the contract have been made and no one has caught on to them yet." Snapping the case closed, he gathered his coat and headed for the door.

"You have just under a month to figure out how Halsey is going to try to get past the board's demand for his resignation," the woman on the phone snapped. "The damned contract doesn't interest me at all."

"It should." Victor rolled his eyes as he snapped off the light and headed down the hall toward the elevator. "With the changes I put in after the negotiations were concluded yesterday and everyone signed, you'll be making a tidy little profit off the losses Halsey's going to have."

"I don't need more money; I want Halsey's shut down. Gone."

"That's what you'll get," he assured her.

"Considering that's what I hired you for, I'd better get it."

Victor didn't curse the dial tone that buzzed in his ear. Sliding his cell phone into his pocket, he rode the elevator to the underground garage. There was something going on. He could feel the undercurrents in the office as Jacob Halsey's retirement drew closer. Toss in some of the whispers coming down from the owner's offices, and Victor was pretty sure Halsey was making plans regarding the warning his father had given him less than a week ago. Members of the board were whispering, and Jacob was sporting a smug expression that didn't bode well for the Makepeaces' plans.

Getting into the pants of Halsey's administrative assistant should make sniffing out the secrets a little easier. Her protests and hard-to-get attitude would only last so long, and then he'd have her eating out of his hand. His grin faded a bit as he slid behind the wheel of his Jag. The warning he'd gotten the day before was unexpected. He knew Halsey took care of his employees, but Victor never thought the man would be interested in his secretary's personal life. Maybe there was more to Mattilda than met the eye. A little sifting through files should help solve the riddle.

* * *

The last of her climax shuddered through Mattie, leaving her limp, draped across Bryce's desk, and cognizant of the fact that she'd intentionally let herself come to see what Bryce would do. The spanking the previous day had left a tingle in her pussy for hours after she'd gone home. Now, she wanted to see what other punishments he had in store for her.

"Not good, Lawrence."

The rumble of disappointment in his voice was so heavily laced with amusement Mattie couldn't feel bad about misbehaving. Working her way back onto her elbows, she watched him rise over her, his mouth damp from her body's climax. Dropping her gaze to the thick wedge of flesh pressing against his trousers, she bit her lip to keep from moaning. It had felt so good under her fingertips. And the flavor of his cum had her mouth watering for more. She'd always thought the stories about women who liked to swallow were male fantasies until now.

Lifting her eyes to his, she didn't bother hiding her smug grin. "What?"

"Did I give you permission?" His hands assisted her in sitting upright and then lifted her to stand against him beside his desk.

Attempting to adopt a contrite look, Mattie shook her head. "No. Sorry."

"Pushing, baby?"

The challenge in his tone had Mattie's body on alert. Meeting his gaze, she realized though the amusement was still there, it was banked beneath the firm resolve he often displayed when entering into hardball negotiations. What she wasn't sure of was just how far he'd allow her to push. She dropped her eyes again to the bulge behind his trousers. The evidence of his arousal had moisture gathering between her thighs. That brief touch hadn't been enough, and here he stood, taunting her.

Lifting her eyes to his, she offered a chagrined look. "Is there any way I can make it up to you?" Allowing her fingers to drift over his firm chest, she waited, holding his gaze until her hands reached his waistband.

"Are you suggesting a bribe, Lawrence?"

She shook her head. "No, not a bribe. More like an incentive." She licked her lips as she glanced back at his face.

His fingers threaded through her tangled curls, tilting her face to his as he lowered his lips to hers. "It would depend on just what you have to offer."

The stroke of his tongue over her lips had Mattie's eyes falling to half-mast. Her fingers fumbled with the belt, button, and zipper on his pants, but she was able to gain access to the heated length of his cock. The smooth crown was damp against her fingertips, the evidence of his arousal leaking in tiny pearls from the slit. Keeping one hand around his crest, she smoothed her thumb over and around the soft flesh, while her other hand gripped his shaft with the firmness he'd shown her earlier and massaged his length from tip to base.

"Mmm." She purred against his mouth as his lips parted and his teeth nipped at the swollen curve of her bottom lip. "Would you like me to demonstrate?"

Taking a last swipe of her mouth with his tongue, Bryce smiled and lifted his head. "Please do. I'm interested in seeing if I'll like this incentive as much as you appear to."

His fingertips flexed against her scalp as she caressed his skin with her mouth. First, she moved over his chin, her teeth scraping at the beard stubble along his jaw, then farther down, sampling the taste of his skin along his throat. From there, Mattie investigated the texture of the firm brown disks on his chest, dusted with white blond curls. She discovered the application of her teeth and some suction yielded even more fluid from his cock, easing the slide of her hand up and down the shaft.

The tip of his erection was almost even with his navel by the time Mattie had settled on her knees in front of him. Abandoning the salty flavor of his skin, she focused her attention on the thick evidence of his arousal. In slow, smooth swipes, she learned the full length of his penis. From base to tip, she investigated every vein, ridge, and wrinkle using her lips and tongue. Again and again, she bathed his flesh, licking away the creamy residue he produced and murmuring her enjoyment of its flavor.

The smell of his skin intoxicated her. The taste had her thighs streaked with her own juices. If he'd let her, she could easily lose herself for hours just learning about this part of him. When the back of her hand brushed the heated sac beneath, she moved her mouth down as well. The scent was heavier, and a light dusting of curls covered the skin as she licked at the pouch before taking part of it into her mouth and suckling it.

Above her Bryce cursed, his fingers twisted in her hair, pulling at her scalp. The pain sent heat shooting directly to her pussy, increasing the juices flooding her channel and seeping onto her thighs.

"Fuck!" Bryce was mesmerized by the sight of his woman going down on him. The fierce hold he had on her hair eased as he realized it was actually painful to her when she moaned against his flesh. A strange emotion stirred in the back of his mind, sending a twist to his gut as he pondered which of her previous lovers had taught her these tricks. Who had shown her that pressure applied in just that spot could make a man's eyes roll back in his head?

Despite his years of training, he fought the urge to explode as she worked his balls with her mouth, rolling and sucking on first one side, then the other, before releasing them to return to his shaft. "You keep teasing me like that, baby, and I'll add another punishment to the one you've already earned." His threat was couched in a throaty rumble. Even he had a hard time recognizing his own voice.

Slumberous chocolate brown eyes blinked up at him as she lifted her head. The dazed look in her eyes had another curse slipping free. Taking his own cock in his hands, he rubbed the tip along her bottom lip, coating the pink curve with his seed.

He had to once again fight shooting his load when her tongue whispered over her lip before scooting around the head, lapping up the droplets slipping free. "Goddamn it, baby, just suck it!" He growled, pressing his cock forward, easing it past her lips, then cursing again as it butted up against her teeth.

The wet suction of her mouth morphed his curse into a groan, as she moved forward, taking as much of his length as was comfortable. Wrestling the need to thrust hard into the wet cave of her mouth, Bryce used every focusing method he knew to regain control. The stroke of her hand against the remainder of his shaft worked in tandem with the roll of her tongue around the part she suckled in her mouth.

Again his fingers clenched in her hair, adjusting her movements to draw out the sensations curling through his balls and winding up his spine. "That's it," he encouraged, his gaze reading the bliss spreading across her face. The concentration evident in her ministrations was visible on her face. With his impending climax near, he halted her motions.

"Lawrence," he rasped. "Look at me."

Her moaned protest had him fighting a smile. "Baby, I'm gonna come," he warned her. "Look at me," he ordered this time. Her eyes lifted to him. "You need to take it all. Don't waste a drop."

A short nod was her only response before her hands and mouth resumed their attentions. Short moments later, he allowed his release to roll through him. Trying to control the speed and amount of ejaculate he spilled, Bryce watched as Mattie received it without difficulty. She followed his directive and never spilled a bit as the spurts neared their end. He eased his still-firm penis from between her lips.

Drawing her to her feet, he walked her away from his desk to the leather sofa. Settling her on a cushion, he crossed to the wet bar to pull a bottle of water from the minifridge. After twisting off the cap, he took a quick swig, then returned to her side to hold it to Mattie's lips. When she lifted her hands to take the bottle from him, he used his free hand to stop her. "No, let me."

Again, she followed his command without question. Allowing him to set the pace for the water to flow into her mouth, she drank as much as he gave her and only stopped when he took the bottle away.

"That was a very nice incentive, baby." He smiled at her, enjoying the brief glow of triumph that lit her eyes when she seemed to think he wouldn't be meting out a punishment for her orgasm. "But you still broke rule number four."

"No coming without permission," she whispered, resignation in her voice.

But the triumph didn't diminish, making him wonder if she was testing to see if she could sway his decisions. If so, she would soon learn there was little he wouldn't do and very little that would draw him away from his course.

Easing his cock back into his pants, he fastened them before pulling his belt free. "Hands." He waited for her to comply.

Holding her hands out to him, he could feel Mattie watching him as he settled the belt around both wrists, then drew it tight. "Does it hurt?" he queried, sliding his fingers along the edge of the leather, checking to see if it bit into her skin.

Her hands twisted and tugged lightly. "No, it doesn't hurt." Her voice was soft, almost as if she was somewhat dazed.

Pulling on the belt, he drew her to her feet and led her to the cushioned ottoman. Grabbing a decorative pillow from the chair, he tossed it onto the floor. "Kneel." He watched her carefully lower herself to the floor with her knees sunk into the soft cotton. Dropping the belt, he returned to his desk and retrieved the items he'd purchased for her.

Her eyes followed him as he returned to sit in front of her on the ottoman. Each item was carefully scrutinized as he set it on the floor beside him. "Look at me, Lawrence." He kept his tone steady and firm. Guiding her through the next challenge would determine the depth of her trust in him. When she raised her gaze to his, he ordered, "Tell me our safe word."

"Pirate." She didn't hesitate.

"And when should you use it?"

Her eyes seemed to search his for a clue as to why he was asking these questions, before she answered, "I should use it if I become frightened or if what is happening goes beyond what I'm comfortable with."

"Very good." Bryce held up an item for her to see. "Do you know what these are?"

Mattie nodded. "They're nipple clamps."

"Sit up and hold your hands above your head." He waited until her bottom came off her heels and her hands rose above her head to move the belt aside. Leaning forward, he cupped one round globe in his hand and lowered his lips to the soft red tip. Taking his time, Bryce suckled and laved the tip to a stiff peak, her breast swollen with arousal and her breath hitching with each pass of his tongue over the crinkled bud. While it was still damp from his lips, he fastened the thumb ring over the turgid bead and then lowered his mouth to the other crest. Treating it to the same attentions, he drew back when the tip was swollen and hard and then slipped the second thumb ring over it. Dangling between the two clips was a thin platinum chain without adornment, merely connected to the base of each clip.

Smoothing his hand down her belly, Bryce grinned and marveled at the amount of moisture she'd produced between her thighs. "Does it feel good, babe?" he queried.

Eyes half closed, Mattie smiled. "Yes," she murmured, her hips undulating against his hand.

"Nuh-uhn," he warned, pulling his hand back to land a firm swat against her nether lips.

A shudder trembled through her body. Fists clenched, eyes squeezed shut, Mattie moaned, her body arched toward him, and her breathing stopped for the barest moment before resuming. "Again."

God, she looked beautiful, the heat of excitement flushing her body, her breasts adorned and her pussy wet, dampening his hand and her thighs as she sought another tempered blow. But he had other plans. "No."

From the floor, he retrieved the next item and held it up for her perusal. "Are you familiar with this?"

The trembling of her body increased. For a moment he wondered if the safe word would slip from her lips, but when she lifted her eyes to his, Bryce's erection surged to life within his confining trousers. The pupils had expanded, leaving thin rings of chocolate around them.

"Yes."

He waited as she swallowed and seemed to draw a deep breath, as if trying to calm herself.

"It's a flogger."

Oh Lord, the thoughts ran through her head, making her sway as she knelt before him. The sight of his dark, tanned chest, his cool green eyes assessing her every response, had her teetering on the verge of another orgasm. The sting of the clamps on her nipples had the muscles clenching in her womb. Her bound hands only increased the stimulation.

Now this. She was sure to earn another punishment if he applied the flogger to her ass. In her research about BDSM she'd read about their use and construction. Some could be inexpensively made with leather or suede and a wooden dowel, while others could sell online for hundreds, if not close to a thousand dollars. The one Bryce teased her with was one of the less-decorative designs. A simple black leather handle with a multitude of tails dangling below. Some braided, terminating in thick little knots, while others were flat, half-inch-wide strips of hide.

Taking his time, he rose from the footstool in front of her.

"Lower your hands." His order was cool as he gripped the dangling end of his belt.

Her teeth nipped at her bottom lip as she followed his directive. The jostling of her breasts by the movement sent another zing of sensation through her body.

"Lay across the stool, Lawrence. Breasts over the edge."

The wide, cushioned top was soft, cradling her body from ribs to midthigh. As she watched, Bryce deftly fastened the belt around the thick metal leg of the ottoman, allowing her to use her hands against the carpeted floor to brace her upper body, if necessary.

"Since you only disobeyed once, baby, I think we'll keep this part of your punishment to ten."

She couldn't look over her shoulder to read his expression. Her hair, left loose, had fallen forward to blanket her head in soft brown curls. When the first blow landed, she gasped and squirmed against her cushion. No harder than the strike of his hand against her ass, the flogger's different tails stung, but the same stirring of arousal tightened in her core.

"Call off each one, Lawrence."

Following his direction, she called out, "One."

The next one struck lower, just below the curve of her ass and with more force. "Two." She called off the next three in quick succession as the flogger landed heavily against her right cheek, her left cheek, and then both. The feelings coursing through her were nothing like the fear her father's beatings had instilled. Unlike her father, Bryce controlled his strikes, never allowing more than a small measure of his strength to power his blows. Body shaking, breasts heaving with each sobbing breath, Mattie waited for the next one, anticipating the thud and the resultant pain-pleasure melding with the burn in her nipples.

When it still hadn't come, she let the words loose that she battled against. "Please, more, Bryce. Again."

"Are you sure?" His hand stroked over the heated curve of her ass, pushing between her thighs to spread the swollen lips of her pussy.

She knew her juices had spilled free, soaking her curls and staining the expensive leather beneath, but she didn't care. Only the pleasure enfolding her made sense, and the means of maintaining that sensual fire dangled from his left hand. So close. "God, please, Bryce. Five more. Just…" Her back arched, ass pushing upward as if seeking the caress of the flogger.

Instead, the slow stroke of Bryce's tongue moved from the top to the bottom of her slit, lapping up her cream, teeth scraping over her swollen clit, and then nipping at her labia. The pulse of her orgasm started in the flutter of her pussy lips. Wrestling to contain it, Mattie clawed at the carpet beneath her fingers.

"No coming without permission, Lawrence," was growled against her pussy just before Bryce shifted away and the sixth slap of the flogger was laid across her bottom.

"Oh God, thank you, yes! Six," she cried out, barely aware of her words as the climax receded beneath the wave of pain-pleasure. The remaining four were given in quick succession, her voice going hoarse as she fought the orgasm building inside.

Chapter Eight

Bryce watched her move around her office the next morning as he leaned in the doorway. The burgundy blouse tucked into a narrow gray skirt accentuated the full curves that had stirred his interest when she first barged into his life eight years earlier. The swish of her braid had him grinning as he recalled the muttered curses from the night before when she'd attempted to regain some control of her wild curls.

"Lawrence," he called out, keeping his expression neutral even as his cock hardened at the sight of her body freezing in place. "My office."

He didn't check to make sure she followed. Leaving the door open, he waited until Mattie had crossed the threshold before using the intercom. "Dana, hold all calls for the next thirty minutes, please."

"Yes, sir." The crisp response of the receptionist preceded the *click* of the door lock sliding into place.

Collecting the nipple clamps from his desk drawer, he circled the desk and leaned against the front of it. "Blouse, bra, skirt, and panties, Lawrence."

In the same order he'd given, Mattie slid the buttons free on her blouse, shrugged it from her shoulders, and carefully folded it before handing it to him to place on the desk. The pale pink lace bra, gray skirt, and matching pink lace thong were quickly handed over, leaving her clad in sheer stockings and high-heeled gray pumps.

Spreading his legs, Bryce eased her to stand between them, admiring the steady way she awaited his next command, her arms still at her sides. The urge to smile was pushed down as he watched her breasts flush, the nipples growing hard beneath his gaze. Lifting his eyes to the tiny triangle of skin at the base of her throat, he studied the increase in its flutter as her heartbeat accelerated and her breathing grew rapid.

Raising the fingers of his left hand to her breast, he circled the areola, thumbing the hardening peak before pinching it between his forefinger and thumb. "Sore?"

"Ju—" She cleared her throat. "Just tender."

"Hmm." Taking his time, Bryce played with the tender nipple, tugging on it, giving it a little twist, gauging her response to each action. "Have you been thinking about your decision?" He kept his tone conversational, casual, the complete opposite of the intimate way in which he fondled first one breast before taking the crest in his mouth and turning his fingers loose on the other tip.

"*Ummm*...yes. I still...*ahhh*, I still need time."

Her breath hissed through her teeth as he attached the rings to her taut nipples. Her hands clenched into fists, but she held still. "Understandable, and there are three days left for you to think." Bryce rose from the desk and settled his hands at her waist. "But while you think, I've made an appointment for you at the spa. Sarah couldn't fit you in until Friday, but she is the best aesthetician as well as being the owner."

"The spa?"

The fingers of his left hand tugged at the dark curls between her thighs, drawing a heady moan from her lips. "I told you last night we needed to have this pussy trimmed."

"I can—"

"Uh-uh, baby," he whispered in her ear, his teeth nipping the lobe as he drew more moisture from her. "Waxed, not shaved. I want all but a little patch to be smooth as silk. No stubble."

Something in her eyes had Bryce waiting. She seemed reluctant to ask for several long seconds, before she finally blurted, "And my legs?"

He found it difficult to stifle his laughter, but the grin on his face must have revealed his amusement. The fire in her eyes and the way she crossed her arms beneath her breasts had Bryce fighting laughter again. "Of course, Lawrence. What else is a day at the spa for if it's not to pamper you?"

"Pamper, my ass." She snorted under her breath. "Try torture."

"Torture?"

She gave him a look so full of sarcasm, Bryce again found himself stifling his guffaws into sedate, tactful chuckles. "Torture, how?" he queried a second time.

"You lay on a cold, leather-padded table. Bare-assed naked, except for some stupid paper gown." Leaning against him, Mattie continued, "Just to have some strange woman slather your legs and pubis with hot wax and then rip it all off five minutes later."

Bryce winced. "Yup"—he nodded—"I have to admit that does sound a bit like torture."

"So, why don't you just—" Mattie smiled at him.

"No. Sarah is the best; she'll take good care of you."

"Yeah, right," Mattie groused.

"Yes. Now let me take a look at your ass."

Taken aback, Mattie gazed at him, not sure what to expect. "Excuse me?"

"Lean forward, hands on the desk," he directed, "and let me get a good look at your ass."

Not sure how serious he was, Mattie waited, sobering. "I don't…"

He shook his head at her. "Ah, be careful," he warned. "A refusal could be construed as breaking a rule. There are no employees around, and one of my responsibilities as your master is to inspect your body to make sure no damage was done last night."

She'd read about inspections but had assumed they were primarily a determination of whether the sub or slave's appearance and body met with the approval of a Dominant or master. Mattie had never considered it to be a responsibility of either party, but considering the paddling she'd taken the night before she could understand Bryce's concern. Hell, she'd had the same concerns herself this morning. Biting her lip, she asked, "What do you consider bruises?"

All teasing left Bryce's face. "Damn it, Lawrence. Bend over." He didn't even wait for her to comply. Moving to her side, he pressed against her upper back with one hand, while the other smoothed over her bottom.

Bracing her forearms on the polished mahogany, Mattie interlaced her fingers and waited. She winced at the colorful profanities Bryce spit out as he inspected the few bruises dotting her bottom and the skin just beneath it. When he pressed against the only dark one, despite her resolve not to, she flinched. Her eyebrows rose, and she couldn't help but glance over her shoulder at the inventive combination of curses that spilled out.

"You know"—she grinned back at him—"it's okay."

"Yes, bruises heal," he agreed. "But I'll have to remember…"

"Remember what?" She tried to rise, but his hand against her back halted her.

"To remind Richard."

"Why?"

"When he punishes you, we'll have to be careful not to bruise you too badly."

The mention of the company's vice president and director of mergers and acquisitions had her heart hammering in her chest as she recalled Bryce's comments about enjoying the feel of a woman sandwiched between him and another man. Her own mind had conjured images for years when she'd first heard the rumors, but fantasy was nothing like reality. She'd discovered that last night when he'd used the flogger on her. Yes, she'd enjoyed it, but the feelings it stirred also frightened her. It was possible the same could happen should she ever live out her fantasy of being the filling in a sandwich between Bryce and Richard. "Why would Richard punish me? He isn't part of our arrangement."

"He will be if you decide to become my sub, Lawrence," Bryce informed her coolly, his green eyes boring into hers.

"I..." Mattie wasn't sure what she was going to say, but the words froze at the chill look from Bryce.

"Don't play shy, Lawrence. You knew exactly what I meant when I discussed the manner in which I treat my submissives. That's what this entire week of experimentation is about." His hands smoothed over her ass, kneading the firm globes, before one dipped lower to delve between her labia, coating his fingers in the warm syrup of her arousal. "Preparing you for all the things I could expect of you."

Taking his time, Bryce used her own cream to lubricate the tight pucker of her rectum, sliding around the tiny hole, then over it with his wet fingertips. She waited, anticipating the initial penetration of his finger into her bottom, but it didn't happen.

Instead, he confused her momentarily with a directive. "Go into the bathroom. Top drawer, right side of the cabinet. Bring me the white tube."

Moving into the bathroom was easy. She used each step as a means to draw a slow breath and exhale, bringing her body under control. It was only after she realized what he'd had her retrieve that crossing the room dressed only in her hose and heels, with his crystal green gaze following her every step, grew difficult. Returning to his side, she held the lubricant out to him, heat flushing her face and coloring her breasts and chest as she contemplated what he might do next.

"When you agreed to marry me..."

"I told you I wasn't sure about being able to submit," she reminded him, her breathing tight, shallow, but not with fear.

"You still know what I am, Lawrence." Tilting his head to the side, he watched her cheeks flare with color. "You admitted you've heard the rumors. I never lied to you about the things I expect from my bed partners. I assured you that if you couldn't commit to a D/s relationship I could live with that decision."

"Yes, but..."

"But what? Did you think I'd ignore your choice and try to force you into agreeing?" His eyes narrowed as he stepped closer, towering over her. "Is that what you were afraid I'd do? Even after these last few days?"

Mattie grew flustered, her pulse jumping, her breasts hurting. "Yes... No... I..." she stammered, her mind whirling at the images his warning had stirred up, the smell of Bryce so close presenting its own distraction.

Anger flashed in his eyes, so she pushed aside the swirling emotions and held on to the fact that his behavior seemed to challenge her determination, her intent to see if she could take on the role of his submissive. Poking her index finger into his chest, Mattie snapped, "Don't you try to bully me, Halsey." She glared up at him, refusing to admit that no amount of prodding was going to move the man in front of her. "If you think you can scare me into changing my mind about this, you're wrong. This isn't some whim of mine. This isn't 'test the big, bad Dom.' I'm trying to make sure the marriage you and your father think you need to keep control of your company is sound enough to handle any conflict Frieda and her little minions decide to throw at us."

Bryce grasped her wrists. Effortlessly, he maneuvered them behind her back and held them with one hand. Leaning down, he gripped her chin between the thumb and forefinger of his free hand while his green eyes bore into hers. "I've never tried to intimidate or bully you, Lawrence."

"Oh yes, you…" she began, but his grip tightened fractionally, and he tipped her chin until she could feel the tension in her neck.

"No, Lawrence, I wanted to fuck you." He waited while her stunned mind absorbed his admission. "You waltzed into my office, calling me a pirate and condemning me for buying your foster family's boatyard, completely oblivious to how quickly my cock sat up and took notice of you."

She could feel the color fill her cheeks.

His fingers smoothed down her throat before sliding over her breast, tugging at the platinum chain. "While you stood there berating me in front of Gino, I entertained visions of fucking that vicious mouth, stripping you naked, tying you spread-eagle to the top of the conference table, and riding your lush little body until you couldn't scream anymore."

Mattie's lips moved, but no words came out. Her tongue stuck to the roof of her desert-dry mouth as his revelations sent pictures skittering through her mind, each more graphically arousing than the last. Bryce didn't seem concerned with her sudden speechlessness. His grip tightened on her wrists as his other hand drifted from her breast to the curve of her hip.

"You weren't ready for it eight years ago, Lawrence. You weren't prepared for what I would demand from you. Not then. You had your little-girl infatuation with me, but you're over it. More matured. Now, though"—his hand palmed her ass, squeezing appreciatively as he easily lifted her in his arms and moved toward the broad sofa—"now I've shown you some of what I'd like from you." Before she could react, Bryce released her wrists and had her laid out on the soft cushions clad only in her stockings and heels, her hands stretched and pinned above her head as Bryce settled into the space he made between her thighs.

"You…you agreed," Mattie whispered, her mind tumbling over itself trying to decide if her request to not have sex had been as wise as she'd thought it was. If he'd always planned on having her submit to his dominance, then maybe he'd always considered her capable of fulfilling that need.

"Yes," Bryce admitted, his lips lifting in a wry smile as he focused his attention on the quivering flesh of her full breasts. "And I'll stick to that agreement, babe." He lowered his lips to whisper across a taut nipple cinched by one of the purest metals in the world. His free hand caressed the curve of flesh. "That doesn't mean I won't spend the next two days preparing this sweet little ass to take my cock."

Mattie shook her head, not in denial, but in an attempt to focus her thoughts. She could feel her pussy pulse with arousal at his words. Scenes flashed through her mind of

Bryce bending her over the polished mahogany desk in his office and shoving his cock up her ass, or having him push her to her knees and slide it past her lips so she could suck him off. Remembering the flavor and feel of him in her mouth, against her tongue, her arousal grew with each consecutive thought, soaking her curls and tightening her nipples.

Bryce must have misread her motions, Mattie thought as his eyes narrowed and the tightening of his jaw emphasized the high, sharp angles of his cheekbones and patrician nose. Lifting his hips from between her thighs, she watched as he worked the thin leather belt from the waistband of his trousers. He had her hands bound and secured to the decorative wrought-iron post on the sofa before she even suspected what he had planned.

"Don't try to make me believe you don't know what I want from you, Lawrence," Bryce warned as Mattie tilted her head back to blink in amazement at her immobilized wrists. Though he settled his hips over hers, Mattie knew Bryce must have held the majority of his weight on his forearms as his hands framed her head and stared into her eyes. "No coming, Lawrence." His breath caressed her face. "Not unless you want a repeat of last night."

Leaning down he pressed his lips to hers, his eyes holding hers as he seduced her mouth open. His tongue slipped inside to explore.

Mattie's eyes closed as the warm mint and honey flavor of his mouth filled hers. The feel of his broad chest, still clad in a silk dress shirt and unbuttoned suit vest, teased her clamped nipples, the sensitive peaks swollen and aching.

Bryce eased his hips deeper between her thighs, pressing the hard evidence of his arousal against her mound, drawing a needy moan from deep within her.

Her mind still fogged by his touch, the caress of his lips as they slipped from hers and moved along the pulse pounding in her throat, Mattie voiced the only question that swam through her thoughts. "Why?"

"Because I want to taste that sweet little pussy."

Shaking her head, Mattie swallowed past the soft cry that left her lips as his fingers tugged at the taut peaks of her breasts, trying to remember the question that was so important to her. "No." She gasped, her legs drawing up to hold his hips close to hers. It was so hard to focus with her body's responses overwhelming her mind. "Why wait eight years?"

Lifting his gaze to hers, Bryce's expression was deadly serious. "Eight years ago what I wanted would have resurrected too many memories. It would have driven you away. But now your body craves what I can give it." He squeezed and twisted her nipple to create just the right amount of pain to heighten her pleasure.

Again he tugged and Mattie felt a gush of cream drizzle from her pussy. "The need to give up control to someone else isn't abhorrent to you, is it? It arouses you. Makes you wet." One hand slipped to the wet curls covering her mound. Moving lower on the sofa, Bryce used the breadth of his shoulders to keep Mattie's legs splayed while his hands returned to cup her breasts. His tongue dipped to taste the moist pink flesh held open and on display for him.

Mattie felt as if her mind exploded. The warm rasp of his tongue through that sensitive slit stole her breath and what little control she still had over her body. She could feel every stroke, each lick as he lapped at her swollen clit before moving on to circle the weeping entrance. She was barely cognizant of the wet suckling sounds, the low hum of appreciation and husky compliments Bryce voiced as he fed on her cunt, while the coil of arousal tightened deep in her belly.

"Always such a good little admin," Bryce teased as he lifted his head, his lips and chin wet with her juices, meeting her eyes as he parted the plump lips of her pussy and slid a finger into her tight channel.

She could feel the firm, callused digit delve deeper, pressing into her. Her belly tightened, her sheath pulsed around the alien presence. Then he touched something within her that made her gasp and groan aloud. Her hips lifted of their own volition, thrusting against his touch. His eyes held hers as he dipped his mouth back to the pink flesh spread before him.

A second finger pressed into her, causing her back to arch from the cushions, making her cry out softly at the pleasurable pain the stretching of her tight sheath induced. Bryce pressed a kiss, then lapped consolingly at the knot of nerves peeking from beneath its hood. "You're so fucking tight, Lawrence. Even after the last few days."

The wet sucking noises her pussy made as Bryce finger fucked her registered in a distant part of her brain. The rational, quiet part of her cringed with embarrassment at the base behavior, the animalistic pleasure coursing through her veins, while the hidden sexual being within her gloried in every sound, every gasp.

With each thrust of his fingers, Bryce pushed the rational part further and further away and imbued the sexual part of Mattie with strength and power. Confidence. Enough confidence that the sounds sliding out of her mouth changed from gasps and moans to words and demands; her hips kept pace with his hand, and her fingers curled around the cold wrought-iron bar, reveling in the feel of the leather binding her wrists.

"Oh God, faster, Bryce." Her voice was quiet but strong in the room. "Please fuck me. Fuck me!"

His throaty chuckle and the nip of his teeth on her nipple had Mattie's eyes snapping open. "No fucking until you make your decision." His lips and chin glistened as he lowered his mouth to hers. Mattie could taste herself on his lips. The smell of sex filled her nostrils as he ate at her lips, his tongue imitating the same thrusting motions as his fingers, the pace the same, just enough to keep her poised on the edge of orgasm, but not enough to push her over.

Against his lips she sobbed for release, she twisted beneath his fingers, but he wrenched control from her by lifting her hips. Only her upper back was still in contact with the sofa beneath her. Again he chuckled at her need, his lips leaving hers to smile down at her.

Frustrated and emboldened by the release of her vixen self, Mattie growled at him. "Bastard. Prick. Quit teasing and fuck me."

A thin white blond brow rose in challenge over Bryce's left eye. "Oh no, Lawrence. We made a deal, no sex—

fucking—until you decide yes or no. What we're doing here and for the next two days"—he easily maneuvered her belly down on her knees—"is making sure…"

She could feel him draped along her back, his hands gripping her hips. The solid length of his aroused cock stayed firmly secured behind the straining fly of his trousers. A subtle thrust of his hips and the column of hidden tissue parted the damp globes of her ass, the moist evidence of her passion having dripped into the crevice, lubricating the dusky flesh.

"This tight little ass is all ready to take my cock for a long, hard ride."

Mattie groaned as her pussy pulsed, empty and desperate to be filled again. She didn't move, not sure if her body would fly apart if she shifted even an inch, when Bryce's weight lifted and moved away from her. She heard the rustling of paper, a soft snapping sound, then the warmth of Bryce's hand settled on her bottom.

"I'm just going to make sure you're ready for that ride, Lawrence." His voice was deep, throaty with passion as his thumb and finger parted her cheeks. Mattie shivered, her nipples scraping the leather beneath her as she unconsciously swayed forward, trying to move away from the cool plastic he placed against the tight hole of her ass. In her mind she could see the nozzle of the tube of lubricant pressed against her, she'd imagined this scene for years. In the various books she'd read, and even when she used her own toys, it was always his touch, his face that preceded the first stinging stretch.

A little nudge, a gasp from her, a whispered word of praise from him, and Mattie could feel a generous amount of cool gel filling her. Still more gel was applied to the tight rosette before the cap was snapped shut and the blunt tip of Bryce's finger massaged the exposed puckered flesh.

"Should I remind you that sharing you with Richard has always been part of my plan?" Bryce suggested as he slowly circled, then pressed against her. "Don't fight it, Lawrence. Push back a little as I press in."

Mattie heard herself whimper, but it wasn't a pained or frightened sound. It sounded to her more like a pleading sound. She was surprised at the anticipation spiraling through her as she did as Bryce told her and pushed back as he pressed his finger into her ass up to the first knuckle. Sensitive tissue protested the invasion, but the sound of Bryce's voice as he began to speak distracted her.

"Over the years he and I have discussed it."

Mattie's head snapped around to meet his gaze over her shoulder. The motions of his finger as he pressed it deeper, massaging past gripping muscles, weren't nearly as distracting, nor as arousing, as the look she saw reflected in Bryce's gaze while he watched himself slowly, seductively accustom her back entrance for his use.

Looking up to see her watching him, Bryce nodded at her. "I'd always imagined fucking you here." His finger pressed deeper, spreading the lubricant as it advanced. "The tight grip, the expression on your face. I could see those. But the realization that you might take to your training so quickly, that I wondered about. There are other things we have yet to try."

He clucked his tongue at her and eased his finger out, then back in, sending a shiver rippling down Mattie's spine. As she bit her lip, he listened to Mattie attempt to stifle the moan building in her chest at the same time she became aware of the growing heat in her pussy, the tightening tension low in her belly.

"Take a deep breath, baby," he warned. A second finger began working its way in to join the first. The moan broke free and slipped past Mattie's parted lips while her need to push back, aiding the penetration of his fingers, increased.

"You take well to the flogger and my hand, Lawrence. The next thing you need to work on is your ability to hold off your orgasm. Your pleasure isn't our primary concern. You've read that, I'm sure." Her gasps and moans made his dick twitch, protesting its confinement, but Bryce ignored it. "As master, my needs supersede yours. Pleasing me is what should bring you pleasure." He watched as he buried both fingers in her tight passage, her hips rocking beneath his hands, part of the rhythm he'd built. It would probably take more than the remaining two days to prepare her, he reminded himself as he scissored his fingers inside her, stretching the passage gripping him.

He continued his instructions. "Although I enjoy watching you come"—at her confused look, he smiled—"breaking you of the habit of climaxing when you want should prove to be very satisfying for both of us."

Breathless and fighting the knot twisting in her belly, Mattie asked, "Do I always have to ask permission to do something?"

Bryce didn't hesitate in his answer. "No. Permission is only necessary as it pertains to the rules we've established."

"Meaning, if I'm going to go somewhere with men, I can't be alone with any of them?"

"Yes."

"And I can't masturbate or come without gaining your approval first."

"Yes."

Remembering his comments about whose pleasure was more important, she asked, "What if the thing I want to do brings me pleasure?"

"Is it likely to make you orgasm?"

Recalling the sensations she'd experienced as she sucked him off, she nodded, then groaned as the increased pace of his fingers in her ass had her clutching at the iron bar on the sofa frame. "Y…ye…yes."

"Then you would have to consider carefully before doing it."

"And if I wanted to bring you pleasure?"

"Permission wouldn't be necessary. Unless seeking your own satisfaction is the primary motivator for pleasing me."

Mattie whimpered, her mind spinning with the concepts as well as the sensations racking her body. "I…I don't know… I can't…" She wasn't sure what she was trying to say and that very frustration had tears clogging her throat.

"Shhh." He soothed her, the pace of his thrusts slowing as he leaned over her. "As your master, it's my responsibility to guide you, baby. To show you how to exceed the limitations you've placed on yourself. All you need to do is trust me."

Mattie could feel the anxiety ease, the slow stroke of his fingers over her head and along her back, coupled with the rhythm of his fingers in her ass, calmed her despite the building need to come rising within her.

"Was there something you needed?" Bryce queried.

Mattie refrained from saying what she was thinking, but just barely. It wouldn't serve her plans if he was forewarned of her intent. The man was brilliant. He didn't need to know what she planned. "No," she assured him.

* * *

Having planned his approach carefully, Victor was taken aback when he stepped out of the elevator on the executive floor and spotted Bryce Halsey in the doorway between the reception area and Mattilda's office. Another nagging call, this time from Lionel Makepeace, had him stepping up his plans to ingratiate himself with Mattilda. He was sure the old bitch had put her husband up to making the call. If she'd just back off for one fucking minute, things would all fall into place. But she had her damned panties in a wad over this retirement business...

His thoughts veered from Frieda and Lionel to Halsey when the other man started to turn around. The whisper of the elevator doors behind him followed by the distinctive sound of the car descending blocked that avenue of retreat.

Around the corner was the entrance to the stairwell, if he hurried... Keeping one eye on Halsey, Victor barely made it to the door before the older man headed for the double doors to the hall with his administrative assistant at his heels.

Keeping out of sight, Victor followed their progress along the hall and then cursed again when Halsey headed for the door he hid behind. Taking the stairs two at a time, he barely made it to the next landing before the door below opened. With the door to the private apartments on the top floor locked, Victor was trapped until Halsey had gone down to the next floor or two. Why the bastard had to be so health conscious...

"Baby, I'm already late."

Halsey's voice floated up to Victor as he rested on the stairs. The throaty rasp could in no way be considered businesslike. Leaning to the side, he watched as the target of his employers' wrath backed Mattilda into the corner and kissed her. From above, he could clearly see the open blouse and bra, and the way Halsey's hands fondled her breasts.

Hell. Victor adjusted his thickening cock. If he'd known her tits were that nice, he'd've done more than just cop a feel the other day. His arousal grew when he spotted the flash of metal and realized that the woman who wouldn't even allow *him* to stroke her thigh had clamps on her nipples.

"I'm not the one who dragged you in here," Mattilda moaned as Halsey released her.

"Self-preservation." A hum of appreciation floated up to Victor along with a gasp from Mattilda when Halsey tugged on the nipple chain before righting her bra and blouse.

"Leave this on for another ten minutes, then take it off." His head dipped for another kiss. "No coming."

"I remember rule number four, Bryce." Her tone was more compliant than sarcastic, surprising Victor.

"Don't forget your appointment with Sarah at the spa." Halsey smoothed his tie and jacket before tugging open the stairwell door. "I won't be in at all tomorrow."

Mattilda nodded. "I remember the meeting in Andevine. I don't know why you..."

"If I had you along, Lawrence"—he eased the door shut, pulling Mattilda close—"I'd be spending the entire time trying to figure out a way to finger fuck you under the conference room table."

"Please." The moan in her voice assured Victor that her plea was an approval rather than a denial.

For several minutes after the door closed behind them, Victor remained in place. Not because he worried about being discovered, but because the beginnings of a plan had begun to surface. If the Makepeaces wanted Halsey off-kilter, focused outside the business, perhaps Mattilda Lawrence was the tool to make that happen. Victor rose, brushing the seat of his pants off and descending the stairs slowly. If he wasn't mistaken, Halsey was working on his own method of circumventing the worries the Makepeaces had stirred up with the board.

Bypassing the doorway to the executive level, Victor went down another level and exited the stairwell. Pulling his cell phone from his pocket, he hit the redial and waited. Before the person on the other end could say more than "hello," he asked, "What information can you get me on Mattilda Lawrence?"

"Why?" Lionel's nasally voice whined in his ear.

"Because I think Bryce Halsey's resignation is going to be a moot point in the very near future." He grinned at the invectives spilling from the other man's mouth. "Get as much dirt on her as you can, then call me." Victor slid the phone closed as he pressed the elevator call button.

During his time working for Halsey's, he'd discovered there were a number of people who enjoyed humiliating others. It should be easy enough to use them to get what he needed.

Chapter Nine

"You know," Lyssa whispered in Mattie's ear as they approached the doors separating the reception area from the main lounge of the Diablo Blanco Club. "If you wanted to find the perfect way to piss off a Dominant, I think this would be it."

"How so?" Mattie couldn't stem the excitement shivering through her. Eight years of curiosity were about to be satisfied, and all Lyssa wanted was to discuss Bryce's possible reaction. Stifling the snort of exasperation, she reminded her sister, "I've been invited here several times over the years."

"To the annual 'select a sub' night," Lyssa retorted.

"The Midnight Masquerade on Halloween is not"—she stopped, then revised—"okay, it may be a night where any unescorted or unclaimed submissive is available for the taking, but not without that sub's permission." Turning back to her sister, she grinned. "Besides, you've been just as curious as me. Admit it."

Lyssa didn't bother to answer. Instead she rolled her eyes. "Just open the damned door already."

The door swung open silently as Mattie twisted the antique crystal knob. At first it reminded her of Bryce's home, Pirate's Folly, with the crown molding, high ceiling, and distinctive early-nineteenth-century design. But the differences soon became apparent. The lounge would have easily made up the formal parlor, sitting room, and dining room at the Folly. The furniture, though comfortable looking as well as tasteful, was definitely contemporary rather than the antiques that decorated Bryce's home.

Then, of course, there were the numerous guests sprinkled about the room and the bar. Settled between the curving staircases that formed a unique X as they led down from the second floor and met in a wide landing before splitting again into two separate staircases, the bar was a beautiful, polished teak expanse, easily twenty feet long with only a few bar stools arranged around it. As she and Lyssa entered, several heads turned, both male and female.

"I feel like someone just announced, 'fresh meat,'" Lyssa groused as she settled beside Mattie at the bar.

"And you are," a friendly voice teased.

The deep red, green, and royal blue lettering on the coasters he set on the bar held Mattie's attention before the bartender set two tall tumblers over them. Looking up, she couldn't shake the disturbing notion that she'd met him before. The amusement in his gray eyes and the cheeky grin on his handsome face only reinforced her suspicions.

"So, what can we expect?"

Lyssa's query intruded on Mattie's mental shuffling to try to fit a name to his face.

"Nothing."

"Nothing?" Mattie could have cursed at the sound of disappointment filling her voice. It didn't help that the gray eyes twinkled even more brightly with amusement at her response.

"Because you're first timers, other members will hover and maybe ask a few questions, buy you a drink or two, but nothing will happen unless you indicate you're interested," he assured them, before stepping away to help another patron at the other end of the bar.

"Well, that blows all my preconceived notions," Lyssa grumbled as she lifted the glass to her nose and sniffed.

Mattie did the same as she carefully surveyed their surroundings.

"So, Miss Mattie." The blond bartender leaned against the counter and grinned at her. "What brings you to the DBC without the boss man in tow?"

"You know me?" Mattie still couldn't place his face, although he seemed so familiar.

"Six months ago, I treated you for a mild concussion after one of Bryce's horses threw you," he reminded her. Looking at their untouched drinks, he assured them, "The drinks are safe, I promise. Just soda and ice. No alcohol. Club rule."

"What do you mean?" Lyssa asked.

"You're a doctor?" Mattie was surprised.

Both of them spoke at the same time, pulling an amused chuckle from the bartender. "No, not a doctor. A physician assistant." Holding out his hand, he reintroduced himself. "Ben Murphy."

Mattie took his hand, surprised at the restrained strength and the calluses that neither medicine nor bartending would have created. "So I guess being a physician assistant doesn't pay enough?"

Ben laughed. "Nah, I just like to blow off a little steam here." He nodded toward a woman settled on the lap of one man, his long, dark hair pulled back and secured in a ponytail with a leather tie, and a goatee framing his sensual mouth, lips curved in a wry smile. The woman's skirt was pushed up around her hips, her blouse hung open. The hands caressing her breasts looked dark against the pale mounds. Bent at the waist, she seemed to be enjoying herself while her mouth worked voraciously on the thick cock of another man who stood in front of her. His faded jeans were open, allowing her access to him, but the blue and black flannel shirt remained buttoned. The broad shoulders and straight stance of the man identified him as young, belying the impression his collar-length gray hair gave.

"What do you mean about no alcohol?" Lyssa asked again.

Mattie heard her but was still watching the threesome across the room. There was something familiar about the men, but she couldn't quite place it. Turning back to the bar, her mind still churning through the faces she saw on a daily basis, Mattie couldn't help but grin at the response Ben gave her sister's question.

"Inhibitions. Decisions here need to be made with a clear head. First-time visitors are only allowed nonalcoholic drinks until they've decided if they're going to stay or leave."

"And then what?"

"If you leave, no problem. If you stay and are interested, you can negotiate a scene with a member. After you make your decision, then the Club rules say you can have no more than two drinks with alcohol—but nothing that would impair judgment."

Drink halfway to her mouth, Mattie hesitated as she realized she knew both of the men and the woman they were engaged with. Turning back to the trio, she had to stifle her amusement at the realization of who they were.

"What's so funny?" Lyssa leaned over to ask.

Mattie gestured over her shoulder to the threesome. "I just figured out who they are."

"And?"

"The guy with the ponytail is a private investigator. David Henderson. Bryce sometimes uses him and his brother to process background checks for new employees."

Lyssa turned to look at the trio. "Interesting. What about the other two?"

"I think you'd recognize the woman. She's a model. Bryce dated her for a few months about three years ago. I'm not sure, but I think her name is Terese or LaTreace."

A sharp cry from the woman had both Mattie and Lyssa turning. Body arched, face suffused with color, it was obvious the blonde was in the throes of climax as David held her still on his lap. The man in front of her had obviously finished and was righting his clothes.

"This gets better and better." Lyssa swallowed another sip of her soda as she turned back to face Mattie. "So who's the other guy?"

Amusement twinkled in Mattie's eyes. "Dayton Kringle."

"You mean *the* Dayton Kringle that everyone calls the Santa of San Diablo?"

Mattie grinned.

"My, oh my." Lyssa took a moment to watch the group, heat stealing into her cheeks. Mattie noticed when David looked their way and gave them a wicked smile and a wink.

Turning back to the bar, Lyssa swallowed some of her soda and chuckled. "Wonder what it must be like to be caught between a private dick and a hard Saint Nick."

Even Ben laughed. The cheesy grin Lyssa gave as she glanced back over her shoulder and lifted her glass in a silent toast had the private investigator nodding even as his hands smoothed the edges of his companion's shirt back over her bare breasts.

Looking around the room, Mattie realized how many people were either watching the threesome or were participating in their own activities. Several times she noticed the various collars adorning the throats of the members. Some resembled jewelry, while others were similar to leather dog collars. Some even sported gleaming spikes or studs. In many cases, matching bindings were attached to wrists and even ankles.

Noting her curiosity, Ben sipped at his own glass of water. "Interesting collars, huh?"

"Collars?" Lyssa voiced the question for her.

"The neckwear some of the members have on." Ben shrugged. "They identify who the owners are."

"Owners?"

Ben looked at Lyssa's stunned expression. "You really are a virgin to all this, aren't you, sweetheart?"

Lyssa choked on her drink and turned red as she tried to regain her breath, but she nodded. "I've only skimmed a couple of books on the lifestyle." Her elbow dug into Mattie's side when she started to laugh.

"The collars are visible proof of ownership that a master will provide for his or her slave. Here at the Club, many of the members choose distinctive styles to identify their slaves to the other members."

He glanced around the room and continued, "Without looking too hard, any collared slaves can safely be left alone and none of the other masters will approach them. No matter how they might beg for attention." Dropping his gaze to Mattie's throat, then her sister's, Ben grinned. "If it weren't apparent that you two are newbies, any number of masters would be clamoring to claim you."

Curious, Mattie asked, "So each of the masters has a distinctive collar?"

"Depends on the master." He nodded toward Dayton. "Kringle doesn't collar his subs. The Hendersons, on the other hand, they both have a penchant for velvet and leather." He subtly pointed out a petite blonde with a man, nearly twice her size, settled at her feet like a pet. "Mistress Lana likes the studded leather."

"What about Bryce Halsey?" Lyssa asked.

Mattie could have reached out and smacked her, but her own curiosity was demanding an answer to that question as well.

Ben chuckled. "Now, that's a man with style." He gestured to the blonde sprawled in David Henderson's lap as he whispered something into the woman's ear. A delicate diamond chain winked at the base of her throat. "Most of the time it's diamonds. Once it was rubies. He never goes for the functional collars, only decorative."

"Are you saying she's his sub?" Mattie demanded. Angry and humiliated that Bryce would have the audacity to approach her when he was already involved...

"No, no. She's old news when it comes to Halsey." Ben excused himself to grab a drink for another patron.

Mattie avoided looking at Lyssa, knowing in her blue eyes would lurk a hint of compassion and curiosity for her. Absently, her hand strayed up to her throat and stroked the bare skin there until she realized what she was doing and immediately dropped her hand to grip the half-empty glass of soda.

Ben returned and continued as if the conversation had never been interrupted. "No, Halsey's collars carry a small lock on them. Once he's released a sub, he removes the lock, and they can choose to keep the collar or not." Motioning with a nod to the blonde whose breasts were now being fondled by David, he said, "She just hasn't found the right master yet. She tends to drift from member to member more than some of the others."

"You mentioned some of the slaves beg for attention?" Lyssa appeared confused. Propping her arm on the bar and her chin in her hand, she asked, "If they're owned by one master, why would they beg for attention from another?"

Ben smiled wickedly. "Some of the masters test their friends by seeing if they can coax them into breaking one of the Club's hard and fast rules."

"What rules?" Mattie turned away from the sight of a collared male clad in little more than a black leather thong meticulously lapping at the exposed pussy of a woman sprawled in a chair.

"The rules that each member agrees to when they join the Diablo Blanco Club," Ben informed her.

Her expression must have reflected Lyssa's confused one, which seemed to amuse the bartender as he smiled and ticked off several rules on his fingers.

"The number one rule is, no messing with another master's slave, unless given permission by the master." With a shrug, he added, "The second most important rule is, what happens in DBC stays here. After that the rest of the rules are relatively common: no abuse, no blood play, no forced play."

"Those sound rather vague," Lyssa muttered.

Mattie watched her sister lift her drink only to halt it halfway to her lips. Before she could follow the direction of Lyssa's gaze, she was distracted by the answer the man in front of them was offering.

Ben shrugged. "Most of the members have their own rules that they use. The Club rules supersede those, which makes everything run smoothly." A call from a customer at the end of the bar had him excusing himself again.

As he moved away, Mattie swung her gaze upward toward the spot Lyssa seemed fascinated with and cursed silently. There, on the landing above the bar, stood Bryce's brother. She'd forgotten Mike was still in San Diablo. That he was a member of the Club wasn't a surprise, but apparently it was news to Lyssa. The glare she received from her sister had Mattie fighting her grin.

"I thought you said he was out of the country," Lyssa grumbled before she swallowed the last of her drink and set the glass close to the inside of the bar, signaling her request for a refill.

Mattie finished her own drink and winced when she turned her attention back to Mike—only to find him descending the stairs, his cell phone pressed to his ear. "He came back into town earlier this week. I didn't mention it because it slipped my mind."

"I am so killing you when we get out of here, Mat," Lyssa promised. "If he even hints at wanting to take pictures of me, I swear I'll scream."

She couldn't stifle the chuckle at her sister's displeasure. "Nude or dressed?" The pinch Lyssa gave her beneath the edge of the bar made her wince, but Mattie couldn't help but notice the flush on her sister's face as she watched Bryce's brother approach.

***

Fingers working the supple black leather, Bryce relaxed in his chair, his gaze focused on the painting he'd left propped on the easel. With the oils dry to the touch, he would be able to finish attaching the bindings to the painted rope wound around the image of Mattie's hands. In less than twenty-four hours she'd be making her final decision, and he had no doubt it would be a yes. Once he'd convinced her that submitting to him would enhance their marriage, it wouldn't be much longer after that the image he'd long imagined and committed to canvas would be enacted.

The ring of his telephone drew his attention from the painting. "Halsey," he answered, glancing at his watch, surprised at the late hour.

"Do you know where your fiancée is?" Mike queried.

"Considering it's after ten o'clock, I'm assuming she's at home. Why?"

Mike's chuckle vibrated against his ear. "If she is, then her twin and her sister are cozied up to the medic behind the bar here at the Club."

Bryce cursed beneath his breath. "How long?"

"I have no idea. I just came downstairs and found them. Ben seems to be keeping them entertained, but there are a few sharks circling your tuna."

"I'm leaving now."

"Should I try to keep them here?" Mike asked.

"Definitely. And tell Ben I'm going to need room three." Snapping the cell phone closed, he set the rope on the table, took one last look at the painting, then shut off the light and left his studio.

Chapter Ten

"Lawrence."

The cool drawl had Mattie stiffening in her seat. Even though she'd been careful to avoid being touched by any of the men who had approached her and Lyssa as they chatted with Ben at the bar, Mattie still knew she'd skirted the rules by coming here. The hope that Bryce wouldn't discover her little excursion was too much to hope for, especially after Mike had taken up residence on the stool beside her sister twenty minutes earlier.

Taking a moment to prepare herself, Mattie settled her glass very carefully on the coaster before turning. The expression in his cool green eyes sent a shiver of arousal through her.

"Come here."

Several patrons shifted in their seats to view the exchange. Mattie could see most of them in her peripheral vision. The hush was filled with the rasp of her slacks against the leather of her bar stool as she stood and followed Bryce's command. Beside her, she watched her sister's instinctive shift to protect her forestalled by Mike's grip on her arm. Moving the few steps separating her from Bryce, Mattie held his gaze despite the urge to drop her eyes.

"Would you like to explain yourself?"

He towered over her, his muscular thighs straining the worn jeans, broad shoulders stretching the black T-shirt over his chest like a second skin. The way he held his legs braced apart and his arms folded across his chest, Mattie was reminded of a pirate steadying himself on the deck of a storm-tossed ship. Even the shadow of his evening beard and the way his hair settled around his shoulders had her seeing him clad in leather with a cutlass at his waist.

She realized she hadn't responded in a long time when he snapped, "Key!"

The bartender tossed something to Bryce.

Snagging it out of the air with one hand, Bryce gripped her left arm above the elbow and turned her toward one of the staircases. A gush of fluid and heat spilled through her center, wetting her panties and hardening her nipples, so they scraped erotically against the silk of her bra.

She should have known Lyssa wouldn't take Bryce's handling of her calmly.

"Now, you just hold on…"

"Stay out of it," Mike cautioned Lyssa, his grip on her shoulder keeping her on her stool.

"It's okay, Lys," Mattie assured her at the same time.

Bryce ignored them both and continued towing her up the stairs.

"Bryce," another male voice interrupted, but Bryce didn't stop their ascent.

Glancing back toward the double doors leading from the reception area into the lounge, Mattie flushed with embarrassment to see Richard Bennett watching them.

By the time they reached the landing, Richard's voice echoed again, this time the tone more determined, if not demanding. "Halsey."

Swinging to face his friend, Bryce hauled Mattie around too. His expression alone must have warned Richard, but it didn't deter the other man from continuing.

"The rules? No forced play, remember?" Richard's gray eyes drifted from his friend's face to Mattie's, then back again.

Mattie waited for Bryce's response.

He looked at her. "Tell them."

Looking up, she met his gaze for a moment, seeing the heat of arousal and the barest hint of amusement causing the green of his eyes to fluctuate between forest and emerald. Swallowing, she turned to face the audience below. She could swear her face burst into flames from the attention directed her way. Focusing on reassuring both her sister and Bryce's vice president and best friend, she met each of their gazes and spoke as clearly as her dry throat would allow.

"He's not forcing me."

Richard's stance relaxed, but Lyssa kept pushing at the grip Mike had on her. Wanting her sister to settle down, Mattie called down, "Lyssa, it's okay—" Bryce propelled her up the second flight of stairs before she could finish reassuring her.

Just before they rounded the corner to head down the hall, Mattie looked back toward her sister and winced. Apparently, Lyssa still hadn't believed her and must have tried following them, but Mike had decided on an unusual method of stopping her. The last thing Mattie saw as Bryce hauled her down the passageway was Lyssa held close to the younger man's chest, her fists pressing against his shoulders but gaining no ground as Mike kissed her.

Yup, she thought. *I'm gonna pay for this one. Lys is never gonna forgive me for getting her mixed up in this situation.*

Bryce pushed open a door and pulled her inside. The *snick* of the lock engaging registered in a distant part of Mattie's mind, but the rest was occupied with taking in her surroundings. Low light spilled from two black-shaded lamps. The one closest to the door sat on a small table and was joined by the key to the room, while the other graced one of the matching nightstands beside a large four-poster bed.

"Strip."

Bryce's order broke her stunned appraisal of the room. Mattie slid the buttons of her blouse free. Knowing it was useless to deny her arousal, she continued to remove her clothing, taking the time to fold each article before setting it on the floor beside her.

Once naked, she bent to retrieve her clothing and met his gaze. "I haven't done anything wrong," she assured him, even as she calmly handed him her slacks, thong, bra, and blouse.

"Nothing wrong?" He turned his back to set the clothing inside a black-lacquered armoire.

With his back to her, Mattie took a moment to reexamine the room. She fought the grin tugging at her lips, knowing Bryce would not take her amusement well, but she couldn't help it. It was so over-the-top with its black padded leather walls, and a black suede duvet spread across the twisted, black wrought-iron four-poster bed. The smile flattened out when she identified thick silver chains dangling from eye hooks bolted into the ceiling.

"Did I tell you to come here?" Bryce faced her again, eyes carefully examining every inch of exposed skin.

When they halted at the juncture between her thighs, Mattie swallowed heavily, realizing one moment of truth had presented itself. Now she'd find out his reaction to her overriding his instructions to the aesthetician at the spa.

If she'd expected a response, she was disappointed. He continued his discourse as if the waxed, smooth surface of her mound was nothing new. "Did you or did you not draw the attention of nearly every man in this place?" He waited patiently for her answer.

"Not every man. There were a few who approached me and Lyssa, but when we said we were just checking things out…"

"That's one."

"One what?"

"Rule you've broken."

"No, I didn't…"

"Were you or were you not alone with another man?" Bryce demanded.

"No." Mattie met his gaze without flinching. "My sister was with me at all times."

"Not good enough, Lawrence."

Planting her hands on her hips, she glared right back at him. "No way, Halsey. You said rule number one was that I can't be alone with any man or former lover. I wasn't. My sister was with me at all times."

"Not. Good. Enough." Stepping up to her, Bryce gripped her chin, his pale green eyes boring into hers as he retorted, "Alone means without your master, Lawrence. And since, for all intents and purposes, during this trial week I am your master, you were here alone."

From the bed, Bryce grabbed two black leather cuffs. "Hands."

Mattie didn't bother fighting him. Hell, her tits were getting warm and her nipples were hard as pebbles at the thought of the black leather in his hands. Verbal resistance was one thing, but physical? No. Especially since the idea of his delivering another spanking had her so aroused she was already reminding herself she wasn't allowed to climax without his permission.

She watched Bryce take his time buckling each of the black leather cuffs onto her wrists before he grabbed another set and fastened them around her ankles. Bryce returned to the armoire to remove a few more items, all of which had Mattie breathing just a tad more quickly.

He tossed the length of black leather with silver clasps at each end on the bed, along with two shorter silver chains sporting the same clasps at each end, and had her shifting her feet to ease the ache between her thighs. In his hands he carried an unusual black belt, easily three inches wide with small stainless steel O-rings attached at intervals around it.

Without a word, he threaded it around her waist and cinched it closed. Running a finger between the belt and her skin, Bryce seemed to be checking to make sure he hadn't made it too tight. She didn't protest anything he did. Her curiosity overrode her fear as much as her arousal was driving her need to find out what he had planned for her.

Stepping away from her once he'd cinched the belt at her hips snugly, Bryce motioned her to follow him toward the bed. Gathering the black leather strap from the mattress, he pointed at the floor directly in front of the high-perched bed.

Feet planted where he directed, Mattie waited, silently fuming over his stubborn point of view. At the same time, she couldn't still the zing of arousal tightening her nipples into stiff peaks or coating her sex with cream that threatened to leak onto her thighs at any moment.

"Hands," he ordered again.

Holding her hands up, Mattie watched as Bryce secured the clamp through the steel D-rings on the cuffs. "This isn't fair," she muttered, unable to keep silent as he moved away from her.

The leather strap landed on the bed again, but remained there only long enough for Bryce to round the end of the bed and pick it up. Facing her across the black suede expanse, he didn't bother responding to her comments. Instead, he tugged on the strap until Mattie found herself bent over the bed, the suede soft against her sensitive nipples, the pinch of the plug she'd put in place before leaving to pick up Lyssa sending a jolt of arousal through her ass and into her pussy.

Opposite her, Bryce squatted beside the bed. The sound of metal and leather scraping against each other had her pulse racing. He'd actually bound her to the frame of the mattress. Pulling back slightly, Mattie realized there was very little play in the strap securing her in place.

The stroke of his hands along her arms and over her shoulders had Mattie staring up at him. "Not too tight?" His touch smoothed between her belly and the comforter she rested on, before skating upward to cup her swollen breasts and lightly pinch the firm crests of her nipples.

"Bryce?" She swallowed again, hoping the crack in her voice didn't betray the strange mixture of arousal and fear snaking its way along her spine. "What are you going to do?"

"Spanking doesn't seem to be working on you, Lawrence." His tone was casual as he eased onto the bed, his fingers threading through her hair, pulling it away from her eyes and off her neck.

She couldn't see what he was doing. From the swish and sway of her hair against her back and the occasional tug on her scalp, Mattie guessed he was fashioning a braid out of her hair. But for what reason, she didn't know. As for his assumption that spanking didn't work on her, he was wrong. Dead wrong, she admitted as a gush of moisture flooded her pussy at the thought of his callused hand falling on her naked butt or the application of his flogger again.

So caught up in the memories and images the thought of his paddling her again conjured, Mattie almost missed the rest of what he was saying.

"So I'm going to have to try something a bit more extreme." A soft *thump* punctuated his words before he slid from the bed.

Pushing herself up onto her toes, Mattie was able to raise herself onto her elbows and follow his progress from the bed to the armoire. The brush of her hair against her shoulder distracted her long enough for her to confirm that she'd been correct. The disorderly curls had been wound into a neat, uniform braid and secured with a length of leather. By the time she turned back to where Bryce had been standing, he was gone.

A door beside the armoire stood open, a soft light spilling into the shadowed room as the sound of drawers opening and closing filtered out to her. The straining muscles in the back of her calves and thighs protested her position. Flat-footed once again, Mattie rested her cheek against the duvet and watched as Bryce approached the bed. The low-wattage bulbs in the lamps beside the door and bed cast a soft glow through the room.

Oh, cripes. She could feel her eyes going wide at the things he carried in his hands. It wasn't fear but nerves that had her belly quivering. The tube of lubricant was familiar, as was the silver vibrator he'd begun using on her two days earlier. Her pussy heated and cream oozed onto her thighs at the memories that slender silver wand conjured. But the most arousing and unnerving item Bryce carried was a butt plug. Only this one was larger than the one currently in residence up her ass.

"Bryce, I..." She didn't know what she'd been about to tell him, but the single negative shake of his head halted her words.

"Not interested, Lawrence." Setting the items on the mattress, Bryce moved to stand behind her.

Mattie waited, eyes closed, forehead resting on the duvet as Bryce's hands smoothed over her hips, onto her bottom, and halted. In her mind's eye, she imagined the red base of the plug she'd used looked incongruous nestled between the curves of her butt.

"That's two rules, Lawrence." His words were husky, as if arousal and amusement vied for supremacy, and neither won.

"Two?"

"Rules one and two." Bryce slid his hands over her butt and into the crease between, before tracing the base of the plug visible between the round cheeks of her bottom. "No other men—"

"Wait," she interrupted, twisting just enough to watch him over her shoulder. "I still say I wasn't alone with another man at any time this evening until you brought me up here."

"—and no self-stimulation," he finished, ignoring her.

"Self-stimu—" Her questioning tone was choked off in a quick gasp as Bryce pulled on the device, sending an unexpected splinter of pain and pleasure through her body.

When he tugged on it a second time, a shiver coursed through her body, stopping her breath and sending the muscles in her belly twitching in time with those deeper inside her pussy.

"Let it go," he urged, pulling carefully at the lodged plug. "Easy now." His voice was smooth, quiet in the still room as he took his time coaxing the thick rubber device free.

A whimper slipped past her lips as the tip left her body and the emptiness registered, but it was short-lived. First one, then a second finger, liberally coated with lubricant eased passed the outer muscles before retreating.

Mattie couldn't stop from calling out, her voice tight with need. "No!" Fighting the pressure he applied to her lower back with one hand to keep her still, she tried to push back.

"Stop." The command was firm and accompanied by a sharp slap to her bottom. A second smack on the opposite cheek had her squirming, but the attempts to draw him back halted.

Quivering, her body desperate for release, Mattie fought her growing climax, knowing another punishment would be handed down if she came without permission. Considering what he was putting her through, she didn't think she could handle a third.

Shifting her grip, Mattie latched on to the leather strap securing her to the bed, her eyes squeezed tightly shut as she burrowed her forehead into the bedding and waited. When it finally came, she could have wept and screamed at the same time, instead she moaned, enjoying the sting of the thick tip of the plug Bryce pressed against her rear opening.

"Push back, baby," he purred.

He'd seen the wide-eyed look filling her face when she'd caught sight of the large butt plug, and the smile on his lips had to have been disconcerting, but it wasn't nervousness or fear—no—he'd forced his excitement down when he realized anticipation filled Mattie's expression. He lubed the plug, then set the tip in place. As he pressed forward, he didn't need to prompt Mattie. In the cheval mirror, he watched her eyes close and her mouth open in an excited gasp as she pushed back, relaxing her muscles so that the first bulb of the toy slid into place. Watching the first rounded tip slide inside had his cock leaking in his jeans.

As the base grew larger, her gasps came more rapidly. He watched her fingers grip the leather her bindings were lashed to. Sliding one hand between the covers and her pussy, Bryce slipped his fingers between the drenched, weeping petals and circled the taut bundle of nerves. Fingering her clit, he pressed the next two bulbs on the plug into place, then felt her spasm against his fingertips as Mattie fought the orgasm winding through her.

Her body shuddered beneath him, cries pouring from her lips, juices wetting his hand and dripping onto the soft black suede of the duvet. Leaning over her, Bryce crooned quiet sounds into her ear, soothing the fear he recognized on her face. Part of him was worried at the look. With the cataclysm pulsing through her body, desperate for release, and the source stemming from the alien feeling of her ass being penetrated, he'd known other lovers to balk and run from him once they'd regained their senses. He knew—hoped, prayed—Mattie wasn't one of those.

It took everything he had to keep from ripping open his pants and filling her pussy. The wet, red lips throbbed beneath his fingertips as he stroked her folds and waited for her ragged breathing to subside. He waited for her to regain control of her body before he continued pushing the remaining few inches of the plug into place.

By the time the sixth and largest curve slipped inside, he was sure he would explode. More than the sight of the small red plug had aroused him. Knowing she'd intentionally defied him by overriding his instructions at the spa had his Dominant nature rearing up. He knew he'd judged her correctly as a woman willing to challenge him on every level. After this evening, she would have little doubt who was the master in their relationship.

With the plug in place, he moved away from the bed, carrying the toy he'd removed into the bathroom and set it in the sink to clean later. Grabbing a clean cloth from the pile on the vanity, he ran warm water over it and squeezed out the excess before returning to the room and Mattie's trembling form on the bed. Quick, smooth swipes of the hand towel removed the additional lubricant glistening on her skin.

The scent of her arousal filled his nostrils, making his mouth water at the thought of her cream wetting her pussy, sliding down her thighs. Fighting the urge to turn her onto her back and bury his face between her thighs, Bryce stripped off his T-shirt, the need to feel her skin against his overriding caution. Draping his larger body over hers, his legs forcing her open, he let one hand caress her white-knuckled grip on the strap, while the other insinuated its way between her shivering belly and the suede cover, damp from her sweat.

Setting his lips close to her ear, he whispered, "When you come into our bedroom after we marry, Lawrence"—he waited for the soft whimpers to grow quiet; then, slipping his hand from her stomach to the bare, swollen folds between her thighs, he stirred the warm fluid pooling there—"this sweet little pussy won't last for very long." One finger, then a second, delved between her puffy lips, teasing the hardened knot before sliding into the tight sheath. "And after I've worn it out with my attentions, I'm going to start on this sexy ass."

Shifting his hold from her hands and sex to her hips, he pulled her back just enough so she couldn't gain purchase on the bedding. With her legs already spread to accommodate him, he thrust his hips into hers, butting up against the solid base of the plug and pressing it deep. Mattie cried out, incoherent mutterings, as Bryce shifted away, releasing the pressure before he moved forward again.

This time her words weren't muffled by the bedding. Twisting her head to look back at him over her shoulder, Mattie demanded in a hoarse, passionate voice, "Harder."

Her body tried moving backward toward him, but the way he had her stretched across the mattress, she had no leverage to work with. Leaning forward, his hips grinding hers into the soft duvet and firm mattress beneath, he growled, "What, baby?"

"Oh God, please, harder, Bryce," Mattie sobbed, trying to press back against him.

Again he controlled her body, keeping her from shifting away or toward him.

"Like this?" he taunted. Using the ridge of his swollen cock and the thick fold of material over the zipper of his jeans, he was able to shift the base of the plug while thrusting forward.

Head arched back, hands fisting over the black leather strap, Mattie sobbed, "Yes, please, more."

Slipping one hand beneath her again, he found her swollen wet petals and parted them, exposing the taut kernel of nerves hidden there. Against the backs of his fingers, he felt the hard bend where the mattress ended. Moving between her legs, he spread her feet and adjusted her position until that sharp edge, blunted by the covers and the suede-wrapped duvet, ground against that most sensitive bit of flesh. Bracing her in place, he rocked and circled his hips against hers, pushing and rubbing that firm point against her body until her cream coated her thighs, soaking through the denim of his jeans, and she sobbed, begging for release.

Pulling away, he deftly flipped her onto her back and spread her thighs before stepping between them. Face flushed, tears streaking her cheeks, Mattie trembled, her body quaking with arousal, desperate for the release he refused to give her permission to have. Stroking his hands slowly from her wrists to her shoulders, he soothed her, settling soft kisses against her cheeks. Licking away the salty tears coating her face before he moved to her thighs, he murmured soft reassurances to her but did nothing to reduce the need within her.

The flavor of her juices and scent of her desire filled his head, but didn't sway him from his purpose. Spanking hadn't worked—she enjoyed the feel of his hand or the flogger on her round ass too much. Hell, she'd intentionally thwarted his instructions a time or two in the office just to have him paddle her ass. Not that he didn't enjoy it himself, but if she was going to submit to him, she needed to understand that some punishments were supposed to be just that—punishments. Refusing to let her come after bringing her to the edge was one of the best methods he'd found to discipline a recalcitrant sub.

Lapping up the cream coating her thighs, he moved to the nude flesh of her mound. Easing first one leg, then the other onto the bed, Bryce secured the D-rings on the ankle cuffs to the belt using the short lengths of chain he'd dropped onto the mattress. Now, spread for his pleasure, there was little his sexy little sub could do but let him play.

"You didn't follow instructions."

"I...I wasn't alone," she argued, her voice raspy as she arched toward the hand stroking her mound.

"Was your master with you?" He held her gaze, waiting for her response.

She shook her head. "No."

"Then you didn't follow instructions."

Again, she refused to admit it. "I did. I wasn't—"

The crisp sound of bare flesh on bare flesh echoed in the room as his hand landed firmly against her naked pussy with just enough force to stun rather than harm. He repeated his comment. "You didn't follow instructions."

The sight of his hand lifting for another strike must have been all the convincing Mattie needed, despite the way her hips arched toward him desperate for the blow to land. "Yes." She spat through gritted teeth. "I didn't follow instructions."

"And?" He made sure no emotion or inflection leaked into his voice as he prompted her to respond.

"And—" Defiance and fire blazed up at him before she forced her eyelids to drift closed. "And I need"—the rebellion was still there in her eyes as she met his gaze again, but banked now, behind curiosity and need—"to be punished."

"Yes, baby." Bryce let his amusement slip free briefly. "You do."

Over the next two hours he stroked or tongued her to the edge, then stopped. Giving her body time to wind down, but not enough to relax completely, he waited before starting again. Three times he brought her close to climaxing before stopping, leaving her aching, desperate to come.

No matter how she begged, cried, or pleaded, Bryce refused permission. By the third time, her eyes were glaring at him, but her words had gone silent, replaced by the steady moans and muffled cries of need.

She seemed to know satisfaction wouldn't be given no matter how long or hard she begged. Resigned to make it through the punishment he'd chosen, Bryce had watched her utilize every possible method of relaxation or slow breathing to combat the quivering need coursing through her body.

Her nipples were flushed and angry red, swollen and hard from the suckling of his mouth and the pinching of his fingers. Even the lightest puff of breath across them had her holding her breath.

Taking his time, he loosened the restraints binding her. First the chains securing her ankles close to her hips and then the strap holding her to the bed. Helping her to her feet, he set her clothes on the bed beside her. "Dress," he ordered before he tugged his own T-shirt over his head. While he returned the belt, cuffs, and chains to the armoire, Bryce watched her careful movements in the cheval mirror beside the bathroom door.

The plug was still in place and perhaps more awkward than the one he'd removed. From the slow and steady way she bent in order to step into her thong, it was apparent she was trying to adjust to the larger toy. Leaving her to finish, Bryce stepped into the bathroom.

When he returned from cleaning the plug he'd removed, she'd barely donned her undergarments. Her breathing was unsteady, and her body swayed as she stood beside the bed trying to fit the front clasp of her bra together. Standing in front of her, Bryce eased her hands out of the way and deftly fastened the garment. "Did you enjoy your first visit to the Diablo Blanco?" he asked, wondering if she would respond with her usual fire or if the lesson he'd given her would temper her tongue.

The humor and spirit were evident in her gaze as she reached for her blouse, her gaze holding his. "Some parts of it were fun, while others were"—she paused to draw a slow breath—"enlightening."

The trembling in her fingers made securing the buttons impossible, but again, Bryce saw to them. Shaking out her slacks, he held them so she could step into them. Pushing her hands away, Bryce eased them over her hips, his fingers taking their time to slide along her curves. As she reached to close and zip them, he stopped her. His left hand slipped inside her pants and beneath the wet silk of her panties. "Was your visit enlightening enough to remember what my five rules are?"

"Oh God, don't," she begged, her fingers clutching at his forearms as her head came to rest against his shoulder.

The damp lips of her pussy pulsed beneath his touch. The need trembled through her as warm cream coated his fingers. "What's rule number one?"

"N-no other men." She gasped, her fingers digging into his flesh at the stroke of his fingers around her clit.

"Very good. And rule number two?" He eased one digit into her sheath, fighting back his own curse at the heat and tight grip he found there.

She cleared her throat and drew a deep breath. "No...*oh*, no self-stimulation."

Pressing deep, he waited, then eased a second finger into her. Her breath hissed out between her teeth, and she arched onto her toes, grinding her forehead into his chest with a shaky sob. Sliding his other arm around her back, he caressed her from shoulder to waist in slow, steady strokes. "Rule number..."

"Three. No restrictions on where and when you can touch me, as long as no employees are present." Her words came out on soft puffs of air as if she fought for each one. Not waiting for him to ask, she continued, "Rule four, no orgasms without your permission. And five, use the safe word…" She shifted down, moaning as her body pulsed around the two fingers lodged within her. "Use the safe word," Mattie repeated, "if I need to."

Lowering his lips to her ear, Bryce whispered, "Very good, baby. But don't come; I haven't given you permission." Easing his fingers out of her, he took a step back. With her gaze locked on his, he slid his wet fingers into his mouth and savored the taste of her arousal.

After licking every bit of her cream from his hand, Bryce swiftly fastened her pants and waited as she slipped her feet into her shoes. Placing a steadying arm around her waist, he led her out of the room, extinguishing the lights and locking the door behind him.

Fighting the urge to swing her up in his arms and carry her back to Pirate's Folly, Bryce forced himself to keep one arm around her waist and take each step slowly. Descending a set of stairs with a seven-inch butt plug up your ass and a body clamoring to orgasm, he reasoned, was likely to make anyone unsteady.

There were still several patrons left in the Club as they moved toward the bar. Ben Murphy still held court, chatting and joking with Dayton Kringle as the younger man leaned on the teak bar, sipping at a squat tumbler of scotch. Mattie's grip on his hand had him looking down at her as they neared the pair. Dipping his head toward her, he waited.

In a soft whisper, she asked, "Lyssa?"

Knowing she was concerned about her sister, Bryce looked toward Ben. "Ben," he called. "Where'd her sister go?"

Dayton rather than Ben answered, "If you mean that cute little blonde Miss Mattie came in with, last I saw, Mike was trying to keep her from following you two."

"I need to find her," Mattie announced.

"I'm sure Mike is taking care of her. He'll make sure she gets home okay."

"But, I—"

Mattie tried to argue, but Bryce overruled her. Steering her toward the door, he reaffirmed Dayton's assurances to her. "She's okay, Lawrence. Let's get you home."

Chapter Eleven

"You can't hide in there forever, Mattie."

The humor in her sister's voice had Mattie sticking her tongue out at the mahogany-paneled door. She took one last look at her reflection before exiting the private bathroom attached to her office. Mattie loved the gown, despite the unease it made her feel. Just like all of Lyssa's unique designs, the close-fitted silk sheath enhanced her full figure. Her plump breasts and rounded hips appeared sophisticated rather than overblown above and below her narrow waist.

The fitted bodice hugged her torso while leaving her back bare to the dimples above her bottom. A built-in shelf bra supported her breasts and clear plastic straps secured the dress in place by curving over her shoulders and fastening with hidden hooks beside her breasts.

The twelve strands of faceted amber crystal beads complemented the deep burgundy silk as much as the triple row of matching beads at her throat emphasized the ballet neckline of the gown. Bare from nape to the small of her back, only the cool brush of the crystals against her skin covered her.

"I really think this is just a bit much, Lys," Mattie hinted as she exited the bathroom.

Keen blue eyes assessed every centimeter of the gown, carefully analyzing the way the material clung to her skin. "Hmmmm."

Mattie watched her sister's approach. Leaning forward, she whispered, "I mean, really, Lys. I can't even wear panties."

"Not supposed to," Lyssa muttered absently as she smoothed a fold before dropping to her knees to examine the slit in the skirt that allowed for smooth strides rather than hobbling her movements. Moving on to the hem, Mattie watched her sister's blonde head bend to assure herself that none of the tiny stitches were in danger of becoming snagged in a shoe heel.

"Lyssa," Mattie groaned as her sister rose and gave a last smoothing pat to the fabric.

Eyes filled with resolve, Lyssa met Mattie's gaze. "Listen, tonight's the last night, right?"

"Yes."

"You've made it through seven days." Lyssa adjusted one of the dark curls framing Mattie's face. "Do you think you can handle the demands he'll make?"

Remembering the events of the past week and the punishments she'd been subjected to, not to mention the arousal, Mattie nodded. "I believe so."

"So once you're married, if he asks…"

Mattie nodded slowly, unsure of the look in her sister's eyes. "I'll say yes."

"So you might as well have a killer dress to make sure he's paying attention." Lyssa waggled her eyebrows.

Mattie couldn't help but laugh. "Lys, he's definitely paying attention." Her smile faded, though, when her sister's eyes moved to the necklace she'd chosen to wear. Matching dangling earrings glittered with the faceted crystals. After what they'd learned at the Diablo Blanco the night before, Mattie was more than conscious of the bare expanse of skin around her throat.

"Do you think he'll give you a collar as well as an engagement ring?" Lyssa voiced the question Mattie had been pondering all day.

She shrugged. "I don't think so, since I haven't told him my decision yet."

"Do you want him to?"

Again Mattie shrugged, but she avoided listening to the small voice inside that whispered, "yes." Wanting to avoid any further mention of collars, Mattie asked her own question, "You aren't staying for the party?" Her sister's jeans and sweatshirt seemed out of place in the office. "I gave you the invitation."

Lyssa shook her head as she gathered up the few items she'd brought on the off chance that the dress needed slight alterations. "No, I can't stay. I have some designs to finish."

"Lys." Mattie watched her sister's fingers pleat the sleeve of her sweatshirt. "You never told me what happened last night."

The heat creeping into Lyssa's cheeks had Mattie fighting a smile. Perhaps the kiss had gotten out of hand. She hid her disappointment when her sister shrugged.

"Nothing happened, Mat. After Bryce dragged you upstairs, I...hung around for a while, then M-Mike gave me a ride home."

"I saw him kiss you," Mattie teased.

Lyssa rolled her eyes at her. "Oh, for God's sake, he's a kid!"

Mattie laughed. "He's my age, Lys."

"Exactly. He's six years younger than me and spends all day ogling naked women."

"I do not ogle naked women." The curt response had Mattie turning to find Mike lounging in her doorway, his black tuxedo looking startlingly sexy against his dark hair and tanned skin. But the heat in his brown eyes as he watched Lyssa had Mattie wondering if her sister was keeping something from her.

She didn't have time to contemplate the idea before Bryce strode through the door, his gaze on his watch. "Lawrence, we're going to be late. Are you...?" His words trailed off as his gaze skimmed her gown, paused on the jewelry at her throat, before halting on her face. "Definitely ready," he murmured.

Ignoring his brother and Lyssa, Bryce slowly circled Mattie, his eyes like a caress sliding over her skin, settling at the sensitive dip above her bottom before rising to take in the elegant knot confining most of her hair and the dangling curls framing her face. Turning to Lyssa, Bryce grinned and surprised everyone in the room with a courtly kiss against the back of Lyssa's hand. "My compliments, Miss Lawrence, on an incomparable dress."

Setting his hand at her waist, Bryce urged her toward the door. "Now, Lawrence, we need to get moving. Mr. King is due any moment, and I want to make sure we are downstairs waiting for him when he arrives."

Glancing back at her sister, she worried at the expression on Lyssa's face as Mike stepped in front of her, blocking her exit from the room. When she tried to get Bryce to stop, he ignored her protest and ushered her into the elevator.

* * *

"So, are you in?"

The mingled noise of party chatter, soft music, and laughter from a nearby couple would have made it impossible to hear if Bryce hadn't been standing just behind the group of five men, his presence hidden by the broad leaves of a potted plant. He recognized the voice of Davis Daniels from his company's marketing department. The other four were also familiar. Victor had his back to him, but he recognized the man's cocky stance and dark hair. After the episode in Lawrence's office, he'd checked into the rumors circulating about the brash attorney. He wasn't liking what he was hearing, and the stories being told by some of the members of the Diablo Blanco Club were merely reinforcing the objections he'd heard Lawrence voice numerous times.

"In on what?" The query came from Richard Bennett, the only man topping Victor's six feet. He stood at an angle to the rest, his shrewd gray eyes watching the men and then looking back at the milling party guests.

"Victor has a pool going." Charles Winthrop was quick to explain, his brown eyes and boyish looks well-developed weapons when he was sent to negotiate mergers. The look within those eyes reminded Bryce of something feral, almost vicious, sighting its prey.

"A pool for what?" Roger Vincent from the accounting department was the last of the five men. He hovered at the edge of the group, looking as if he regretted having stopped and ready for any excuse to escape the small cluster of men.

"How long it's going to take him to bang 'Ice Queen' Lawrence." Davis chuckled nastily.

Victor's expression must have been one of cool confidence, even smugness at Davis's revelation, because Richard's attention was immediately focused on the younger man. The very stillness of his body warned Bryce his friend was battling the same need he had to take Victor aside to enlighten him as to whom Lawrence belonged.

"Mr. Halsey's Lawrence?" Roger stammered, his body edging farther away from the group.

Richard's face would have been impossible to read if Bryce hadn't known the man for nearly thirty years. Anger and disgust narrowed his gray eyes and thinned his full bottom lip. He remained quiet, letting the other men dig their graves.

"Yeah." Charles snorted. "He thinks he's got it made."

Roger shook his head. "I don't think so. Mr. Halsey thinks very highly of Miss Lawrence."

In Bryce's mind, that response earned Roger job security for as long as he ran the company.

Richard nodded in agreement. "I would be very careful..." he warned.

Victor interrupted, arrogance oozing from his every word. "I've noticed distractions in the boss's office. That magazine article has had so many board members in a tizzy, Halsey has been working overtime to smooth the ruffled feathers."

Based on the way Richard stiffened even more, Victor must have given some kind of look or signal to remind his friend about the meeting in his father's office and the request for his resignation. Bryce wondered just how the attorney could believe he'd actually sit back and let Frieda and Lionel Makepeace and their lackeys drive him out of the business he'd been born to run. Everything was going according to plan, and once Lawrence slipped his ring on this evening, the board wouldn't have any other objections. He didn't see how Victor could have gotten the mistaken notion he would allow another man to walk away with his woman. Perhaps the warning he'd given the little snot outside Lawrence's office earlier in the week hadn't been forceful enough.

The group of men turned their attention to someone across the room as Victor continued burying his career. "All you have to do is look at her." He gestured to the woman smiling and chatting with the guest of honor.

"Before tonight I would have thought she wasn't much to look at." Charles snorted, sipping his scotch and soda.

"You haven't 'bumped' into her in the elevator, have you?"

Bumped? Bryce imagined the excuses Victor had come up with to bump into Lawrence. He wondered, his gaze drifting back to her, if she'd failed to mention any further incidents to him. Knowing how vocal she was in her dislike for the attorney, he had to guess she hadn't. Shifting his position, but remaining hidden, Bryce was able to see Victor's profile, and the expression on his face had Bryce setting aside his glass before he ended up crushing it.

"Nice, tight ass, tits that just beg to be squeezed. Her hips could be a little smaller, but they're something to hold on to when push comes to shove." Victor laughed, his black brows rising knowingly over his eyes as if making sure his audience got the right message.

"You should watch what you say," Roger warned.

"Nothing that hasn't already been mentioned." Victor brushed aside the warning. "Give me two weeks, three at the most, and little Miss 'Ice Queen' will be begging for some of this." His hand dropped to cup his cock.

Bryce let his anger simmer. It would be useless to rip Victor's throat out in the middle of the party. Too many employees would be speculating over the reason why. He'd spent the last eight years watching, preparing, arranging to bring Mattie under his control, and the juvenile bragging of a wannabe lothario was insufficient reason to endanger his plan at this late date. Hell, he already held her in the palm of his hand. She'd already agreed to marry him, and once they exchanged the vows, he didn't doubt her introduction to his lifestyle would begin in earnest.

"This sort of speculation borders on sexual harassment, don't you think, Victor?" Richard queried, sipping his drink.

Bryce noticed Richard's attention straying to him as he eased away from the wall. The briefest of signals passed between himself and his friend before Richard returned his attention to Victor's response.

"...broads to overhear and it's just us men, Bennett. Come on. You can't tell me you haven't once thought about having Mattilda go down on you? Or tossed the idea around with the boss? I mean, the two of you have known each other for so long."

Before Richard could reply, Charles again demanded of the other men, "So are you in?"

Roger Vincent shook his head. "I don't think it's an appropriate thing to participate in." He walked away, taking a hefty swallow of his beverage, before any of the other men could respond.

Davis Daniels pulled his wallet from his inside jacket pocket and fished out a twenty. "I give her two weeks from Thursday." He handed his money to Charles with a nasty chuckle.

Winthrop tucked the bill with the small stack he'd collected from other men and jotted down the date on the slip of paper before turning his attention to Richard. From his own wallet, Richard slid out a twenty, passed it to Winthrop, and predicted, "Not a chance in hell he'll get to first base with Mattie, let alone into bed."

Bryce's grin deepened at the flush of anger sliding across Victor's face as Winthrop took the money.

"By the way"—Richard nodded toward the small collection of money—"just how many men have 'contributed' to the pool?"

"About ten," Winthrop replied, making notes on the slip of paper. "Stanson and Little from accounting; Renner, Dawson, and Stillman in mergers; you, Daniels, Prommer, me, and Tenley in advertising."

Victor watched Richard for a moment. "Just some of the guys, you know," he offered with a shrug as if suggesting the pool was as harmless as the ones that occasionally cropped up during the football, basketball, and baseball seasons.

Richard nodded, lifting his scotch to his lips as he moved away from the three men.

Bryce made a mental note to discuss the employment histories of the men who'd contributed to the "bet" with Richard as he turned away from the group as well.

* * *

"You really must see Sydney, Miss Lawrence." The smile and sexy Australian accent would have probably swayed her if it weren't for the fact that she was in love with Bryce, Mattie thought.

"It's on my list of places to see, Mr. King," she assured him with a matching smile.

"Ian," he corrected her. "I'll probably be ringing you up daily with one question or another."

The feel of a hand sliding beneath the draping of beads to caress her back alerted Mattie before Bryce's voice reached her ears. "And she'll be directing your calls to me, Ian, so don't try to charm her away."

Mattie looked over her shoulder at her employer as he moved up behind her. "Mr. King was just giving me some tips on the sights to see in Sydney."

"Ian," the other man urged again, his smile widening.

Bryce's smile was just as knowing. "I know exactly what Ian was trying to do, and I'm not letting him seduce you away from Halsey's." Nodding toward a petite brunette having words with Richard across the room, he suggested, "See if you can get Becka to quit talking numbers with Richard, Ian. I need to have a word with Lawrence."

"Why do you insist on calling her that, Bryce?" Ian shook his head, seeming to accept the brush off with equanimity and wandered toward the corner where Richard and Becka stood.

"I don't know where you got the crazy notion…" Mattie began.

"Because the man has been charming women out of their clothes since he was in his teens." Bryce took the champagne flute from her hand and finished the golden liquid inside. "Ginger ale?" Setting the empty glass aside, he kept his hand at her waist, his thumb stroking along her spine in soft, slow movements.

"You know I don't like to drink." Trying to think what glitch in the party could have brought the annoyed look to Bryce's face, she asked, "Is something wrong?"

"Not particularly, but I would like to speak with you a moment." Bryce looked around the room before nodding toward the open garden doors. The ground-floor ballroom led into an enclosed arboretum situated in the center of the high-rise tower.

Once away from the party and the jumbled noises, Mattie breathed deeply, enjoying the scent of the roses and the subtle hint of night-blooming jasmine just opening its petals since the bright overhead lighting had been extinguished. The fluorescent shine had been replaced with the softer glow from fiber-optic tube lights lining the pathways winding through the trees and shrubs.

His hand on her lower back guided her as they moved along the path, easing deeper into the greenery.

"Have I mentioned that you look beautiful this evening?" Bryce asked as he turned into a secluded area.

Mattie's heart fluttered. "No."

Bryce stopped just short of a cushioned bench and turned Mattie to face him, his hand riding the curve of her spine, where the dress dipped lowest. "Well, you do. Look beautiful. In fact, if it weren't for the hundred or so guests mingling in the banquet room, I'd spread you out on a table and spend an hour or so eating you for dessert."

Her heart hammered in her chest at the heat his palm exuded. "Lyssa is starting a line of evening and formal wear." Remembering his compliment to her sister earlier, she said, "Thank you for letting her know you liked the dress."

Bryce smiled and moved around to examine the gown, his hand skimming the warm flesh exposed by the backless design. The beads of crystal tinkled and clicked together as he dragged his finger along her spine from waist to nape, then back again. "Very…elegant," he murmured as he moved to stand in front of her, both hands now settled at the base of her spine beneath the draping beads. "Very sexy." His hands tugged Mattie a step closer. "In fact, it's just perfect for what I have planned this evening."

Mattie had to swallow several times. She braced her hands against Bryce's broad chest as she teetered nervously on her heels. "A-an-and what do you ha-have…ah, planned?"

"You have a decision to make." Bryce smiled down at her, his hold on her tightening subtly.

Mattie's heart thundered in her ears. She squeezed her eyes closed, willing herself not to be swayed by his words. She nodded. "So do you."

"Me?" He seemed a bit surprised at her comment.

"I wasn't the only one involved in this little test, Bryce." Mattie stepped out of his hold and moved to sit on the cushioned bench.

"I had little doubt in your success, Lawrence." Bryce reassured her as he released the button on his jacket, pushed the sides back, and slid his hands into his trouser pockets.

"True," Mattie admitted, but she held his gaze. "But I sense there were moments when you weren't quite sure…"

"Never." His tone and stance communicated his irritation at her assumption.

At least that was how she interpreted the narrowed-eyed glare and tight expression. "I'm sure there were moments…"

"Let me make something abundantly clear, Lawrence." He leaned over her, one hand slipping beneath the loose curls at her nape. "You were the one who wanted the trial period, not me. *You* wanted to be tested."

Releasing her and stepping back, he continued, "If we had done things my way, you'd be well and thoroughly fucked by now, and we would have flown to Vegas to say 'I do' the afternoon you agreed to marry me." Arms crossed over his chest, he demanded, "So what's your decision?"

"About what, Halsey?" She was as annoyed as he'd ever made her. She stood facing him, hands on her hips. "You haven't offered me anything."

"You damned well know what, Lawrence."

"Tell me again. Remind me why it's such a great idea to submit to you when I'll already be shackled to you for the next five years." Mattie could have cursed her temper and the anger stirring it.

It had been this way for years. He would poke and prod until she exploded. At first she'd kept it inside, slinking away to her office to blow off steam, typing up her feelings, then deleting them. Until she'd learned that yelling back at him wouldn't produce the beatings she'd gotten for contradicting her father. She learned it was okay to argue with Bryce as long as her defense was strong and she kept her words rational.

But this time it was different. This time it wasn't about some business deal or donation to a charity. This time it was her future, her life she was talking about. In the week she'd spent discovering her sexual nature and the intensity of emotion and feeling to be found in surrendering control to him. Mattie had admitted to herself that Lyssa was right. She was in love with Bryce Halsey and probably had been since the first day she'd barged into his office. Marrying him was only part of her dream. Having him accept her as his submissive was the other. Some part of her, a niggling bit of doubt, whispered that she'd never see that dream realized.

"Why?" He seemed surprised at her question.

The very lack of emotion in his voice was frustrating to Mattie. The rest of his words merely reinforced her fears that his confidence in her might not be as strong as her own.

"Because you care about the company as much as I do. You don't want to see Frieda and Lionel Makepeace tear it apart simply because I couldn't assume my rightful place due to some misplaced fears and archaic perceptions on the board of directors' part. You have the right image and confidence to reassure those undecided members of the board." Bryce moved close, his breath washing over her lips. "And last but not least," he growled, "you want my cock slamming into your tight, wet pussy so bad that if I bent you over in the middle of the ballroom and fucked you, you wouldn't care who was watching."

And the fact that what he said was true only made Mattie wonder how long she'd tolerate half a relationship with this man. Was she willing to set aside her dreams and hopes in order to see that his needs were fulfilled?

"It's nice to know I'm good for something."

Bryce didn't take the bait. His eyes flashed a darker green for a moment, but it could have been a trick of the subdued lighting.

"I know you agreed to marry me on Saturday, Lawrence, but are you ready to finally announce it to the company?" Bryce asked.

The thought of standing before the ballroom full of board members and company employees had Mattie trembling. Saying yes to being his wife was one thing, but facing the assessing stares of everyone was something else entirely. But it had to be done. She nodded. "Yes, I'm ready."

"Good." Ever the decisive and well-prepared businessman, Bryce pulled a small black velvet ring box from his pocket and opened it. "You'll need to put this on. We need to get back to our guests. We'll make the announcement to the board and the department heads inside; then we can contact the newspapers in the morning. Have you already started on the arrangements?"

Mattie didn't get a chance to see the ring before he slipped it onto the ring finger of her left hand and turned her back toward the party. She kept pace with him by taking two steps to his one, thankful Lyssa had cut the back of her skirt to allow for full strides. "No, I haven't. I've had other things on my mind this past week." Mattie winced at the sarcasm in her voice.

Bryce stopped, his grip on her waist tightening to keep her beside him. The sound of guests was still muted, the ballroom hidden by the garden's vegetation. "Is there a problem, Lawrence?"

"No."

Turning her to face him, Bryce secured Mattie's attention by settling his hands at her waist beneath the beads again. He didn't say anything for a moment, just scrutinized her face before speaking. "You don't seem to understand something, Lawrence."

"What am I not getting?" Mattie responded. "You're marrying me because I know what your job is like, I know the business and your responsibilities, and because I reflect the perfect image to reassure the board that you're settling down? Right?"

"Correct."

"So what do you think I'm missing?"

"This." His hands pulled her close as his head dipped and his mouth captured hers.

It wasn't a probing or tentative kiss. His firm lips demanded a response and her body gave it. His tongue traced the seam of her mouth before sliding past and exploring the moist confines within. He twined his tongue with hers, drawing a moan from somewhere deep inside.

Visions of her body wrapped around his, his cock sliding, thrusting into her in the same rhythm as his tongue, had Mattie's breasts swelling, her nipples peaking, and her pussy plumping up and preparing itself for his attention. Remembering the feel of his lips against her naked mound, the advance and retreat of the vibrator and his fingers in her pussy, the press of the plug in her ass, Mattie wondered at the anger that refused to go away. She was getting what she wanted, wasn't she?

Pulling away, Bryce watched her with a wry grin. "You've spent the last week sampling what I expect from you. Learning what is and isn't allowed and experiencing the type of punishment disobedience can result in. What makes you think marriage to me is going to be any different?"

Mattie couldn't think for a moment. The way she felt, she imagined her expression was passion dazed. A week earlier, his words would have had her lips opening and closing in stunned disbelief until she stammered her understanding even though she didn't. Now, having felt his hand on her ass, his fingers preparing her for his cock, there was little about his sexual needs she didn't know. And wasn't eagerly looking forward to experiencing.

What she also wanted were his emotions, confidence that his commitment was as strong as her own. The cool Master Dom gazing down at her now was in no way the man she had come to know over the last eight years.

"Do you, Lawrence? Let me remind you the rules are still in effect." Bryce again dipped his head, but instead of kissing her, he settled his lips just below her left ear and whispered, "If you ever again go out in public sans panties or bra, without permission…"

Mattie could feel the warmth of his exhalation against her neck. Her breath stopped as a work-callused palm slipped beneath the draped edge of her gown. It settled on her naked bottom, then lightly squeezed.

"Last night's punishment will seem like a walk in the park."

His warning had anticipation stirring within her. The gush of sudden moisture flooding her pussy didn't surprise her, considering how long it had taken her to calm down last night. The sensation increased as Bryce slid his fingers over her ass and between her thighs. Her face heated as two nimble digits explored the moisture coating her flesh while his thumb stroked over the base of the plug he'd inserted earlier, before Lyssa had arrived.

His darkening gaze held hers as he tested her body's response to his promise. A white blond brow quirked up, and his lips lifted in an almost-sinister grin. "It excites you, doesn't it?"

Understanding how a bird trapped in the mesmerizing stare of a snake felt, Mattie nodded.

His fingers dipped farther into her wetness, parting the lips of her pussy and rimming the entrance to her body. "I wonder how long you can wait before you have to climax? Were you up all last night? Did you ache, waiting for permission to come?"

She swallowed and nodded. Holding her breath waiting for his next comment or touch, Mattie wondered at the feasibility of her plan. The smell of night jasmine, moist earth, and her own arousal filled her senses. The rush of blood through her veins, the thrum of her heart, everything was registering but muted. All those feelings were so easily overridden by the sensation of his touch and the wicked glint in his eyes.

Damp fingertips drifted back, playing with the plug while moistening the flesh around the base with the juices collected from her body, before returning to the damp crease between her thighs. The pressure of his thumb against the toy had her arching farther into his arms, her eyes captured by his in the shadows surrounding them. The glint of his smile grew wicked as first one, then both fingers dipped into her pussy at the same time his thumb shifted the base, pressing against the taut ring of muscles.

"Hmmm," he purred, his voice a rumble against her breasts, stimulating the already-hard peaks into even tighter beads. "You're still so tight, Lawrence, but this ass…" He pulled her close. Holding her gaze, he stroked his digits in, then out, and then back in. "We don't want it too stretched. Tight makes for a much better ride. For both of us."

Chapter Twelve

The breeze blowing up from the ocean had helped keep the wedding guests cool beneath the warm Southern California sun. Despite being late spring, the heat had climbed to just below eighty degrees, making the formal wear uncomfortable until the breeze picked up. The tang of salt water had been refreshing.

Once they'd announced their engagement, things had rapidly fallen into place. With only a few family friends to invite, her dress to be finished, and the menu to approve, Mattie had had numerous tasks to occupy her time outside of the regular routine of the office. In the end, Jacob had stepped in to assist with the few items she'd been unable to complete. Bryce's only contributions to the plans had been to recommend the gardens at Pirate's Folly as the setting for the ceremony and to escort her to city hall to obtain their marriage license.

Ironically, just as Bryce had predicted, within hours of their engagement being announced in the newspapers, the phone calls, e-mails, and unwanted visitors had slowed to a trickle. The IT department was satisfied at the level of voice and e-mail traffic through the servers. Security had seen fewer visitors streaming into the building, so the increased personnel on each shift had been reduced. Tempers had cooled and numerous board members had seen their way to the office to congratulate her. She cringed to think of the number of times she'd been told she was perfect for Bryce. "Just the right calming influence, Miss Lawrence." That was the favorite phrase of many of the board members and their spouses. After giving their opinion, their wives would admire her unique engagement ring.

Even she had to admit, if given a choice, she would have selected it. It was intricately carved, and though small, the details were stunning. Set in the center of the petals of a rose in full bloom, a dragon's claw held a black fire opal that shimmered when the light hit it. She assumed Jacob must have picked the platinum ring, since knowing Bryce as she did, she couldn't see him selecting such a fanciful design.

What she had missed this past week were the heated interludes Bryce had arranged when she'd been determined to find out if she could submit to his Dominant nature. It seemed as if the same intensity of attraction that would result in sweaty sheets and limbs tangled in Bryce's bed on the night they announced their engagement was just as easily turned to anger when she'd demanded a prenuptial agreement. The cold-shoulder routine had begun once he heard her demands.

"Ridiculous," he'd snapped, glaring across the desk at her as they settled in his office after the last of the employees and guests had gone and the caterers had packed away the dishes.

"Why? Because I'm willing to look at this from a logical perspective?"

"Because Makepeace will wave the damned prenup at the board, and they'll demand I step down the instant your five-year deadline is revealed."

"There is nothing in my request that says we have to divorce in five years, Halsey. Just that we reevaluate our relationship at that time and determine our next step." Mattie fought the need to back down. Hell, she hated the thought of examining the marriage after any amount of time, but it only made good sense. "Think about it," she urged him, leaning forward in her chair and bracing her clasped hands on the table. The ring on her finger felt odd, foreign, but she tried to ignore it as she worked to make the stubborn man understand. "In the eight years I've known you, Bryce, not one of your relationships has lasted longer than nine months. A year at the most, if you and the woman were traveling and more apart than together."

"What about us, Lawrence?" He motioned between the two of them. "Explain how our relationship has survived for eight years?" The green of his eyes blazed with repressed irritation and anger.

"No sex."

"What do you call the last week? You wanted a test. I gave it to you. Now you want limitations and checkpoints." Rising from his seat, he leaned forward, bracing his hands on the table, daring her to argue. "What next, Lawrence? A timetable as to when I can fuck you and where?"

Swallowing her own irritation and the hurt his derisive tone shafted through her, Mattie shook her head and leaned back in her chair, arms crossed over her chest. She was glad she'd removed the gown and replaced it with the slacks and blouse she'd worn to work. The more casual business clothes afforded her a sense of objectivity. "No—"

Bryce interrupted her. "Wanting to take on the role of Domme now, babe?"

Unwilling to let him badger her, she shoved out of her chair and met him head-on. "Get over yourself, Halsey. If you'd take one blasted second to listen to what I have to say, you'd realize I'm just trying to save us a lot of pain when you get bored and want out."

That seemed to take him aback. Mattie watched confusion suffuse his features, but it was quickly wiped clear of any emotion. "Bored?" Shoving his hands into his pockets, he shook his head. "I didn't realize you had such a low opinion of me, Lawrence."

Not wanting to read any more into his lack of expression, Mattie closed her eyes and rubbed at the ache building behind them. Her other hand rose to rub at the tension knotting the muscles in her neck. "Listen, Bryce. I'm tired. It's been a long day. Let's just table this discussion—"

The firm clasp of his hand around her upper arm had her looking up at him. "One more thing we should discuss before we table our conversation." His eyes held hers as he pulled her closer.

"Wha-what's that?" she stammered, not sure if it was his gaze or his touch, but the words that he spoke next sent ice cascading through her body.

"Kids."

Wrenching her arm out of his grasp, she moved away from him. "No." There was no yielding in her tone. Just the thought of bringing a child into an unstable relationship had her belly in knots.

"What do you mean no? No, you don't want any? No, you can't have any?"

If there was one thing she desperately wanted and dreamed of most, it was carrying his child, but there was no way she was going to risk having a baby without knowing if she could trust in a future with this man.

"I'm almost forty-one, Lawrence." His eyes studied her as he made it clear what he wanted. "I intend to be involved and able to enjoy my children's growing up. This company will need someone to take over after I've retired, just as I'm taking over for my father. Can you give me some clue as to what exactly you mean by no kids?"

Shaking her head, she told him, "Not in the first two years. Maybe…" She swallowed, her arms wrapped around herself to fight the chill brought on by memories. The screams, the dark, cramped closet she couldn't get out of, the accusations. Drawing a deep breath, she forced them back into the corner of her mind and focused on remaining calm.

"Maybe, what? You will or you won't, or you can or you can't? Give me some clarification here," he snapped, stepping close, holding her gaze.

"I—" Mattie ran her tongue over her dry lips before finishing. "I can have children. And I do want to have your baby. I just want to wait. I want to be sure."

Something in her face must have warned him not to push the issue. And he hadn't. Every other issue and suggestion she'd made, yes, but not her decision that children should wait. Now, a week later, the deed was done.

The vows had been spoken, and she and her husband—*oh my God...* She took a deep breath to still the nerves in her stomach. She and Bryce had said their good-byes to the guests.

Here she stood, her belongings stuffed into closets and drawers, barely filling a third of the space allotted her. The rest of her things, furniture, books, everything either settled in some other room in the house or placed in storage here on the property. Running her gaze over the furniture surrounding her, Mattie shook her head. This was so much more than what she was used to.

The silk veil had been removed hours earlier. Her sister had helped loosen the complex knot of interlaced braids created by the hairdresser Jacob had hired. Untangling each of the braids and brushing her hair had taken only a few minutes, but it didn't settle the nerves that jangled and jumped.

Still, even as comfortable as she was with Pirate's Folly and the nearly two-dozen rooms that made up the mansion, she couldn't bear to remain in their room a moment longer. Slipping out the dressing room door of her suite, she hesitated, wondering if Bryce would be near enough to catch her, or if her sister might find her wandering the halls in her wedding gown. Each thud of her heels as she crossed the carpet runner had her wincing. Kicking them off at the base of the spiral staircase leading up to one of the turrets, she gathered her skirts and hurried up the steps.

Having never been to this floor in the house, Mattie paused in the arched doorway of the staircase. Another archway stood across the wide hallway diagonal from her position, but only two doors opened into the area. Both were closed. Moving to the one closest, she tested the knob and found it locked.

The other door opened easily.

Fading sunlight filtered through the twin sets of French doors and the skylight above, casting a crimson glow over the canvases stacked against the wall, the few chairs tucked into corners, and the paint-spattered table covered in a jumble of brushes, tins, bottles, and palettes. Set between the French doors, not against the wall or near the center of the circular room, but halfway between, was a wide bed with four thick posts supporting the iron canopy; white silk sheets covered the high mattress and a mound of pillows lay scattered at one end of the bed.

She knew about Bryce's interest in painting. The nautical scenes decorating his office and hers were his work, but she'd never been into his studio. In the center of the room, directly beneath the skylight, a painting rested on an easel. It was larger than any she'd ever seen in the offices and the braided black leather framing the canvas piqued her curiosity.

With the light fading through the windows, she reached for the switch beside the door. Lamps, scattered around the room, offered only a dim glow, but it was enough as she stepped around the easel and froze. Her heart stopped, then resumed thumping in a ragged, excited beat. The heat between her thighs and the gathering moisture had her cursing the overactive imagination that allowed the image before her to come to life in her mind.

* * *

The brief summary spelled out his suspicions in black-and-white.

"Sorry it took so long to get the information, Bryce." David Henderson turned from his examination of the books on the shelves to meet Bryce's gaze.

"I understand," he assured the investigator before his gaze dropped to read the last line of the report for the third time.

As confirmed through interviews and information filed with subject's personal physician, subject has never participated in sexual intercourse with any partners, male or female.

"You'll send the bill to the Folly." He closed the file and slid it into the desk drawer before rising from his chair.

"Of course."

The hesitation in the younger man's voice had Bryce pausing to sit on the corner of his desk. "You have something to say?"

David scratched at the neatly trimmed goatee framing his mouth, seeming to debate whether he would voice his comment. Apparently his need to say it overrode his caution. "I figure if you act fast, you can have an annulment wrapped up before the end of the month."

Bryce fought the urge to laugh. He'd trained this man, so he understood David's misconceptions. Without realizing it, his right hand moved to worry the ring on his left. Its unfamiliar weight was strangely comfortable. "There won't be an annulment, David."

The younger man stared at him. "But your rule…"

Bryce shook his head. "No annulment."

David seemed to think about it for a moment before he shrugged, his hands tucked into his dress slacks. "At least she was conscientious about birth control."

"Explain." Even Bryce was surprised at the irritation filling his voice at this information.

"According to her doctor's records, Miss Lawrence can't use birth control pills. Something about side effects. So about two weeks ago, she was fitted for a diaphragm. It came in day before yesterday and she picked it up."

He didn't ask how David had gained access to the confidential information about his wife. The man's covert skills were something he'd admired and relied on since David had taken over Henderson Investigative Services when David's father retired three years earlier. Instead Bryce nodded and thanked him before following the younger man out of the study.

The stairs leading up to the family bedrooms stood to his right as he watched David let himself out the front door. They'd seen most of the guests off before Lawrence and he had drifted toward the stairs. David's request to talk to him had caught him halfway up, so he'd left his bride to go to their adjoining rooms alone.

Bryce controlled his need to curse. Her damned stubborn refusal to wait before having any children would drive him insane. More than likely she would relent on the time frame she'd given, but he didn't want to wait. A child would connect them. It would forge a link she couldn't walk away from, no matter how hard she might try. He could read the mistrust she carried about his commitment to their relationship, but he wouldn't allow her to hide from it.

Since their confrontation over the prenuptial contract, he'd been contemplating actions that would test their relationship but at the same time solidify Mattie's connection to him. With this last bit of information, he was pretty damned sure, distasteful as it may be, it could be the only move left for him. Turning away from the temptation to join his wife, Bryce entered the formal sitting room.

"You don't look like a man anticipating his wedding night," Richard teased from his seat on the sofa.

Anticipating, hell, Bryce thought. His cock was hard and more than willing to spend the next week sating every need he'd held in check for most of the last decade. In answer to Richard, he smiled. "Just making sure the guests have been seen to."

"With the way you've been plotting this, I'd've thought guests would be the last thing on your mind."

An unusual anger slid through him. "Worried you'll have to wait longer than usual to fuck my woman?"

The very stillness that surrounded Richard had Bryce cursing silently. Setting his glass on the table, Richard rose and crossed to face him. "Do you want to say that again, old friend?"

Thrusting his fingers through his hair, Bryce shook his head. "No. My apologies, Rich."

"I'm not the one you should be worried about, Bryce." Shaking his head, Richard stood beside him, arms crossed, eyes carefully scrutinizing him. "You don't actually think you'll be able to share her, do you?"

A part of him wanted to growl at the very thought of letting another man touch what was his. With the report confirming his suspicions about his wife's virginity, a primal part of him reveled in knowing that he was the first to bring her to orgasm, and he would be the first to slide deep into her tight, wet sheath. Another part whispered just how much more intense her climax would be when he introduced her to the pleasure to be had from a ménage.

Shoving that possessive beast down deep, he faced his friend and business associate. "Of course. How is this any different than any of the other women we've shared?" Even with the words spoken, he could see Richard doubted his assurances.

"This is Mattie we're talking about, Bryce," Richard reminded him, returning to his seat to retrieve his drink. "She's not like any of the subs we've trained or the women we've been involved with before."

"She's more, Rich." Bryce smiled as he recalled the various punishments his woman had endured during the trial period she'd insisted on. "I've never seen a woman who was more perfectly suited as a submissive than Lawrence."

"And a ménage?"

"That as well." Bryce forced the words out despite the twisting in his belly. "She'll take to it as naturally as she took to spanking."

"But what about you?" Richard asked. "Will you be able to handle the repercussions?"

For that question, Bryce had no answer.

"Answer something for me, Bryce?" Richard asked, leaning back in his seat.

"If I can."

"Why do you always call her 'Lawrence'?" Richard chuckled. "Since the first day she started working for us, I don't think I've ever heard you call her by her first name."

Bryce actually had to laugh as he contemplated how to answer. Tucking his hands into his trouser pockets, he shrugged. "It was safer to call her by a man's name."

"Why?"

"Keeps me from having to hide a permanent erection." His grin had Richard laughing. "I figured if I called her by a man's name, it would give me just enough time to keep from imagining her naked and spread out for my attentions; then I could control my cock enough to avoid getting into too much trouble."

* * *

The sight of her shoes halted his hand as it reached for the bedroom doorknob. Discarded at the base of the stairs leading up to his studio, Bryce couldn't stifle the grin at what she would have discovered if she'd entered the room. Bending to collect her heels, he moved up the steps, careful to make as little noise as possible. The glow of the lamps and sunset spilled across the honey-colored wood floor as he crossed to the studio door and looked inside.

Mine. The word echoed in his head as he watched her standing before his painting, her gaze focused on the canvas.

The light of the dying sun cast a crimson glow around her body, glinting like flames on the unbound curls hanging to her waist.

In his mind, the years rolled back and the image of another woman in a white gown on her wedding day superimposed itself over the features of his wife. Instead of long, curly brown hair, she wore her soft blonde hair in shoulder-length waves that framed her peaches-and-cream face. At eight, he'd known Miss Helen was beautiful. She was also well loved, not only by his father but also himself. She'd been the perfect mother to him for the eight years before he turned sixteen. It hadn't been until years after her death, when he'd moved to California and inherited Pirate's Folly and the Diablo Blanco Club from his great-uncle, that he'd realized how much his father had loved her as well as his mother.

Neither of his mothers had been submissives or even interested in the lifestyle his father had participated in before his marriages or after their deaths. Jacob's love for both women was deep enough that he'd suppressed the very nature he'd been raised and trained to use. The intensity of his feeling was reflected in the pain his father suffered with each of their losses. A hurt Bryce had felt with Miss Helen's death and which he never wanted to endure again. Bryce slammed the door on his memories and the emotions associated with them.

A master controls no one if he cannot control himself. The phrase ran through his mind, recalling him to his determination for absolute control. He needed to maintain the necessary barrier between his emotions and the women in his life. Mattie would be no different. He would make sure she wasn't.

Blinking, he refocused on the woman he'd exchanged vows with. She belonged to him. Despite her not having said the words, he knew her feelings for him, and he'd be damned if he let her five-year plan take her away from him. No, she'd trusted him to lead her body into pleasures she'd only read about. He wasn't about to let her get away after having waited eight years to have her. As underhanded and devious as it might seem, his action would force one of the boundaries she'd tried to establish, and he decided as he silently set her shoes on a chair beside the door and entered the room, no matter what it took, he'd make sure she never left him.

"Well?" Mattie heard the deep Southern drawl of her husband as she stood before the life-size canvas.

Refusing to turn, she shrugged. "What do you want me to say?" She swallowed to clear the obstruction that made her voice sound like the croak of a sick frog.

The sound of the door closing and his steps as he crossed the room to her side had her heart hammering so hard, she wondered if it would break through her chest.

"The truth." Bryce's voice whispered past her ear as he moved behind her, eyeing the painting over her head.

She could hear the grin in his voice. *You don't want the truth*, Mattie thought to herself as she fought the fire in her belly while examining the artwork. Each powerful brushstroke was evident in the rich earth tones, gold and brown, that accented the subject. The broad canvas, framed with tightly braided strips of supple black leather, stirred her in ways she didn't want to examine. More than any of the things she'd done with Bryce during the week of her testing, this painting frightened her.

It was the focus that caused her heart to stop, then lurch into rapid palpitations at the same time she felt her breasts swell, her nipples peak, and her pussy grow damp as she gazed upon the image of two men entwined around a single woman. The graphic depiction of a ménage wasn't what created the sudden fear and anticipation that flooded Mattie's system. It was the uncanny resemblance the three people in the painting bore to her, Bryce, and Richard.

The woman's hands were bound over her head with a loop painted and attached to the leather framing the canvas and her face turned away from the viewer. The cascade of thick brown curls caught in the tight fist of the man sinking his cock into the woman's ass were similar to the curls she'd just tugged a brush through a few minutes earlier.

The faces of both men were also turned away, with the one in front suckling a breast as he fucked her, while the one behind buried his face in the curls at the woman's nape. The color of their hair was similar to the white blond shoulder-length waves Bryce sported and the mink brown curls Richard kept tamed by cropping them close to his head.

"Lawrence?"

Bryce's voice drew Mattie from the fantasy induced by the image before her. "Yes...well," she stammered, then cleared her throat. She pretended disinterest as she turned away from the painting. "It's...nice." Her nerves had her twisting the wedding and engagement rings on her finger, still not used the weight of the thick platinum bands. She moved toward one of the French doors, wondering if there was a staircase leading down from the widow's walk that she might use to escape.

Bryce's chuckle whispered through the quiet room. He seemed to read her discomfort and moved closer as Mattie watched him over her shoulder. The distance to the door was short, but she knew there was no way she'd make it past him.

Why she would be so frightened she didn't know. In the eight years they'd worked together he'd never once hurt her physically. And the week he'd spent reassuring her that any punishments he meted out she could handle had only proven that the pain he inflicted was more as a stimulant to pleasure than as a means to do harm.

Resolved to overcome this irrational fear, Mattie settled her hands at her waist and turned fully to face him, her mien of bravado firmly in place. If she was going to survive in this marriage, she would have to make it clear that submitting to him sexually was one thing, but knuckling under to his Dominant nature was quite another.

"What else do you want me to tell you, Bryce? That the painting is erotic and a little startling?" She watched him move closer and she took an involuntary step to the side, coming up against one of the posts of the bed. Reaching out, she held the smooth column and waited.

"It is…nice." His voice dropped to a sexy purr. "But, Lawrence, does it make you wet?"

Chocolate brown clashed with ice green for several breathless seconds before Mattie turned away without replying. Her hands gripped the post, and her damp forehead pressed into the cool wood as she fought the arousal his words and the painting stirred. Yes, she was wet, and she knew he wanted her that way, but was it because he felt something for her or because he found it arousing to control her passion? The questions were getting harder to answer, not easier.

The stroke of his hand along the side of her throat didn't help her concentration either. The brush of his lips against her neck as he eased her hair over her shoulder, exposing the back of her gown, had her knuckles going white.

"Did I tell you how beautiful you look today?" he asked, his hands sliding over the ivory silk brocade to the twin pearls holding the Mandarin collar closed.

"Yes." Her breath hitched, then shuddered out of her lungs as the pearls were slipped free. The collar eased open as the callused tips of his fingers traced the narrow triangles of silk securing her long, tight sleeves to the bodice of her gown, while leaving her back bare from shoulder blades to the dimples above her bottom. Only the eight strands of pearls offered any covering as they draped the back of her dress from one side to the other.

"Your sister created the illusion of innocence while acknowledging the siren's power of seduction." His body pressed close. His fingertips drifted across the ropes of pearls, finding the hidden hooks and slipping them free.

Watching him from over her shoulder, Mattie marveled at the heat darkening his eyes as they rose to meet hers. The last and longest strand of pearls pooled in the draped cloth at the base of her spine. The clear plastic bands that had helped to secure the dress snug against her torso had been attached to the same hooks as the pearls. With the loosening of each, only the pressure of the post kept the gown from slipping.

"Now this"—Bryce's fingers pulled aside the last rope and skimmed the silk just beneath the dimples above her bottom—"has tempted me all afternoon."

"How?" The throaty whisper surprised Mattie. Her cheek resting against the post, she gasped at the heat in his emerald gaze as his eyes met hers.

His lips brushed hers as his hands moved up her spine and then slid beneath the loosened silk to stroke her swollen breasts. "Because it's had me wondering, if I bent you over, would it let me have access to your sweet ass without ripping the dress."

Chapter Thirteen

Her gasp was silenced beneath his kiss. The flavor of her arousal mingled with the taste of white chocolate and whipped cream. He hadn't exaggerated. The little drapery of silk had teased and taunted him during the hours they entertained their guests. It also had him wondering if his warning about her undergarments had gone unheeded.

"Tell me, Lawrence," he whispered, his fingers plucking and fondling the taut crests of her breasts. "Are you wearing anything under this dress?"

Her hands had released the post, one covering the silk over his own hand at her breast, while the other clutched at his waist. She pulled him close, her ass squirming against the ridge of his cock, held secured behind the placket of his trousers.

When she didn't answer, Bryce stepped back enough to turn her in his arms. The sleeves of her dress were smoothed away and the gown slid to her waist before she made an attempt to stop it. "Hmmm? Are you trying to hide the fact that you didn't listen to my instructions?" he teased, moving away to shed his tuxedo jacket and drape it over the chaise nearby. His bow tie, cummerbund, and shirt followed.

Discarding his shoes and socks required he sit down and untie them, but his eyes never left her.

The glow of her skin in the pale lamplight made his cock ache even more. Her breasts trembled with her erratic breathing, the strawberry red peaks hard. Tiny white teeth nibbled at her lips, making him recall the light scrape of them the first time she took his shaft in her mouth. Another pulse thrummed through his rigid flesh. "Show me." The command whispered across the room. "Have you earned a punishment, baby, for not following my directions?"

"No," she finally answered, releasing the hold she had on the gown and allowing it to pool around her feet.

She hadn't disobeyed him. Ivory stockings sheathed her legs to midthigh, and the tiniest scrap of silk covered her bare mound with a thin strip wrapped around her hips keeping it in place.

"Very good." He praised her, enjoying the flush that crept over her breasts and into her cheeks as he watched her. "Bring me your dress. We don't want it ruined."

After stepping out of the gown, Mattie bent to retrieve it. The sway of her breasts and the way her hair flowed over one shoulder, hiding, then revealing one globe, gave him visions of that hair drifting down his body. Bryce imagined the tangled curls would feel like raw silk if he wrapped them around his cock. He'd have to see later.

He watched her cross the room, her fingers rehooking the pearl ropes before carefully folding the gown. She held it out as she stood before him, but Bryce shook his head. "Set it here." He patted the worn velvet to his left. His other hand rose to caress the side of one breast, thumb coasting over and around the tight peak before smoothing down to her narrow waist and then farther to her full hips.

It required her to lean across him to access the section of chaise, but she didn't argue or protest. Bent at the waist, Mattie reached to set the dress where he directed. Only his quick shift to grasp her waist kept her from toppling over when his mouth opened on her breast and his teeth nipped at the swollen nipple. When she would have settled onto his lap, he released her flesh and turned her to face away from him.

"Not yet, Lawrence." He noted the husky tone of his voice and slight tremor in his hands as he rose to stand behind her.

Focusing on the tiny bow fastening the bit of silk at Mattie's waist, he tugged it open and quickly slipped her panties off, tossing them onto the folded gown. "Bed."

Mattie gazed over her shoulder at him. "I'm not going downstairs..."

Dipping his head, he kissed her, enjoying again the taste of chocolate, whipped cream, and her. "No." He nodded toward the one across the room. "That bed." As she moved away from him, her steps unsteady, he added, "We'll get to the one in our bedroom later."

The sight of her full curves had his cock straining for release, but he tempered his need. As with every other lesson he'd taught her, he'd slowly been accustoming her to identifying what pleased her most. Even with the report from David still in the back of his mind, Bryce had no intention of going easy. At no time during his lessons had his woman balked at his methods. He wasn't about to slow down now.

She waited for him, legs curled to the side, eyes on him, hands in her lap, the pillows a soft mountain behind her. The ivory stockings blended with the sheets beneath her, but the golden tone of her skin, the aroused flush in her cheeks and breasts, the tight berry-colored nipples made his fingers itch to explore every detail. Maybe, when he'd sated his need, he'd get around to having her pose for him, but he doubted he'd be able to concentrate on putting charcoal to paper when she looked as she did now.

"Spread your legs for me, baby, and lean back against the pillows." Moving forward, Bryce rested his shoulder on the post at the foot of the bed, watching as Mattie followed his instructions and adjusted her position on the bed.

One hand tucked into his pocket, he smoothed his fingers over the perforated edges of the packaged condoms he'd gathered from his room before he'd gone looking for his wife. *His wife.* The words whispered through his mind as he stared at the woman in front of him. Remembering the vow he'd made at his mother's and stepmother's graves, to never love a woman that much again, he had to admit he'd allowed his attraction to Mattie to sway him more than he'd planned.

"Did you enjoy yourself today?" He kept his tone casual, but he was sure the heat of his arousal was evident in his eyes as his gaze lingered on the parts of her body he intended to investigate the longest. The sharp foil edges gouged his hand before he forced himself to relax his grip on the prophylactics.

"Yes." She nodded, her breath hitching as she leaned back on her elbows.

As he watched, her nipples hardened, her legs eased farther open, and her heels dug into the bedding as her hips rocked upward, allowing the moisture coating her plump folds to glisten in the muted light.

Moving his other hand from his waist to stroke down over his erection, Bryce teased her with his smile before pulling the condoms from his pocket and tossing them onto the bed near her feet. With her eyes focused on the six black-foil packets, he shed his trousers and underwear, tossed them onto the nearby chair, and climbed onto the bed. When she would have moved forward and reached for him, he shook his head and ordered, "No, baby. Stay right where you are."

Situating himself directly in front of her, he slid his legs beneath hers so her knees rested over his thighs. The condoms were collected into a small pile, and all but one were set on her quivering stomach. "Tuck these under one of the pillows."

As she shifted to do so, he smoothed his right hand along her leg from ankle to knee, enjoying the heat of her skin through the soft silk. "These are very pretty. But we need to take them off before they get damaged."

Mattie tried to sit up, but again he stopped her with a shake of his head. "No, no. I'll take care of it." Using slow, casual movements, he eased his fingers beneath the wide band of lace at the top and coaxed the stocking down her thigh. At her knee, he paused, raising her leg so her ankle rested on his shoulder, and pressed his lips against the inside of her knee. Setting another kiss on the back of her knee, Bryce finished stripping the stocking from her leg and tossed it over his trousers.

"It always fascinated me, Lawrence," he murmured, his fingers smoothing over her feet, thumbs massaging over the balls of her feet, then downward toward the arch and heel, "that as tiny as you are, you have such long, sexy legs."

"Tiny?" Her denial came out in gasps as his mouth lingered on her instep. "I'm not—"

He leaned over her, pressing her leg back toward her chest. "Baby, you're a good eighty pounds lighter and over a foot shorter than me. That equals tiny in my book." Returning to his upright position, he turned his attention back to her leg. Brushing a ring of kisses around her ankle, he trailed his lips along the inside of her calf to her knee before leaving her limb draped over his shoulder and moving his attentions to her other leg.

Taking his time, he repeated the same slow striptease with this stocking as well, ending with the foot massage and kisses along the inside of her leg. Moving forward, he waited, his lips investigating the sheen of passion coating the tops of her rounded thighs.

The scrape of her nails over the bedding had him fighting a smile as he hooked his hands beneath her ass and lifted her plump, wet pussy to his mouth. The hiss of her breath didn't surprise him. She reacted that way every time, whether he voiced a warning or not. He enjoyed knowing he'd been the first to take her this way as well.

"Hmmm." He hummed his appreciation against the heated folds. "You always taste so…" His eyes held her stunned gaze over the rise of her belly. Taking his time, Bryce dragged his tongue from the bottom of her slit to the top, ringing the hard kernel of nerves before pulling her taste into his mouth. "Good."

With one leg draped over his shoulder and the other settled at his waist, Mattie was open to his attentions, her body quivering with arousal. He watched her scramble to keep her focus and maintain control over the climax building within her.

"You know"—his mouth moved away from her center to suckle the moisture from her thighs—"I've missed this over the past week."

"What?" Mattie rasped, her left hand gripping his ankle as she glared up at him. "Missed teasing me?"

Still my minx, he thought as he eased open her outer lips, exposing the pink inner folds, sensitive bud of nerves, and the tight virgin hole his cock ached to fill. "Tease, Lawrence? I don't tease, baby. I assert discipline." Setting two fingers on either side of her clit, he pinched it between them even as he massaged above and below the pleasure button. His thumb eased inside her channel, pressing against the soft walls gripping him.

"Do you remember what I promised you about tonight?"

Mattie's hips rocked in time to his caress, her moans whispering past her lips, the blissful expression on her face adding to his own arousal. When she failed to respond, Bryce pulled his hand away and administered a soft, firm slap to her delicate flesh that had Mattie arching upward. The pulse of her hips and the flutter of the tiny inner lips of her pussy testified to how close she'd come to orgasm.

"The rules still apply, baby. No coming without permission." He stroked first one, then a second finger into her tight sheath, the passage eased by the lubrication her body provided. "Do you remember what I promised you about tonight?"

"Y-you said you were going to"—she drew a deep breath, tightened, then relaxed her grip on his ankle before tightening it again as she finished—"to ride my p-pussy until it couldn't take anymore, then you were...*ahhh*"—she moaned and arched as he thrust his fingers deeper and scissored them apart and back, stretching the taut muscles surrounding them—"then you were...were going to start on my ass."

"And it feels like it's going to take a while to get you stretched out again, babe." He shook his head as he pulled his fingers free to collect the single condom he'd left beside them on the bed.

Easing her leg from his shoulder, Bryce shifted position until he knelt between her thighs, Mattie's legs draped over his at the knees. He set the packet on her abdomen and stroked his hard cock between the wet folds of her flesh. "Put it on me, darlin'."

Ignoring his instructions, Mattie chose instead to rise up enough to wrap both hands around the thick stalk, her thumb smoothing the pearls of seed oozing from the tip over the hood and down his shaft.

"Baby, either put it on me, or I take you bareback," Bryce growled, his accent slipping free of his control. Stilling her hands on his length, he waited until her eyes met his. "I'd love to feel your wet pussy slidin' over me, Lawrence, and mark you as mine by comin' inside your sweet candy box." He pushed forward, allowing his balls to make contact with her wet opening. "But in keeping with your decision, do you really want my swimmers dancin' with your girls?"

Even as she hesitated, Bryce could tell that some part of her mind was almost visualizing what he'd teased her with. It probably wouldn't take very much coercion, he mused, just a bit more stroking for him to convince her to forgo the protection. In her eyes, he read the same confidence he held that, if one of his sperm did come in contact with one of her eggs, the likelihood of pregnancy was certain. Not that he didn't have every intention of putting his child in her and binding her to him irrevocably long before her two-year deadline, but a semblance of allowing her to set her limits seemed necessary, at least on this first night with her.

In her eyes, he could read the argument brewing. The very fact that she doubted his ability to remain committed to her and their marriage still burned in the back of his mind. Could that be her motivation for waiting? Did she truly not believe in him, or was it that she didn't want his children? Were monsters from her childhood whispering in her mind, reminding her of the abuse and fear she'd experienced at her father's hand? And was she equating his Dominant nature with the overbearing control her father had attempted to exert on his family?

As he watched her mull over her decision, her hands continued to slide over his length, teasing the solid flesh with soft, tender pressure, slow caresses, and the sweet glide of her fingers over the weeping slit.

"Last warning." His words appeared to finally register as Bryce halted her hands again.

Knowing her as he did, it didn't surprise him that in choosing between what she wanted and what was right, his woman would go with what was right. Mattie fumbled the package on her belly, ripped it open, and rolled the condom into place.

He must have let some part of his disappointment show either in his eyes or his expression, because the briefest look of apology flashed across her face. *If the damned woman would just see that my mind isn't going to change in fifty years, much less five, we could get this resolved.* But he didn't begrudge her her fears. Taking into consideration his past, it was only reasonable. Too bad he wasn't going to allow her to avoid those fears. As her master, his responsibility included making her face her feelings of insecurity.

"Bring me home, baby. Show me where you want me most." He smiled down at her, the fingers of one hand returning to hold her intimate flesh open, exposed to his gaze and touch.

The soft, wet walls teased the tip of his cock as she settled his length at the entrance to her body. It wasn't until she tried to shift against him that awareness dawned in her expression just how little control she had in the position he'd placed her. Even as she struggled onto one elbow, flexing her legs but gaining no purchase, Bryce pressed forward, easing past the taut entrance and steadily working his hard length deeper.

"Take it all, Lawrence," he commanded. The thin layer of latex blunted the sensation of heat her tight pussy emitted. The smell of her arousal, the strained awareness darkening her eyes, had him fighting the urge to simply hammer himself deep within her.

Leaning forward, he threw her further off balance, pressing beyond the taut muscles fighting his invasion even as they pulsed with need around him. Feeling her tense beneath him, Bryce waited. Drawing a long, deep breath in order to calm himself, he watched her, searching for any indication of pain or distress. There was none.

Her body tensed beneath him the deeper he moved. The flutter of her pulse could be seen in the delicate triangle of flesh at the base of her throat. The pounding of her heart vibrated the swollen silk of her breasts and was visible in the flush rising over her chest, along her neck, and into her cheeks.

The scrape of her nails against the bedding and the cries sliding from her lips echoed in the quiet room. Holding her gaze, he pushed past resistant muscles until his full length was sheathed within her. The sudden stirring in the base of his spine, the tingling in his balls as they drew close to his body surprised him. None of his other lovers had ever had him on the brink of climax the moment he entered them.

"You're so wet and tight, baby," he whispered, leaning over her, his eyes capturing hers. "Tighter than I expected." Adjusting his focus from the spiraling sensations in his own body to those communicated by his wife's body, Bryce staved off orgasm.

Stroking one hand between them, Bryce eased the swollen petals surrounding him open, exposing the nubbin of nerves to the pressure provided by the base of his cock rubbing over it. Pulling back, he fought the smile threatening to curl across his lips when Mattie protested, her hands leaving the bedsheets to reach for his hips.

"No." He voiced his command at the same time he deftly caught her hands and pinned them to the pillow beneath her head. Grinding his hips into hers, Bryce made sure every inch of his length flexed within her as he advanced and withdrew several times. "You feel so fuckin' good, baby. Six times might not be enough for me tonight."

Even after he settled close, his chest stroking over hers, his hips easing backward and forward, advancing and withdrawing his firm cock through her virgin flesh, Bryce reveled in the clasp of her wet pussy. The gasps of arousal and need spilling from her lips filled the room, but she never begged. When she neared her brink, he could feel the flutter of her internal muscles around his shaft. Her breathing would increase until Mattie regained control of it; then the kneading muscles around him would slow so he could vary his strokes.

"Such a good sub, Lawrence." He praised her as she forced back another orgasm. Sweat slicked their flesh as he settled over her, his hair tangling with the loose curls clinging to the sheen of perspiration on her cheeks. Against her lips, he whispered, "You've got a few weeks to practice your control before Richard joins us."

The widening of her eyes only made his grin broaden. "Oh, baby." Adjusting his hips, he thrust deep. One hand secured her wrists above her head while the other slipped between their bodies to knead a swollen crest, plucking at the sensitive nipple as he added, "It'll be so fuckin' sweet sandwiching you between us."

Dipping his head, he pinched her other nipple between his teeth, tugging at the red peak until his woman arched against him, crushing her mound against the damp curls at the base of his shaft. Releasing the firm bead, Bryce rocked his hips in a subtle circle, massaging her nerve-rich clit squeezed between their bodies and holding her gaze as he continued, "Can you imagine it, Lawrence? My cock buried in your ass, stretching that sweet little rose until you're hovering between pleasure and pain. Then Rich'll slide right inside."

"Oh God." Her plea vibrated against his chest, but the sound was barely audible through the increased soughing of her breath through her lungs. Her thighs trembled around his hips, the muscles flexing wildly.

The cry grew louder as Bryce pulled back, the tip of his cock trembling on the edge of slipping free of her pussy. Her heels dug into his ass as she worked to force him to return. Despite the accumulated heat of the day swirling around them, mingling with the conflagration kindled by their lovemaking, the thought of any man, even Richard, savoring the woman beneath him sent a decided chill snaking its way from his wet cock up Bryce's spine. The flat disks on his chest came alive, tautening into apparent crests just as Mattie struggled to free her hands and tried lifting her hips to his, drawing him back inside.

Instead Bryce waited, wrestling the wayward thoughts back under control and returning his attention to his wife. Once he could feel the rising strength in the pulsing taking place in her most intimate flesh, he pressed inward, tunneling past her soft tissue, forcing the narrow channel to open for him, and finishing his prediction. "He'll fill you up, baby." His shaft rocked back out, then in. "And we'll have you riding our cocks longer and harder than any of the horses we've saddled here at the Folly." He increased his pace. "It'll feel so good, Lawrence. Fucking you front and back. Both of us sliding in and out." He swallowed the bitter taste at the back of his mouth, determined to direct their relationship as he had those in his past.

Out, in, faster and faster, deep, then shallow, Bryce varied the depth and speed, then evened it out before switching up again and this time increasing his thrusts so every word punctuated a stroke in, then out. "Faster and faster, until you won't know which end is up, and your sweet little pussy is begging to come. Your juices coating our thighs, the smell of wet pussy and hot cocks will be thick in the air, and every word will be you begging for permission to come."

"Please." Mattie's voice hovered between them.

His eyes held hers as he used his free hand to shift her hips higher, tighter against his own as he shook his head. "No, baby, hold off. I want to see your pretty brown eyes go black as we ride you through climax after climax. And after each one, we'll remind you about asking permission."

The inevitable happened. The flutter of her flesh around him, the cries sliding from her lips and echoing in the still room erupted simultaneously with the shattering of her body beneath him. The walls surrounding him convulsed, clutching at his length, drawing him deeper, closer. Sobs tumbled from her lips as tears welled in her eyes and spilled down her cheeks.

"Stay with me, darlin'," he gritted out as his own climax released the vise around his balls, arrowed up his spine, through his body, and radiated outward, filling him with heat.

Wits dulled by satisfaction, Bryce hovered over his wife, licking the tears wetting her cheeks. Soft words he was barely cognizant of uttering whispered through the room, easing the ragged soughing of her breath. The trembling of her legs as they fell away from his hips and the cry shuddering out of her as he carefully eased free of her body tugged at the invisible bond building between them. Despite his earlier decision, he was careful to make sure the thin latex protection remained in place as he pulled his still-hard cock free and rolled aside to dispose of the used condom.

Mattie was numb, her mind hovering in a vague cloud somewhere above her shaking frame. One part of her consciousness was aware of the slightest sound, could feel the lightest breeze slide across her damp flesh, while another was finding even the most automatic functions impossible, like breathing. It grew worse when Bryce separated his body from hers and rolled away. Without his solid form keeping her in place, she was sure to float away, her body felt that insubstantial.

The rough pressure of tears pressed against her eyelids, and the ragged sobs were difficult to stifle. Even as her emotions roiled within her, Mattie worked to calm her body. "I'm sorry," she whispered. Curling onto her side, she settled against his back, drawing some satisfaction from the knowledge that though her own climax had been unauthorized, Bryce's control had been just as undermined as hers. The unsteady tempo of his breathing quickly smoothed out. Again she whispered, "I'm sorry."

"It's all right."

The rumble of his voice vibrated through her. The feel of his skin tingled against her palms. Smoothing over the damp flesh, Mattie took her time exploring, stroking along the broad expanse of his shoulders even as he shifted to face her again.

"Get another rubber, baby," he directed, his lips against hers as the slide of his hard cock registered.

Glancing down, Mattie gasped at the firm erection pressed between them, the damp shaft nudged her belly even as she propped herself up on one elbow to retrieve a prophylactic from beneath the mussed pillows. "I...but..."

"Oh no, baby." Bryce shook his head. Gripping one leg, he lifted her limb over his hip even as his free hand moved between them to hold her labia open, allowing his cock to settle into place in preparation for fucking her. "You're allowed one breach of conduct." The head pressed past the opening. "But no more coming without permission. Besides..." He stroked inside, burying himself completely in her wet channel, sending sensations rippling through her body.

She almost didn't hear the rest of his words as she fumbled for the condom beneath the pillows.

"...besides, I'm nowhere near satisfied." Warm lips opened over her breast, suckling the soft peak inside, bringing the sensitive tip to prominence. "I've got eight years to make up for." His hips drew back, pulling his cock free, before hammering it home once, twice, and then a third time as he raised his head, cupped the back of hers, and turned her gaze up to his. "Eight years, darlin'."

Moaning, Mattie stifled the automatic protest rising to her lips as he drew free of her body. Holding the foil packet up, she waited, body trembling in anticipation, knowing nothing would be the same by the time the sun rose again.

* * *

"Are you sure this is all you could find?" Victor thumbed through the file, grimacing at the sparse information within the pages.

"I have no idea what the investigator found, Victor." Lionel's sniff was audible over the connection, as if delving into the past of Halsey's new wife was beneath him.

"Well, it took him long enough." A note at the bottom of one page drew Victor's attention. He'd grown used to the condescending attitude of the Makepeaces, so the derision in the older man's voice was nothing new. "They were just married, so the investigator was a little late to make this information of any use."

"Well, since you couldn't stop the nuptials, you'll just have to make yourself useful and get rid of the bitch before the board meets to give Halsey control." Lionel's tone was especially cold. "It's your job to make sure he doesn't take his father's place." The older man's reminder was couched in his perpetually annoying whine.

Victor ignored it as he read the last few paragraphs of the page. "We have three weeks."

"No, Victor," Lionel reminded him. "*You* have three weeks."

Victor barely noticed the abrupt termination of the call as he reread the single-page, copied article and the neatly typed notes beneath it.

"Hey, Victor." Charles Winthrop stepped into the office and dropped onto the chair in front of the desk without waiting for an invitation. "I just talked to Daniels."

Careful to keep from drawing attention to the file, Victor closed it and set it beneath the blue folder containing another background report on Richard Bennett. "And?" Not that he was really interested in the other man's information, but keeping the sheep placid helped in gaining him access to information he needed.

"Bennett is demanding the money from the pool." The smirk on the younger man's face grated on Victor's nerves. Winthrop wouldn't have a job if he had his way. And with things falling into place the way they were, it wouldn't be long.

"Yes, I am." The cool tone of Richard's voice filled the office as he leaned in the doorway. "Although I am impressed at how late you've decided to stay."

"Wedding over already?" Victor chided. "That certainly didn't last long."

Richard tucked his hands into the pockets of his tuxedo pants, the jacket unbuttoned, and pushed back as he moved into the room and settled onto the corner of Victor's desk. "Let's just say the bride and groom had other things on their minds than partying with their guests."

"How inconsiderate of them." Victor sneered, leaning back in his chair.

"The bet, Victor?" Richard ignored his comment. "Knowing Bryce as I do, and Mattie as well, there's no way in hell you've gotten anywhere near her since the party. So pay up."

Nodding at Winthrop, Victor watched as the Richard collected the money and counted the bills carefully. "I'm sure it's all there, Bennett."

"Just checking." Richard folded the bills and tucked them into his pocket. "By the way, I would suggest curtailing your interest in making bets of a similar nature in the future. If I hear even a whisper of a rumor that you and your pals are laying odds on sexual conquests, your asses will be on the street so fast, your heads won't have a chance to begin spinning."

***

He knew the lighting was poor since the clouds had rolled in during the night, obscuring the moon, but it didn't matter. From memory, he could identify every curve of her body. The soft rise of her breast, the nipped-in waist, and the full, rounded hips were imprinted on his mind's eye. Not to mention stored in his sensory memory as well. Having explored every inch of her frame throughout the night,

Bryce was confident he could easily recreate an image of her without illumination of his subject. Now, leaning back in his chair, sketch pad on his knee, Bryce worked on committing every curve, each dip, onto paper.

The bedcovers were tangled near her feet. The majority of the pillows littered the floor around the bed, having been pushed there earlier in the evening. The thick length of his growing erection was easy to ignore as he worked on the sketch. Hell, his cock hurt too much to think about sinking into her body one more time tonight.

Involuntarily, Bryce chuckled. He'd been right when he predicted six times wasn't going to be enough for him. After that first bone-melting orgasm, he'd given them only a few minutes rest before rolling his new wife up onto her hands and knees and mounting that sweet pussy from behind. The lush curve of her ass taunted him with every thrust, but he'd waited. He'd waited until after pulling three more climaxes out of her before lubing his cock and breaching the tight entrance and marking his property by coming inside her for the first time.

Just a few hours earlier, he'd been careful to study her reaction when he cursed at the discovery of a torn condom. The flash of worry came and went in her eyes, telling him little other than his attentions had exhausted her. Inside he'd grinned at the defective prophylactic, knowing that its collapse could later be pointed to as the possible culprit if she fell pregnant. Despite his plans to force her to face her fears regarding his commitment to their marriage, he hoped this accident proved a lucky one.

As his hand flew across the page and the image of her began to take shape, he looked forward to the day he could have her model for him. Her body round with life... "Christ," he whispered into the stillness of the room. "You're getting as bad as old Cole himself, my man."

Besides landscapes and portraits of his children, his great-great-grandfather and namesake, Collas Brysson Halsey's favorite subject for his art was his wife, Margaretta. In various states of dress, and at all stages of her pregnancies, he'd sketched and painted her.

Looking up from his sketch pad to the woman on his bed, Bryce had to admit to a similar fascination with his own wife. Hell, how many renderings did he have hidden away in drawers and cabinets? Drawings he'd done every time the need had grown so great fucking a convenient woman wasn't enough to satisfy him. Even as he watched her, imagining the curve of her belly rounding and expanding as his baby developed, he had to admit that the thought of mounting her while she was carrying his children was just as exciting as knowing he was her first lover.

In the insufficient light, his eyes followed the curves of her swollen breasts, peaked nipples, and splayed thighs. Despite the weak light, he could make out the glimmer of juices on her naked mound. He wondered if her dreams were as bawdy as his own had been over the years. When sleeping, did she dream of his mouth settling over her pussy, fucking her with his tongue before replacing it with his cock?

Setting aside his pad and charcoal, Bryce gripped his erection, stroking up and down its length as he watched his wife shift among the tumbled bedding. "Spread those legs for me, baby. Let me see my pussy." Bryce was aware he'd spoken his desire aloud, but it wasn't until Mattie complied with his command that he wondered if she was playing at being asleep or if she really was.

When she rolled onto her side, facing away from him, Bryce had to grin. Even in her sleep, his lady was tugging at her restraints. The ache in his flesh as well as that in his balls had him rising from the chair and returning to the bed. "Roll over, baby," he commanded, making sure to keep his voice low.

Mattie did as he ordered, turning onto her back, hair tangled across her face as she arched into the stroke of his fingertips over her breasts. In her sleep she purred in response to his touch on her nipples, the insides of her thighs, and the bare flesh of her mound.

Easing down onto the bed, Bryce settled between her legs, pressing open her labia to expose the wet pink center. Swollen but shy, her clit barely peeked out at him as he moved forward, sliding his tongue from the bottom to the top of her slit and then repeating the caress. The moment he thrust inside the warm sheath, lapping at the honey her body produced, he could feel her tense, then arch beneath him, signaling she was awake.

Protest hovered on her lips, but she didn't voice it. He could see it in her eyes as he rose over her and slid inside, pushing deep, hissing at the discomfort while savoring the wet, heated walls surrounding him. "God, baby." He chuckled, sliding back, then shoving forward, needing the rasp of her flesh over his. "You're so fuckin' addicting. I'm never gonna get any work done."

"Co-con-condom," she stammered, even as her legs rose to wrap around his waist, drawing cries from both of them as his cock settled deeper, rubbing the one spot he'd discovered could quickly undermine any control she fought for over her body.

"Not this time," he commanded. Leaning down, he kissed her, nipping at her lips, puffy from his attention earlier in the evening. "Swear to God, baby, I'll pull out before I come, but I have to feel this. Feel you, wet and hot around me." Even as he shuttled in and out of her body, his hands gripping her hips, mouth feeding on hers, Bryce worked the logistics out in the small part of his mind not overcome by the sensations making love to his wife induced.

Each thought was voiced aloud as he made the decisions, her every response cataloged to be drawn on later for analysis. "No panties at work, baby," he ordered. "At least not for the first six months. I might"—he shook his head, dipped to nibble on a taut peak before finishing—"and I mean *might* be able to make it through my early morning appointments without bending you over the desk, but don't count on it for the next six weeks or so."

Her mewling cries increased as his hips picked up the pace, circling, then thrusting before switching tempo and depth. "And you better make sure we've got plenty of protection stashed in the desks. Both mine and yours. And the apartment upstairs."

"Yes, yes." Mattie gasped, her hands clutching at his shoulders, fingers pressing deep as she fought the climax he could feel building inside. "Oh please, Bryce, I need... I can't..."

"Do you have to come, baby?" he asked, hands cupping her cheeks, forcing her thrashing head to still and her eyes to meet his. The pupils expanded, swallowing the chocolate until only the faintest ring surrounded the black center.

"Please."

"Then come," he whispered, caressing her lips with his. "Let go, darlin'. I've got you." The press and flex of her internal muscles had him gritting his teeth, fighting his own climax. Seconds after hers started, Bryce began cursing as first one pulse, then a second escaped his control, forcing him to pull free and empty his load over her belly and breasts.

Keeping control was going to play hell with his nerves, but finally taking possession of his woman was going to be worth every second of discomfort.

Chapter Fourteen

"So." Lyssa smiled at Mattie as she set the teakettle on the burner and switched on the stove. "How's married life?"

Mattie watched her sister move around the kitchen, not sure how to respond. She could be honest and say the sex was incredible and nonstop, but she didn't think her sister wanted to hear that. "I've only been married a little over two months, Lys. There hasn't been time for the honeymoon to end."

"Bullshit." Lys snorted, setting the box of cookies on the table. The chocolate and marshmallow confections were Mattie's favorite, and Lys always kept them on hand for her. "You've been to the Club at least twice a week since just after your wedding."

Mattie swallowed the bite of cookie and watched her sister carefully. "How would you know?"

"Let's just say a little bird told me."

"Do you mean a nosy brother-in-law?" Mattie teased, still curious as to what had happened that first night she'd talked Lys into going to the Diablo Blanco Club and her sister had ended up with Mike.

"No." Lys shook her head vigorously and hurried to the stove as the kettle began to whistle. "I've run into a couple of

Club members, here and there. And I found out a certain bartender lives in the house three doors down."

Mattie could tell Lyssa wasn't quite telling the truth, but she wasn't about to call her on it. "Okay, so you know Bryce has taken me to the Club."

"And?"

"And what?" Mattie fingered the handle of her cup wondering just how much information Lys had wormed out of her contacts. It wasn't that she was ashamed of her time at the Club, she just wasn't sure how Lys would take finding out about some of the things she'd done there.

"Are you feeling pressured to go?" Lys asked as she set the steaming teapot on the table between them.

Mattie took a moment to think about it. "No." Taking care to pour the hot tea into her cup and then Lyssa's, Mattie continued, "I like the Club, Lys. No one pretends to be someone they aren't there."

"And you? Do you enjoy being on display?" Lyssa sipped her tea, her blue eyes steady as she watched Mattie.

Mattie didn't turn away. In the weeks she'd been married to Bryce, she'd discovered things about herself that she'd never suspected. "It's not what you think, Lys." She leaned back in her chair, her cup cradled between her palms. "The first night Bryce took me to the Club, all we did was talk to and watch some of the other members."

"Like that sexy Santa and his private eye friend?" Lyssa waggled her eyebrows.

She couldn't hold back her laughter. "No, Dayton and David weren't there the first night, but they have been there together and individually several times since."

"And have they watched you?"

That was a harder question to answer. "I don't know."

"You don't know?"

"How do I explain this?" Mattie wondered aloud. "When I'm with Bryce, nothing exists but him. Everything else blurs around me. I don't know any other way to explain it."

A fleeting look passed over her sister's face, giving Mattie the impression that in some way, Lyssa knew exactly what she meant. "What about being tied up or spanked?" her sister asked. "Do you enjoy that aspect as well?"

This time Mattie didn't have to think about her answer. "I love it, Lys."

The older woman choked on the sip of tea. Setting the cup down, she coughed and sputtered for a moment before Mattie took pity on her and stopped laughing. "You are twisted, little sister."

"No"—Mattie grinned—"I've just learned that it can be very freeing to have someone else call the shots. That it's okay not to be in control as long as you trust the person who is."

"And you trust your husband?"

Mattie nodded.

"But you still don't have a collar?"

The fingers rubbing along the base of her throat stilled, as Mattie realized she'd once again reached for the missing object. "No." She slowly lowered her hand to cradle her cup, but she didn't drop her gaze. "He hasn't mentioned it yet."

"And have you talked to him about it?"

Again she shook her head, but Mattie wasn't sure just what Lyssa wanted to hear. "I don't want to have to ask for it, Lyssa."

"What? Are you trying to earn it or something?"

Setting her cup aside, Mattie stood up from the table and paced toward the door leading out to the screened-in porch. "I don't know." Not wanting to see her sister's expression, especially since she feared it could hold a measure of pity Mattie didn't want to experience, she continued staring out the window set into the door. "I have a feeling Bryce never really expected me to indulge his dominance as much as I am. I told him when he first proposed I was curious about bondage, but I think he's just waiting for me to voice the safe word."

"And if you use this safe word, what do you think he's going to do? Leave you? Go to another woman?" Lyssa sounded worried.

Shoving her hands deep into the pockets of her jeans, Mattie shrugged. "I keep hearing this little voice in my head telling me that he isn't serious. That he's just waiting for me to say the word so he can tell me 'I knew you couldn't handle this' or 'Why don't you go back to playing pretend and let a real woman take over.'"

"Mat, I don't—"

"It's the only thing that makes sense, Lys." Turning, Mattie met her sister's concerned gaze and didn't attempt to hide the tears streaking her cheeks. "Jacob's retirement party was weeks ago. He's had plenty of opportunity to present me with his collar, but he hasn't."

"Are you still worrying about what happened at Jacob's party?" Lyssa asked.

"Yes," Mattie admitted. Just thinking about the painful confrontations from that night had her stomach churning.

"Now you're letting what Charlene said—"

"Tell me you wouldn't be just as upset to have some skinny, redheaded model slobbering all over your husband and flaunting the diamond collar he gave her last year. Then to have her laugh about how I don't measure up to her. To *her!* You're damn right I'm letting what Charlene said get to me. She has his fucking collar and I don't!" Brushing at the tears soaking her face, she continued, "Add to that Frieda and her snide little comments about me being 'not their kind,' it makes me sick. And think that maybe they're both right."

"Don't pay them any mind."

Mattie nodded, but she didn't feel convinced. "I tell myself they're wrong. That Bryce is satisfied with me. I just have to stop to remind myself to give it time."

"So give it time," Lyssa encouraged.

"I want to. I try to." Mattie turned back to the view of Lyssa's backyard, her arms crossed over her stomach. "But the longer he goes without saying anything, the larger my doubts become."

"Until he says otherwise—" Lyssa began.

"I don't think he will." The laugh she gave sounded more despaired than amused. "Hell, it could be years before he'd ever admit our marriage was a mistake."

"Now you're being ridiculous," Lyssa snapped. "When you first told me about his proposal, I was worried you might end up hurt. But I've watched the two of you together. Seen how he acts around you. If he doesn't love you the way you love him, he at least cares about you."

"Yes, he does," Mattie admitted, though that niggling voice in the back of her mind taunted her that caring didn't equal love.

"So what's the problem?"

"I want more," Mattie declared. "I mean, I thought I could handle the situation if he could see me as his submissive. But now that I'm actually involved, I'm finding I want more."

"You'll always want more," Lyssa warned her. A shadow hovered in her blue eyes, and she rubbed her stomach. "It's the nature of being in love, Mat. You want what's best for the person you love, but you also want them to feel the same way about you."

Leaning against the door frame, Mattie shook her head. "Every time we make love, I have to stop myself from telling him how I feel. I keep thinking about the reasons why he chose to marry me, and I wonder if he'll ever be able to care about me, beyond just being his lover."

"And how will getting his collar help? What would it mean beyond him staking his claim on you?" Her sister motioned to the platinum rings on Mattie's hand. "You're already wearing his rings. Aren't those proof enough?"

Mattie traced the edges of her engagement ring, her eyes drawn to the threads of fiery red and iridescent blue flashing in the black stone. "It should be, but I need something more."

"*You* need?"

"Yes, me," she declared, crossing her arms over her chest. "I love the damned man and have loved him for years. If he can't love me, he can at least show the other members of the Club that I belong to him. He can at least show me that he values me."

"Is that what you think his giving you a collar would mean?"

Mattie nodded. "For me, that's what it means." Shaking her head, she returned to the table. "Why can't the blasted man see that?"

Smiling, Lyssa reached out to pat her hand. "Because, sister dearest, he's a man. Clear, concise explanations are best." Pulling her hand back, she cradled her cup in both hands. "Tell him what you want."

"No." Mattie shook her head. "I want him to give it to me on his own. It has to be his decision."

"And you're afraid he'll never make that decision?"

Reluctantly, she nodded. "Yes, I am. I want him to recognize my worth and show me that he sees it."

"By having him give you some bit of bling like every other woman he's slept with?"

"Not every woman. Just those he considered capable of meeting his needs as a Dominant." Finishing her tea, she added, "I already have his respect in the workplace. What I'd like is for him to trust me to be able to fulfill him sexually."

"And getting him to give you a collar will do that?"

"To me, yes."

"So make him give it to you. You made him accept you as his submissive, right?"

Mattie nodded.

"Okay, so make him see collaring you is the best way to keep you both satisfied."

"How do I do that?"

Lyssa groaned. "How the hell should I know, Mat? You're the one doing the freaky-deaky, kinky stuff with him; you figure it out. I don't think he'll do it…"

"Why not?"

Lyssa rolled her eyes and rose to put her cup in the sink. "Because I think he already thinks he's got you tagged as his." Motioning to her rings, she snorted. "The second he put those on you, he was warning every other man around to stay back."

"It isn't that simple."

"I bet it is." Leaning against the sink, she grinned. "In fact, I'll bet you that he won't give you his collar because he already considers you marked."

"And if I can get him to give me his collar?" She knew this was Lyssa's way of getting her to face her fears and see that they were unfounded. Much as she appreciated making a contest of getting Bryce to give her a collar, some part of her still worried that her husband didn't consider her capable of sustaining the role as his submissive.

"If you can get him to give you his collar, great. You win. But if he doesn't give you his collar, without you asking for it, you have to leave."

"What?"

"You heard me. Leave. Divorce his ass and walk away."

"Are you nuts?" Mattie snapped. "I tell you how much I love this guy and what I wouldn't give to have him love me back, and you tell me that if I can't get him to recognize me as his slave, I'm just supposed to walk away?"

"Yes."

When she stepped toward her, Mattie nearly turned away, but when her sister cupped her cheeks in her hands, Mattie couldn't look away from the caring and concern in her blue eyes.

"I love you, Mat. And I know that if you stay after trying so hard to get him to give you this one little thing, it's going to eat away at you. Every minute of every day, you'll be dwelling on what you did wrong. What you could have done to change his mind. And why just you and how much you love him weren't enough to get him to see what was right in front of him." Pressing her forehead to her sister's, she continued, "I don't want you doing that. I want you living your life, not withering away like Mom did. If you can't get him to give you his collar, swear to me you will leave. Get a divorce. Find a job somewhere else. But don't stick around here and dwell on what you couldn't have."

Wrapping her arms around her, Mattie hugged Lyssa tight. "Do you still have the dreams?" She felt Lyssa tense against her, then nod. "They've been getting worse." She rested her head on Lyssa's shoulder. "I keep hearing Daddy calling me names. Telling me I'll end up a whore just like her."

"Don't, Mat." Lyssa squeezed her. "He was crazy. Sick. Nothing he said was true."

"But I look like her. Don't I?"

Lyssa cupped her cheeks again and smiled. "Yeah. You look just like Mama."

"Do you hate that I let you take the blame—"

"Hush." Lyssa cut her off. "I didn't blame you then, and I don't blame you now, Mattie. So just hush. I want you to be happy, Mat. You know that, right?"

"Yes."

Pushing a loose strand of blonde hair behind her ear, Lyssa asked, "Do you think I could be like Dad?"

Mattie shook her head and gripped Lyssa's hands tight. "Never, Lys."

"I look like him, Mat. If I had a baby, I could end up hurting it just like he did us."

"No. Lyssa, you could never hurt anyone. You could never be like him."

"But I would hurt you. By making you leave Bryce if he didn't give you his collar, I'd be hurting you."

"No, you'd be protecting me. Just like you always have." Mattie didn't doubt her answer, and the disquiet acknowledging how right Lyssa was made her stomach churn. Thoughts of actually leaving Bryce had her shivering. "I really hate that I can't hate you, Lys."

Lyssa squeezed back, then let go. "Yeah. Kinda sucks when the big sister is right and you have to admit it, huh?"

Mattie nodded, wiping at the tears on her cheeks. "Yup." Taking a deep breath, she collected her cup and the teapot from the table. She really needed to lighten the atmosphere before the tears started up again. "Okay, you want me to divorce Bryce and leave San Diablo if I can't get him to give me his collar."

Lyssa nodded. "It would be for the best."

"I can see that, Lys. I really can. It kills me to think of walking away, but I could do it." Setting the dishes in the sink, she added, "What are you going to do if I win? If I can get Bryce to give me his collar, without asking, what forfeit are you willing to give?"

"I'll make all your babies' clothes?" She grinned.

Mattie laughed. "You would do that anyway. No"—she grinned and nodded—"I know. If I win, you have to pose nude for Mike."

"No." The amusement drained from Lyssa's face. "Nuh-uh. I'm not posing in any way, shape, or form for that man."

"I think you doth protest too much," Mattie teased.

"I do not!" Lyssa's face grew red, and she kept her attention on thoroughly cleaning and rinsing the dishes before putting them in the drain rack.

"Listen, Lys, if I'm willing to pack up and leave a man I've been in love with for eight years, the least you can give up is your clothes and body to art."

"That kid is not an artist. He's a photojournalist."

"According to the awards he's won and the magazines begging him for his photos and articles, he's an artist." Taking hold of Lyssa's arm, she made her turn around. "I mean it, Lys. If you're expecting me to walk away from my marriage as my forfeit, you better be ready to pony up something important too."

"Okay." Lyssa nodded. "I'll do it."

* * *

Despite the reasoning Lyssa had given, the teasing, and their bet, as Mattie pulled into the detached garage at the Folly an hour later, her mind hadn't changed about the reason Bryce hadn't offered her his collar. Clearly, there was something Bryce could sense about her that made him reluctant to accept her completely.

Settling the strap of her tote bag over her shoulder, she exited her SUV and headed for the side door. On the path to the house, she spotted Bryce in the corral working with Jezebel, the long, yellow lead connecting horse and trainer. In much the same way as he trained his horses, Mattie knew he used just as gentle, but firm, a hand in leading her through the various steps of her own submission. Leaving him would be difficult, but if the results from the package in her bag turned out to be positive, it would have to be a choice she'd need to face.

Just inside the door, her cell phone rang, the distinctive ringtone associated with Bryce's cell making her grin. He'd obviously seen her return. "Hello?"

"Have a good time?"

The sound of metal on metal and the snort of a horse assured Mattie Bryce was finishing his workout. "Yes. Are you finished with Jez?"

"Yes. Did Lyssa have any plans with you for tonight?"

"No. She has a design she needs to finish, so we're going to see about getting together later next week."

"That's good to hear, because I have a little something special in mind for tonight." The sexy chuckle had Mattie squirming.

The last surprise he'd given her had left her barely able to move after her fifth orgasm. Not that she was complaining. "Hmmm, that sounds...interesting."

"Give me a few minutes to get Jez bedded down; then I'll be inside to tell you more."

"Will I have time for a bath?" Imagining a warm bath waiting for her had helped soothe her frayed nerves after she left Lyssa's. Mattie still longed to immerse herself in the Jacuzzi tub upstairs, despite the arousal his teasing was stirring.

"Not too long, babe," Bryce warned before disconnecting.

That could mean any number of things, Mattie mused as she hurried up the stairs. In the bathroom, she began filling the deep, round tub. As she settled on the raised platform surrounding the minipool, the bottle of Bryce's cologne caught her eye. Though he only wore it at work and on formal occasions, Mattie loved the distinctive scent. Before she could rethink the impulse, she crossed to the vanity, collected the jar, and drizzled some into the bathwater.

Turning on the jets, she returned the bottle to the counter as the scent-filled steam rose from the tub.

Thinking of Bryce's reason for her last surprise, Mattie shed her clothes, working hard to avoid caressing her body. Pleasure from punishment was becoming hard to control, she admitted as she conjured the memories of a special luncheon at La Paloma. The elegant Italian restaurant was one of her favorites, which was the primary reason Bryce had selected it for her introduction to risk-taking public displays.

Having had an audience when Bryce had received and given oral pleasure at the Club, Mattie had believed that the sensation of risking getting caught in public doing the same wasn't much different. She was wrong.

Stripped of her clothes, Mattie settled into the swirling water, her hair held on top of her head with two lacquered hair sticks, and recalled every detail of that day just a week earlier.

She'd been nervous, seated between Bryce and Richard in the restaurant, diners at the various tables around and in front of them. After they'd given their orders to the waiter, Bryce had settled his clasped hands on the table and spoken, his voice firm but never reaching beyond the island of their booth. "When in my presence, if I give permission for another to touch you, you need to accept it."

Knowing it was the master speaking, Mattie nodded. "I understand."

"Did you leave your panties off before we drove to work as I instructed?"

Again, she nodded. "Yes."

"Very good." Bryce's gaze had shifted from her face to his friend. He nodded and then returned his eyes to hers as Richard shifted closer on the curved bench seat of the booth. "Richard is going to adjust your skirt to better accommodate your instruction. Lift up, so he can settle it around your waist."

The slide of Richard's hand along her thigh had been a warm and somewhat alien feeling. The calluses were not as pronounced as those on Bryce's palms and fingers. His touch was tentative, not as firm as Bryce's, and didn't heat her core the way her husband's did. Still, she did as she was told, lifting her bottom to allow the silk skirt to be pulled up. The chill of the leather seat had her stifling a gasp.

Bathed in the warm water, the scent of Bryce filling her nostrils with every wisp of steam floating from the surface of the bubbling pool, Mattie ached to touch herself as Bryce and Richard had during that long, sensual lunch. The memory of the stroke of their fingers up her thighs to the bare mound of her sex had her panting. Remembering how each man took his turn exploring the swollen lips, the wet passage within, and the throbbing protrusion of her clit, had Mattie squeezing her thighs together and arching upward in the rolling water.

Only the knowledge that breaking the rule about self-stimulation could result in even more denied pleasure kept her from attempting to find relief from her growing need. Unbidden, the plea for permission to come whispered from her lips into the empty bathroom even as it had in the restaurant when Bryce had coaxed her to the edge and then slid his hand aside to allow Richard access to her tender flesh.

Though she hadn't expected Bryce to allow her to climax then, she'd been surprised when he'd taken her clenched fist from the seat between them and tugged her from the booth. Sobbing at the delay, she'd barely been aware of him making sure her skirt had fallen back into place, covering her bare skin, before he led her toward the restrooms. Ignoring any chance that the room might already be occupied, Bryce had followed her into the ladies' room, snapped the lock closed on the door, and lifted her onto the counter in one smooth movement. The rasp of his zipper was barely audible over her sobs as he spread her thighs and ordered, "Wait."

Her fingers had clawed at his suit coat, head thrown back as she swallowed her cries with the firm thrust of his cock inside her. The tight clutch of her body had him cursing as he forced every inch of his length home. "Goddamn it, baby, take it. Fucking take it all," he growled, his hand rising to force her head down to watch their bodies connect. Her flesh swallowed his as the last bit sank in, and the fingers of his free hand spread her labia, exposing her clit to the scratch of his pubic curls and the pressure of his pelvis.

Then as now, she hovered, desperate for climax, knowing he could deny her permission. Deny her release as a means of showing her the strength she had in controlling her body's needs. And then, just as now, she both reveled in and despaired over the power he held over her, that she gave to him. Willingly.

Mattie moaned as the heat stimulated her flesh and another drift of steam increased the scent of her husband around her. Her hands continued to clutch at the sides of the tub, desperate to caress her breasts and belly before they slipped between her thighs to test the moist folds hidden there.

From the doorway, Bryce was reluctant to remain silent. Knowing how she loved to take her time in the bath, he'd come inside hoping to hurry her, but now he was hard-pressed not to join her. With her eyes squeezed shut and her body quivering with arousal, he wondered what thoughts could possibly be running through her mind. A wry grin lifted his lips as he gave in to temptation and crossed the cool tile floor on bare feet.

Standing over the tub, he watched her fingers clutching the rim of porcelain, the flex of her thighs as she held them tightly shut, and listened to the tiny, breathless moans issuing from her lips. Each sent a shaft of heat arrowing directly to his groin. Fully dressed, he eased into the tub and whispered, "Lean forward."

Mattie's eyes flew open, mortification mixed with relief in her gaze as Bryce stood over her. She shot upright in the water and tried to scramble out, but his firm grip drew her back. Sliding down behind her, Bryce cradled her against his body as he braced his feet against the textured bottom and slid his right hand over hers, guiding it between her thighs.

His husky whisper drifted through the dimly lit room. "You have my permission to touch yourself." He could feel her heart fluttering furiously and her body tense in his arms. "Relax, darlin'," he crooned, smoothing his left hand down her left shoulder to the fingers tightly clenched against the rim of the tub, he gentled her slowly, back to the aroused state she'd been in before he'd made his presence known.

"Open up a little more," he whispered, lifting his right leg against hers until her foot rested on the rim of the bath. "Good, good. Now." He eased their fingers between the moist petals. When she tried to pull away, he stopped her. "No, let me show you," he urged. Parting the delicate flesh, he kept his hand cupped over hers as he guided a finger from each of their hands into the tight channel within.

"Feel how wet you are?" His hoarse voice whispered over her ear. "How tight?" She protested softly when he slipped his touch from her, but it was quickly stifled as he nudged a second of her fingers into her sheath. "Your hands are so much smaller than mine, darlin'."

With his right hand guiding hers, he taught her the slow, sensual rhythm that would bring her to climax. When her head fell back, cradled between his neck and shoulder, and the fingers of her left hand twined with his, Bryce grinned with satisfaction. He watched as her breasts swelled, her nipples drew to stiff little points, rising above the water like tiny islands. Against his growing arousal, Mattie's hips pulsed in time to the stroking of her fingers.

Hoarse little cries came on gasps of air as Mattie climbed higher and higher. His hand cupped over hers, Bryce drew their tangled fingers to rest on her right breast; he led her fingertips around the taut, berry-sized bead. "You have very sensitive breasts, Lawrence," he told her as he smoothed her hand around first one breast, then the other, squeezing the full globes with his hand over hers before sliding his touch away when she began caressing herself without his guidance.

Slowly, Bryce withdrew his touch until he was once again just an observer, watching over his wife's shoulder as she lay against him in the bubbling water. He watched, his body taut with desire, as her body grew flushed, her lips parted, her thighs quivered, and she whispered a soft plea.

"Please."

"Please what, baby?" He knew what she wanted, needed, but waited for her to ask.

"May I come? Please, Bryce."

He only hesitated a moment. "Yes, baby, you may."

Arching against him, she cried out as her orgasm swept over her. It took everything he had to keep his hands still on the rim of the tub as Mattie's bottom rocked over the swollen length of his arousal, locked within his sodden jeans. Silent, he waited and watched as she gradually returned to Earth, her hands gently stroking her damp flesh beneath its clear liquid cover.

"Better?" His voice was rough in the dimly lit room.

Refusing to feel embarrassed, Mattie nodded. "Mmmm, much." Letting impulse guide her, she braced her hands on the sides of the tub and lifted away from her husband. Turning to face him, she grinned in amusement at the picture he made, arms draped casually on the porcelain rim, wet chambray plastered to his muscular chest, and soaked denim outlining his straining arousal beneath the waves.

When his shoulders tensed, preparing to raise himself from the bath, Mattie leaned forward. "Wait," she whispered, her fingers sliding easily over his buttons, releasing them one by one until the shirt parted, revealing his darkly tanned chest, sparsely covered with pale blond curls, and lean muscles. Meeting his fiery green gaze, she simply said, "May I?"

Bryce didn't have to ask what she meant. She was sure he could read it in her dark chocolate eyes, and the heat in his gaze assured her his arousal had kicked up another notch. Rising, he rested his flanks on his heels, knees spread for balance, facing her. Her hands cupped his, following as he eased open the five buttons holding his jeans closed, then shifted aside the silk covering his swollen manhood. The dual sensations of rolling water and moist, warm air against his penis, along with the feel of her soft hands over his, brought a groan slipping past his lips. Mattie's gentle smile drew a self-deprecating laugh from his chest. "Think it's funny, my little witch?"

"Oh yes." She smiled, her eyes leaving his to watch as his hands caressed the length of his stalk from base to tip, modeling for her what brought him the most pleasure. Beneath her fingers, she could feel just how firmly he gripped and how fast or slow his strokes were. Much as he'd guided her in learning how to bring herself to satisfaction, Bryce showed her again just what was necessary to bring about his climax.

"It's almost like being inside you," Bryce whispered against her hair as she bent over him.

"How?" Mattie asked, her attention focused on the slide of his fingers over his flesh.

Drawing in a deep breath, he laughed, a sexy, dark rumble that made her more aware of the way his scent clung to her. "You are so wet." She watched his eyes close and wondered if he was remembering, like her, the hours he'd spent making love with her on their wedding night and every day since. "Tight and hot. I almost came that first time as soon as I got inside you."

He felt his control slip just a little as he recalled what her body felt like wrapped around his. "Like a silky glove, Mattie; you were wrapped so close I couldn't tell where you left off and I began." His motions grew more rapid as the tingle began in his spine.

Watching her slip her thumb from his to investigate a single drop of milky fluid, Bryce gloried in the pleasure his wife seemed to gain from playing with his secretion. Sliding the pad of her thumb over the thick, bulbous tip of his shaft, he barely gave Mattie time to marvel at the proof of his slipping control when she found herself pulled tight against his body. His hands held her hips as he buried his face against her neck, groaning as his body rocked against hers. The thick length trapped between them, the need to come overwhelmed his control until he felt his body pulsing and wet warmth gushed over their bellies.

From the hall, the grandfather clock chimed six deep, sonorous notes, startling them from their stunned embrace. Bryce was the first to pull away. Grabbing at a pile of towels nearby, he found and dipped a washcloth beneath the water and gently bathed Mattie's breasts and belly, removing the evidence of his passion from her trembling body. Raising his eyes to hers, he wasn't sure what he would have said before she forestalled him by pulling away and stepping from the tub.

"You said you had a surprise?" Reaching beneath the water, she pulled the plug from the drain and wrapped herself in a towel.

Realizing she was trying to avoid his touch, Bryce wondered at the sudden hesitation in his wife. Resolved to follow through on his plans for the evening, he nodded. "Yes. Why don't I get a quick shower while you dress; then we can head out."

"What should I wear? Formal? Casual?"

"Whatever you'd like." He grinned. "You won't have it on for long. I promise."

The laugh Mattie gave seemed almost forced, Bryce decided as he watched her leave the bathroom. Feeling every one of his forty years plus a decade or two more, Bryce rose from the rapidly emptying bath and stripped his wet clothes off. Striding to the shower, he jerked the cold-water faucet on full and stepped beneath the pulsing jets. Gritting his teeth to keep from crying out, he soaped up and rinsed off in record time.

Chapter Fifteen

"Bryce, I'm...I'm not sure." Mattie hesitated on the threshold of the bathroom.

"What is our safe word?"

"Pirate."

"Are you afraid of Richard?" Bryce held his hand out to her and drew her close. When they'd arrived at the penthouse to find Richard already waiting, Mattie had been fine; but when he'd led her into the bathroom to change out of her clothes, she'd begun to balk.

"No, but..."

"Are you afraid of me?" When he moved behind her, she could feel him comb his fingers through her hair, easing the sections free of the braid she'd confined it in before they'd left home.

"Never."

Finished with her hair, he returned to stand in front of her. "Do you trust me?"

"Yes."

Leaning forward, his hands sliding beneath her robe to squeeze her hip and cup her breast, Bryce settled his lips against hers. "I swear, baby," he whispered into her mouth, nipping at her bottom lip, then licking away the sting, "if you get scared, you just use our safe word and he's gone."

Still nervous, Mattie nodded and kissed him back. The ugly whispers trickling through her thoughts sounded so much like the accusations her father used to fling at her mother, it took Mattie several deep breaths to force them into silence. Following him out of the bathroom and into the bedroom, she didn't hesitate in her steps, nor did she resist him when he loosened her robe and smoothed it off her shoulders. Inside, she was glad this hurdle was being done at the apartment and not the Folly. Here the bed was merely a bed, a place she and Bryce had slept and made love, but the Folly was home. It was sacred, a place reserved only for her and Bryce. No one else.

"You know, Bryce," Richard's voice called out from the hallway, "we don't have to—" The words seemed lodged in his throat as stood frozen in the doorway.

Mattie waited, feeling the heat climb from her breasts to her cheeks as Bryce carried her robe to the chaise, leaving her naked in the center of the room. The sun was just sinking below the city's sprawling towers of concrete and glass, casting a reddish glow through the room. In her own defense, she was a bit taken aback at the sight of Richard's bare chest and feet and the faded jeans riding low on his hips.

"Holy Christ, Mattie." The tone of his voice was near reverent as he moved toward her.

Glancing over her shoulder, Mattie sought out Bryce, needing to determine by his expression what her next step should be. Having taken a seat in one of the chairs scattered around the room but close to the bed, he watched Richard approach her. His stoic expression told her nothing as he split his attention between the sketch pad in his lap and her and Richard.

Standing directly before her, Richard seemed to gain control of himself. "I have your permission?" His inquiry was directed at Bryce, but his eyes never left her face.

Mattie could practically feel his gaze caress her skin. Memories of the stroke of his fingers against her clit surfaced, making her breathing hitch. Flashes of that strange lunch meeting had been bubbling to the surface of her mind over the last week, not just this evening. Every time Bryce settled a plug in place, then made love to her, she couldn't help but imagine what it would feel like to have two cocks filling her at one time. Not that she could think of anything else with the heated whispers Bryce constantly teased her with.

It wasn't like Richard wasn't handsome. Hell, she'd had her share of fantasies about the dark-haired man, but she'd grown to know and recognize the difference between desire and love. Richard's touch, his look, the way he treated her, and the way she reacted to his touch at the restaurant all made her know there was little chance she wouldn't be able to maintain control over her body and senses. It wouldn't be like the out-of-control feelings Bryce stirred in her.

Bryce must have given his permission with a silent nod because Mattie didn't hear him say anything before Richard's lips covered hers. His broad hands cupped her cheeks, holding her still as his mouth coaxed hers open. The taste of chocolate and mint filled her senses, and the stroke of his fingers as they drifted from her cheeks to her breasts stirred her senses, but nothing like Bryce's touch.

Just like your mother, a little slut. The voice snarled from the darkness she'd trapped it in. Her body went stiff before she shoved the thought away and concentrated on relaxing, absorbing the sensations Richard's touch evoked.

A part of her mind seemed isolated, cut off from the sensations washing softly through her body. It analyzed the lack of recoil and revulsion. Both feelings had always been present with the men she'd ever dated before Bryce, but not Bryce himself. Although the heat and heart-slamming arousal just the thought of Bryce could induce wasn't present, a bit of Mattie wondered at why Richard's touch didn't affect her the way other men's had.

"Stop thinking, Lawrence," Bryce commanded softly from across the room.

And she did.

Against her lips, Richard chuckled. Lifting his head, he smiled down at her. "I guess he could hear the gears spinning as much as I could."

"Sorry." Mattie blushed, suddenly aware of how aroused this man was, while her own body was showing only mild interest.

"No worries, Mattie." With surprising ease, he swept her off her feet and deposited her on the bed. "It just means I have to work a little harder. And you know I like a challenge."

If she turned her head, Mattie could clearly see Bryce seated beside the bed. The pencil working furiously over the sketch pad, his gaze moving between her and Richard, even as the other man stepped away, shed the loose jeans, and revealed the lack of undergarments and a thick, aroused cock. From the nightstand beside the bed, he drew out one of the black condom packets and began to tear it open.

"No, use the gold," Bryce ordered, his expression tight as he watched his friend over the top of the pad.

Her mind spinning with doubts about her ability to go through with Bryce's request and the increasing taunts in her father's voice, Mattie barely registered the direction.

Richard seemed just as surprised at Bryce's comment, but he shrugged, set the black foil aside, and drew a gold one from the drawer. Mattie watched as he sheathed his cock in latex before moving back to the bed. Easing her legs apart, he settled between them, the warm flesh of his chest stimulating the sensitive skin on the insides of her thighs. The grin on his face grew wider as he drew in a deep breath. "Hmmm, smells like Bryce has already covered you."

Images of the few times Bryce had allowed her near the corrals when one of his studs was servicing a mare ran through Mattie's mind but were quickly dispelled when the heat of Richard's tongue stroked over her damp pussy. Thick fingers parted her bare flesh and teased the nubbin within to life.

Even as her body responded, Mattie had no difficulty controlling her need. Unlike the speedy rise of arousal and the pulsing need to come that always overwhelmed her when her husband made love to her, Richard's touch was soothing, sweet, but not mercurial like Bryce's. She felt none of the separation from reality, the submersion in sensation that being with Bryce brought, but the caress of Richard's hands, the stroke of his lips and tongue aroused her.

Perhaps this is what it would be like with someone I cared about but didn't love?

Again, Bryce seemed to sense her inability to separate thoughts from her body's reaction to Richard. Setting aside the pad, Bryce rose, stripped off his faded jeans, and settled, bare assed, onto his chair. He seemed to wait until she'd gotten a good look at the rising length of his arousal before speaking. "Close your eyes, Lawrence," he commanded.

Mattie complied, her breath hitching as Richard's body shifted over her, his hips easing between her thighs, the protrusion of his erection hot against the moist opening of her pussy.

"Can you feel him against you?"

"Yes." She was surprised at the pressure of tears against her eyes. *He wants me to do this*, Mattie reminded herself as she fought the strange mix of thoughts and feelings bombarding her. That dark little voice in her head taunted that only a slut would allow a man not her husband to touch her intimately. She shivered at the memory of the things her father had shouted when he'd barged into her mother's apartment. The accusations he'd growled and spat at her mom as she cowered against the headboard in her bedroom. Mattie was forced to watch due to the grip he held her arm in.

At the same time, another louder voice reasoned that the pleasure Bryce derived from watching her with Richard was more arousing than the sensations of her own flesh. As she forced the ugly memories into submission and the other, louder thought grew clearer, her body responded, seeming to pick up on the desire filling Bryce's voice as he continued guiding her. This was for his pleasure. It was what her master wanted. If it wasn't as good as when Bryce touched her, made love to her, it was part of her responsibilities as his submissive to place his needs before her own.

"Her breasts are sensitive. Tug on her nipples as you thrust. You'll love the way her pussy clamps down on you."

Even in this her body's response was mediocre in comparison to how it responded to Bryce. The smooth caress of Richard's hands over her breasts, the press of his fingers on her nipples, and the gentle tug and pull didn't stimulate her body the way Bryce's could. In her mind, Mattie tried to convince herself it was Bryce, not Richard, touching her, but her flesh knew differently. It gave only a lukewarm reaction to the same stimulus that usually had her begging permission to orgasm when it was the man she loved.

Richard seemed to sense the distress building within her. Leaning down, his lips smoothed over her cheek and to her ear as his cock stroked in and out of her sheath. "It's okay, Mattie. It's okay. Don't force it if it isn't there."

"I'm sorry," she whispered back, her eyes still closed, awaiting Bryce's next command.

He must have sensed something was wrong as well. As Richard eased upward, the slide of Bryce's hands over her breasts had heat singing through her system. Those distracting, terrifying voices stilled in her head. Every nerve exploded with sensation. The heat in her belly quadrupled, and the glide of Richard's length within her sheath was impeded by the flex of her inner walls.

Breath hissed over her face as both men laughed and cursed at the same time.

"Christ, Bryce," Richard groaned. "I don't know if I want you to keep hold or let go."

"Feel good?"

"Fan-fucking-tastic." He chuckled, his hips thrusting against her, forcing her clutching flesh to relax with every advance and retreat. "Please tell me her ass feels just as sweet."

The grip of Bryce's hands stilled on her breasts, telegraphing his tension to her for a heartbeat or two before fading away; then he assured Richard, "Yeah, just as tight and hot."

The brush of his lips over hers had Mattie reaching over her head, finding and smoothing over the bare heat of his arms, then his shoulders, to his back. The slide of his tongue over hers, the way he coaxed her lips open, Mattie was lost in the sensations of his kiss, the thrust of Richard's flesh within hers only barely registering on her senses.

Her whispered protest was hushed when Bryce pulled away just enough to order, "Make him come, baby. Then I can have my turn."

Knowing the control Richard had over his body, Bryce wasn't surprised at the chuckle his friend gave when he heard what he'd whispered to Mattie. What did surprise him was the way Mattie eased free of his hold and turned her face up to Richard. The determination and gleam of challenge lit her eyes and took both men off guard. With a deft maneuver he'd never seen her use before, Mattie gained control by flipping Richard onto his back and straddling his hips.

Keeping his eyes locked on her, Bryce watched as she flexed and rocked over his best friend's body, her hands smoothing up his sides to his ribs and then over to the dark brown disks buried in the dusting of hair across Richard's chest. Her lips settled over one while the fingers of her right hand plucked at the other.

Bryce stilled the voice that protested the events he'd set in motion. Yes, they'd been married for three months. Every night she lay in his arms sexually sated, yet willing to continue even when exhaustion muted her cries and tears streaked her cheeks from the repeated orgasms he'd wrung from her.

Despite the numerous times he'd sent her to sleep or awakened her with his cock hard and filling her, he still had to coax her tight sheath into accepting him. Even her back entrance remained snug. Allowing another man to experience the heated clasp of her body made him want to howl, but the thought of sinking into her tight pussy as Richard worked his way up her ass soothed the beast within him. He'd done it in the past with other lovers. This time should be no different, he tried to assure himself.

But it was. Pushing away the thought, he watched his wife.

Seeing her focused on following his instructions, Bryce wondered who would win the ministruggle, Mattie or Richard. Just when his confidence would have leaned toward his friend of nearly forty years, he heard curses fill the room.

"Fucking hell, Bryce, why didn't you warn me she could do that?" Even as the outburst left Richard's lips, one hand tugged Mattie's lips from his chest. "Okay, baby, you win this round, but next time, it's my turn." Mingled laughter and groans signaled Richard's climax as he arched beneath Mattie, nearly throwing her off.

Mattie eased away from the other man. Bryce grabbed the black foil packet from where Richard had left it, ripped it open, and carefully rolled the condom into place. He'd forgotten he'd left some of the doctored prophylactics in the nightstand when he'd arranged for Richard to join them tonight. He'd have to make sure he reminded his friend only to use the gold packets.

Kneeling before him on the bed, she held her hands out to him. "Please."

"As much as you want, baby," Bryce assured her. The smile lifting her lips set off a series of explosions in his chest that stunned him. Shaking off the sensations, he pulled his wife into his arms. "You'll have to come quick, Lawrence. Rich tends to recover fast, and the second time around it takes hours to make him come."

* * *

Arms bound to the canopy above her head, Mattie knew the scene would mirror the images on Bryce's canvas. The one she'd seen on their wedding day. Her body quivered with need, having been allowed only one orgasm since she'd met Bryce's challenge earlier. Behind her, she could feel the heat of Richard's cock stroke the lubed entrance of her ass even as Bryce focused his attention on adjusting the grip of the nipple clamps he'd put in place.

"You know what to do, baby," Bryce reminded her, his lips rising to caress hers. "Press down as he goes in and relax."

She couldn't help but laugh at the last. Then she gasped as the first few inches slid inside, even as her body did exactly what Bryce told her. "You relax, Halsey." She chuckled, then groaned, the heat filling her growing to match the pounding arousal the slide of Bryce's fingers between her labia was creating. "You don't have his cock spreading your ass."

That had both men laughing, confusing Mattie until Bryce cupped her cheeks and held her gaze. "Oh, but baby, I have," he taunted her. The smile on his lips widened just as she felt her eyes go round. "He's pushed that bat-sized cock up my ass a few times."

The surprise alone had Mattie struggling to make sense. "But...you're...and..." Then Richard settled the rest of his length in one smooth stroke, leaving her gasping for air at the images flooding her mind and the heat rolling over her body.

Richard's response and the laughter it brought out of Bryce barely registered as Mattie felt Bryce's erection press inside.

"Like that club of yours is any smaller?" Richard eased back, then thrust upward before adding, "Shit, I walked funny all weekend after you reamed me with that beast."

"Why do you think I kept Mattie in bed the first three days we were married?" Bryce assured his friend even as he pushed deep, hissing at the squeeze of her wet walls around him.

Mind spinning with the knowledge that her husband and his best friend had fucked each other as well as with the sensations bombarding her body with the double penetration, Mattie's fingers gripped the leather above her. Aching with the desire building in her center, she wrapped her thighs around Bryce's waist and tried to match the rhythm of the men. As one would advance, the other would retreat, leaving her breathless and confused, but desperate for more. Out of frustration and need, she gave in to the urge and growled, "Why don't you boys quit the reminiscing and...*ahhh, God yes, there, Bryce...*" She gasped for breath. "And just fuck me already."

Richard's laughing response came first. "Hmm, Bryce, sounds like the creamy filling has a few complaints about our sandwich."

"We wouldn't to disappoint, now would we, old friend?" Bryce replied.

Against her ear Richard whispered, "Better watch what you wish for, baby, it may be more than you can handle."

Fingers threaded through her damp, tousled curls just as Bryce smiled down at her. "No coming without permission."

The gleam in his eyes had Mattie crying out. This was definitely going to test her ability to control her body. She shivered at the slide of skin against skin, the sounds of bodies connecting, sheathing one within the other. His pleasure magnified hers and she flexed her internal muscles, caressing first Bryce, then Richard, learning what made each man moan and curse and striving to increase their arousal.

* * *

The room was darker than she ever remembered it being and her place in it was wrong. She should be in the doorway, Lyssa standing beside her as she watched the scene unfold. Instead, she could feel the warmth of Richard's body along the front of her own and Bryce's heat against her back. Within her chest, she could feel her heartbeat increase as the bedroom door slid silently open and a figure moved into the room. Neither man sharing her bed moved as the intruder halted at the foot of the bed. The scream boiling up within her was locked behind her lips, unable to escape.

"You were supposed to be a good girl," the man told her, his voice matter-of-fact, no anger or disgust evident in the tone.

Some part of her knew it was a dream. A nightmare. As each element unfolded, Mattie could see both the memory that created the nightmare and the new elements her mind had decided to include. She watched herself rise in the bed, her bare breasts hidden behind the fall of her hair. "*I am, Daddy. I am a good girl.*"

He shook his head. "No. A good girl doesn't fuck two men. She doesn't allow herself to be used."

"You don't belong here, Daddy. You aren't supposed to be here," her protests began, then turned into a cry of alarm as the man she faced raised his left arm, revealing the pistol gripped in his hand. Both men began to stir in the bed.

The barrel of the pistol shifted its focus away from her. "Which one caused this?" Her father's voice was coldly furious as his gaze moved from Bryce to Richard, then back to Bryce.

"Don't. I'll be good. Just don't hurt them." Mattie could feel herself shaking, trying to think of something to say that would keep her father from using the pistol on her husband and friend.

"Tell me." Her father's voice was cold and unrelenting.

Her trembling increased. "I promise I'll be good. I promise."

Richard's hand brushed her shoulder as he began to rise beside her, and the gun went off once, then a second time.

As his body fell back onto the bed and Bryce's toppled as well, Mattie lunged up, screaming, pleading. "I'll be good, Daddy. I promise." Again and again she cried her promise, her head buried against her upraised knees, her arms crossed over her head as she rocked forward and back on the bed.

Cursing and the sudden wash of light barely registered. Even Bryce's arms pulling her close couldn't drag Mattie from the nightmare's grip. The spray of blood, the loud reports of the pistol, and her mother's screams fading into silence kept playing over and over in her mind.

"It's okay, baby," Bryce whispered, holding her close, his hand brushing through her tangled hair.

She couldn't talk; the sobs rendered her speechless, mute, the memories of what her father had done to her mother and what had come next making it impossible to do anything but burrow closer to her husband's heat.

"What the fuck was that all about?" Richard demanded, his fingers shaking as he raked them through his close-cropped hair before swallowing down half his scotch in one gulp.

Bryce shrugged, his own drink unsteady as he raised it to his lips and sipped. His gaze didn't leave the open door to the bedroom. He shivered at the chill the water dripping from his hair and down his back produced. Twenty minutes of holding his wife under the pounding spray of the shower had finally calmed her enough so he could coax her back to bed. Wrapped tight in his shirt as well as the heavy velvet robe he'd unearthed in the closet, she'd curled into a ball and drifted off.

"Don't go all quiet on me, Bryce. Give me some kind of idea what could possibly make Mattie wake from a dead sleep screaming her head off." Richard refilled his glass at the bar before dropping onto the sofa.

Feeling decades older than his four, Bryce eased into the matching chair adjacent to the sofa. "I fucked up."

"What?"

"I rushed her." He sipped at his drink, processing through the steps he'd taken to introduce Mattie to a ménage. He wondered if his own need to force normalcy into the chaotic emotions jumbling his mind had him ignoring the warning signs that his wife wasn't ready to accept another man into their bed yet.

Richard nodded. "She didn't seem comfortable at first. But later…"

"I should have waited." Bryce rose and paced the carpet in front of the sliding glass doors leading onto the roof garden.

"That still doesn't explain her panic. The screaming."

Bryce watched the shudder ripple through his friend. He suspected he knew what Lawrence had been reliving in her nightmare. Making Richard privy to her history would be necessary if they were to avoid a repeat of the same thing. "It happened when she was eleven."

His tone must have alerted Richard to the seriousness of his information. "What? You said she hadn't been—"

Before his friend could draw the wrong conclusion, he continued, "She saw it all. According to the report I had compiled just after she started working for us, Lawrence's father forced his way into the apartment where she was living with her mother and Lyssa." After refilling his drink, Bryce returned to the chair and sat down. "Details are sketchy, but the police officers who responded reported that Aaron Lawrence was drunk and enraged that his ex-wife was involved with a new man. He dragged her to her mother's bedroom. Shot her mother and the new lover. Lyssa had grabbed Lawrence and ran for the door, but somehow he got in front of them. There was a struggle. Lyssa was shot, but there was a rifle in the closet. Before he could shoot either of them again, Lyssa shot him with the rifle."

"Oh God." Richard leaned back in the sofa, his face pale.

"Neighbors had called the police. They arrived with an ambulance in time to find Lawrence curled around Lyssa in the closet, holding onto the rifle."

"If Mattie was eleven, then Lyssa was—"

"Seventeen."

A soft cry from the bedroom had both men on their feet and across the room. Still curled in the center of the bed, Lawrence shifted restlessly beneath the covers.

"Listen, I'm going to take her home." Bryce was careful to keep his voice quiet.

Richard nodded. "I'll head out too."

"We'll have to—"

His friend waved him off. "No more until *she* says she's ready, Bryce."

Another whimper from the bed had Bryce moving into the shadowed room. "Yes. We'll wait." Settling onto the mattress, he brushed the hair from his wife's cheeks. He didn't pay attention to the sound of Richard collecting his belongings or the whisper of the elevator as he left. Gathering a T-shirt from the dresser, he tugged it on, then his socks and boots. Pulling an extra blanket from the closet, he bundled Mattie up. "Let's get you home, baby."

Chapter Sixteen

"Mattie."

Dana's voice from her doorway had Mattie raising her head. The swimmy feeling was slow to dissipate, but she smiled at the receptionist. "Yes?"

"I'm heading down to sandwich shop for some lunch. Would you like me to pick anything up for you?"

Mattie's cheeks heated at the memories of the weekend. Richard's reference to her being the filling in his and Bryce's sandwich skittered through her mind again, before memories of the nightmare that turned everything upside down prodded her. Bryce had been very careful with her all day yesterday. It had her unnerved and scared that he'd begun rethinking her suitability as his sub. Forcing her thoughts to the present, she nodded, reaching for the drawer she stored her purse in. "Yes, could you get me a ginger ale and a tuna on wheat."

"No pepper jack cheese and spicy Italian?" Dana teased as she crossed the carpet and collected the five-dollar bill Mattie held out to her.

Shaking her head, Mattie grimaced. "No, my stomach is giving me fits today. I'm hoping something bland will help settle it."

"Hmmm, is it possible...?" Dana suggested, her eyebrows wiggling up and down suggestively.

Fighting the fear that had been growing over the last few weeks, she shook her head. "Not likely, I assure you." *Although as soon as you head out, I'll be checking out the box in my bag.*

"Oh, I almost forgot." Dana turned back to face her. "Mark Conlin is on his way up he wanted to talk to Bryce about something."

"Bryce is going to be with his brother at least another two hours," Mattie reminded her.

Dana nodded. "I know. I told him that, but he was adamant that he talk to someone, so he asked to speak to you."

Cursing silently at the delay, Mattie worked to keep her expression unconcerned. "No problem. I'll keep an eye out for him while you're gone." With luck, she'd have five minutes...

"Perfect timing, Mr. Conlin." She heard Dana's greeting through her open door and slid her bag back into the drawer and shut it.

Rising, Mattie was careful to take a steadying breath and wait until her head stopped spinning before moving away from her desk. As Mark Conlin crossed the threshold of her doorway, she fixed a polite smile on her lips and held her hand out. "It's nice to see you again."

"And you." The man smiled, his friendliness genuine, as he gripped her hand and returned her handshake.

"So, you can see my concerns," he told her twenty minutes later. Mark opened the sheaf of papers to several highlighted pages. "My attorney showed me this. At first, I assumed it was an error. When I said that, my attorney assured me it couldn't be. The wording was too precise and subtle."

Reading through the passages, even with her limited understanding of legalese, she could see the discrepancy. "You realize what you're losing out on by showing me this, don't you?"

He nodded. "I know, but that isn't the way I do business, and I have far too much respect for Bryce and this company to let this go."

"I'm sure your attorney advised against you showing this to us."

"Gil has been with me since the beginning. He knows how I feel about this, and I wouldn't be using him as my legal representative if he was willing to let something this damaging slide." He chuckled, his long fingers ruffling his cinnamon-colored hair. "Heck, he was the one demanding I get my ass over here and show it to you as soon as we found it. I made him wait while we did a little investigating."

"How long have you known about this?"

"Almost a month."

Mattie was sure her suspicions were apparent on her face. His expression and the comments he'd made convinced her he'd read her correctly.

"I know I should have brought this to you sooner, but I wanted to make sure I knew who was behind it."

"Did you suspect someone at your company?"

"No. Yours."

Looking down at the documents spread over the conference table in front of her, Mattie could see where Halsey's staff would come under suspicion before Conlin's. The damage to Halsey's wasn't irreparable, but they could have been enough to bring the board against Bryce, since it was his idea to absorb Conlin's company.

Recognizing what repercussions it could have on the company, Mattie immediately dialed Richard's office. "Are you going to be there for a few minutes?"

"Sure. I don't have to leave for my meeting this afternoon. It was canceled."

"I'll be right there."

Turning to Mark, she explained, "Since Bryce isn't due back until later this afternoon, Richard should be able to help you get this taken care of."

"Aren't you curious about who did this?"

Mattie shook her head. "I have a good idea who may have been behind the plan, but since the primary attorney working on the contract was Victor Prommer, I'm pretty sure he's the one who altered the stipulations."

He chuckled. "Bryce always said you were hard to keep up with."

That surprised her. "He did?"

Mark pulled his papers together and placed them neatly in the folder. "Yes. If I'm lucky, I figure I'll find a sub as challenging as you one day."

"Sub?"

He looked at her, head tilted to the side. "I've been a member of the Club for just over five years, about the time Bryce and Richard began my training."

She shouldn't have been so surprised, Mattie decided as she and Mark headed for Richard's office, the files he'd brought tucked under his arm. Many of Bryce's business associates were involved with the Diablo Blanco Club.

Seeming to understand her need to change the subject, Mark smiled at her. "You know, I never did thank you."

"For what?" Mattie pulled her mind from the mental search she'd been doing to determine if Mark Conlin had ever been present at the Club when she and Bryce had been there.

"R and D. I don't think any of my people or I would have thought of that little stipulation if you hadn't mentioned it to me. You didn't have to make the suggestion, and I guess when I found out about the discrepancies in the contract, I felt I owed you something."

"The research you started three years ago was decades ahead of the others out there. I would hate to see it go to waste." Mattie shrugged.

"Still, I appreciate it."

* * *

After leaving Mark with Richard, Mattie hurried back to her office. Dana still hadn't returned so she grabbed her bag and made a beeline for the private bathroom adjoining her office. The facilities boasted a full-sized tiled shower with frosted glass door, gray-veined marble vanity, sink, and toilet. Plush burgundy rugs dotted the cool ivory and burgundy-trimmed tiled floor.

Twenty minutes later, the little pink plus sign taunted Mattie as she stared in disbelief at the pregnancy test stick. "Damn it," she groaned, allowing her head to rest against the cool marble of the sink beside her.

It could be wrong, a tiny voice inside tried to reassure her.

Not when it's the third positive result.

Looking into the mirror above her, Mattie smiled wanly. Fate had a decidedly nasty sense of humor, she determined as she examined the pale cheeks and trembling lips facing her. She could count on one hand the times Bryce hadn't worn protection when making love with her. And the single incident where the condom failed. Other than that she'd been very careful. But not careful enough, obviously.

The bare expanse of skin revealed by the V-neck cut of her blouse taunted her. If he'd given her his collar, this would have been different. If she were more confident of his feelings, this wouldn't require the decision before her.

* * *

Bryce watched from the doorway as Victor focused on the computer screen, his fingers clicking through commands. He wondered if the man was trying to erase evidence of his betrayal or merely trying to appear industrious. Not really caring either way, Bryce stepped inside and signaled the security guards to remain outside the open door. "You need to collect your coat and leave, Victor."

Startled, Victor looked up, his face going pale.

Bryce wasn't sure if it was the expression on his face or the sight of the guards that had the younger man frightened, but he really didn't care.

"Excuse me?" Victor tried to bluff.

Bryce shot him down. "Any personal items you leave behind will be returned to you after security has examined them."

"You can't—"

Bryce laughed. "Trust me, Victor. I can and I will."

"I signed a contract."

"Which clearly stated that immediate termination was possible if an employee is found to be soliciting or selling information that could be ruinous to Halsey's or any of its interests," Bryce paraphrased. "I hope Lionel and Frieda paid you well, because other than your prorated salary for this month, you won't get another dime. We've also reported your actions to the bar association's ethics committee."

Watching Victor, Bryce added, "You let your ego overrule your intelligence."

"In what way?"

"When you weren't caught feeding information to outside companies, you thought you could worm your way into my office through my executive assistant." Bryce shook his head. "You should thank your lucky stars she never heard the particulars of that ridiculous wager you started."

That seemed to annoy Victor. The flush of red stealing up his throat and into his face betrayed his anger. "What about your wife?"

"What about her?"

"Is she being told to pack up her things and hit the road?" Victor sneered.

"She's never betrayed this company, Victor. You have."

Victor's laughter was taunting. "You think she's so innocent, why don't you ask her who put the idea in Conlin's head about taking the position in research and development? Hell, he probably screwed her too to get—"

Bryce's voice overrode Victor's. "I can deal with you trying to steal money from my company and destroy what my family has spent almost two hundred years building. That's just business."

Victor gave a weak grin. "Glad you see it that way. No hard feel—"

His words were cut off when the air stopped flowing. The clasp of Bryce's hand around his throat squeezed off the faint squeak of protest. To make sure the little bastard heard him, Bryce leaned forward. From the expression of fear on Victor's face, the heat in his green eyes must have belied the ice in his voice. "But one more word about my wife, and not only will you be looking for another job, you'll be looking for a new career, Victor."

The look in Victor's eyes warned that he wasn't willing to listen to reason. He tried to speak. "You don't know about her past. She's convinced you—"

Bryce's hand around his throat cut off more than his words. "When you target my woman. My. Wife. In your little schemes. That's where I draw the line, Mr. Prommer. She is mine. To protect, to care for, and to honor. And the machinations of a dried-up harridan and a slimy wannabe lothario can result in much more than a lost job if she is harmed in any way.

"Know one thing, Victor. You will never work in this state again. If you haven't handed your keys to the security guards here and left the building by the time I return to my office, there won't be a job available to you anywhere in this country."

Not trusting himself to keep from harming the young fool, Bryce nodded to the two security guards to watch Victor. "Tell me when he's left the building. I'll be in my office."

It had all been so anticlimactic, Mattie thought as she shut the door to her office and settled behind her desk. The discovery of the problems in the Conlin merger contract had set the wheels spinning. As if choreographed, information had been collected and a special board meeting arranged. Having just left the meeting, Mattie wondered at what would happen next. The machinations of the Makepeaces and their hiring of Victor had been presented to the board. In just twenty minutes, all the reasons Bryce had asked her to marry him, every obstacle her presence was supposed to alleviate, were wiped away. With Frieda and Lionel losing their seats, the primary opponents to Bryce replacing his father were removed.

She smiled at the irony. In twenty minutes, Bryce had everything he wanted, including a baby.

And she was left wanting something more.

Chapter Seventeen

"We're going to the Club after dinner," Mattie told Lyssa as they dried their hands in front of the mirror. Dinner at La Paloma had been a treat provided by Jacob to celebrate the removal of the Makepeaces from the board of directors. He'd included Lyssa in the party, adamantly insisting she deserved to participate since he considered her family. With the meal over and desserts having been ordered, Mattie and her sister had escaped to the ladies' room.

"Are you asking me to come along?" Lyssa teased.

Mattie started to laugh, but the smile faded as she spotted the older woman standing behind her sister. The ladies' room door was just sliding shut. "Hello, Mrs. Makepeace." She offered a brief nod.

"Bryce thinks he's so smart, doesn't he?" Frieda snarled. The smooth, unlined skin of her face attested to the skills of her plastic surgeon, but the bitter look in her watery blue eyes undermined any beauty she'd paid for.

"I don't—"

"You have no place in our world." Her gaze dropped to Mattie's bare neck. "He hasn't even staked his claim, and you think you can ruin my life. Everything I've worked for." Frieda turned on Lyssa. "And you, you're just an overpaid seamstress." Shaking her head, she sniffed. "You're trash. Refuse dropped from the belly of a whore."

The smile lifting her lips was frightening enough that Mattie actually took a step back, trying to put distance between her and the older woman. Her sister moved with her.

"He doesn't know your secret, does he?" Frieda taunted. "Murdering little bitches like you have no place here, and as soon as the Halseys see you two for what you are, you'll be out of my hair. Gone." Pulling the door open, she snorted. "And good riddance."

Mattie didn't know what to say. Standing, shaking, beside her sister, she fought to breathe normally.

The flush of a toilet shattered the silence, startling Mattie and her sister. Stunned, Lyssa and Mattie watched as the blonde from the Club stepped out of a stall. Moving past them, she began washing her hands.

"I wouldn't pay any attention to the old bitch."

"Excuse me?" Lyssa gasped.

Drying her hands, she leaned against the countertop and shrugged. "Frieda has been sniffing after Jacob Halsey for decades."

"What does that have to do...?" Lyssa began.

Feeling unsteady, Mattie moved to take a seat on the tiny sofa in the waiting area, her eyes repeatedly going to the diamond necklace around the woman's throat.

"She strikes back at anyone or anything connected to the Halseys." Dropping the paper towels into the wastebasket, she crossed her arms over her breasts. "I should have remembered that when I accepted the invitation she sent me to the retirement party."

Shaking her head, she followed Lyssa to take a seat on one of the two remaining chairs. "As soon as I saw Char acting up, I knew it was a mistake. But I have to admit, you did scare her when you walked up to her in the middle of the party while she was hanging all over Bryce and told her you'd pull her arms out and beat her with them if she didn't leave your husband alone."

Mattie recalled the comment she'd made to the drunken model. "I didn't mean it," she began, but the other woman's laughter filled the room, warming the chill Frieda's vindictive speech had left behind.

"God, I was hoping you did. The way that tramp tries to steal men from other women, not to mention masters from subs, she'd deserve everything she got and more." Leaning forward, she settled her hand over Mattie's and gave her fingers a reassuring squeeze. She reached up and removed the necklace from around her throat. "Listen, this means nothing to Bryce." Holding it in her hand, she stared at it a moment before tucking it into the tiny purse dangling from a gold chain over her shoulder. "None of the women he gave these trinkets to meant anything to him. As for Frieda's comments about not being claimed"—she motioned to the rings on Mattie's fingers—"those are a truer sign of Bryce's ownership than any bit of glitter he may have handed out before."

Watching carefully, Mattie tried to believe what the woman was telling her, but even she could see a hint of doubt in the beautiful blonde woman's eyes. Knowing how she'd tried to alleviate her doubts, Mattie couldn't begrudge her the attempt. "Thank you."

"LaTreace." She offered her elegant hand in response to Mattie's outstretched one.

"Thank you, LaTreace."

With a smile, LaTreace glanced over at Lyssa. "I know she's already taken, so if you head out to the Club tonight, make sure you keep your hands off a certain blond bartender. I've been trying to tempt him for a month now, but with no luck."

Mattie had to smile at the blush filling her sister's cheeks. Even as she tried to convince herself LaTreace was right, the temptation to cover her bare neck had Mattie clenching her fists to keep them in her lap. *Maybe she's right, maybe I should be satisfied with being his wife. It's the same thing Lyssa told me a few days ago.*

* * *

"Please," she cried, her body quivering, desperate for release as Bryce stroked her breasts in time with each thrust. The full feeling of the plug, coupled with his cock sliding in and out, had left her teetering on the edge for nearly an hour. Each time climax came too close, she'd find some way to hold it off, but now control was too shaky. The wet clasp of his lips over her nipple overwhelmed her senses and left her gripping the restraints binding her to the bed until her knuckles were white.

"Does it feel good?"

"Yes, please, I need—"

"Better than when Richard was with us?"

She could swear there was something in his voice. Forcing her eyes open, she tried to clear her thoughts, read the expression in Bryce's face. Confusion and need fogged her mind, making it difficult to think coherently. "No…yes…I don't know."

Above her, Bryce stilled; his hands rose to cup her face, fingers smoothing the sweat-dampened curls from her eyes. "Explain."

She wondered why he'd ask. "For you."

Holding her gaze, his lips smoothed away the tears she wasn't aware she'd shed. "Why?"

And there it was, the one question she'd asked, her sister had asked. Why would she do these things? And just as simply, the answer came through. "It pleases my master. You're my master. I love you."

His expression was inscrutable. The pride she could read easily in his eyes, but still something was missing.

"You may come." The cool command washed any thought from her mind. The pulsing wave of orgasm moved through her body, flooding her senses, erasing any idea she might have of trying to reason out Bryce's reaction to her words. Or the actual lack of reaction.

The knocking on the door was the first thing Mattie heard as she eased back into herself. The bindings on her wrists had been released, the cuffs still in place. Bryce had removed the plug and bathed her body, leaving her feeling refreshed rather than sticky with sweat.

"All right," Bryce growled, the bed shifting as he rose and tugged on the slacks he'd discarded earlier.

Swinging her legs off the bed, she sat up and reached for the robe folded on the nightstand beside her. Even as she finished tying the belt at her waist, Mattie could hear the commotion from downstairs as Bryce pulled open the door.

"What is it?"

"Lionel Makepeace is kicking up a fuss downstairs." Ben Murphy stood on the threshold, his blond hair tousled. "Richard tried to handle it, but the old fart is refusing to leave until he talks to you."

As Ben shoved his fingers through his hair, Mattie realized the condition of his appearance was due to frustration rather than the attentions of LaTreace. Knowing the woman had been downstairs when she and Bryce arrived, she had to smile.

"Okay, give me a second." Shutting the door, Bryce grabbed his shirt from the chair and pushed his arms into the sleeves. Haphazardly tucking buttons through buttonholes as he shoved his bare feet into his shoes, he paused beside her. "I'm going to go downstairs for just a few minutes. Be right back." Pressing a hard kiss against her lips, he didn't wait for a response before striding out of the room.

Curious, Mattie followed. With the robe snug around her, she leaned against the railing and looked down into the lounge area. Near the double doors, Lionel Makepeace weaved drunkenly. His words loud, echoing off the high ceiling, were slurred and abusive. Unable to clearly make out his complaints, Mattie shook her head and turned back toward the room.

Movement down the hall drew her attention. A woman stumbled and fell against the wall before dropping to her knees. Not sure who she was, but concerned there could be something wrong, Mattie hurried toward her. The woman had gotten unsteadily to her feet by the time she reached her, and Mattie was chagrined to see it was the bitchy redheaded model, Charlene, whom LaTreace had mentioned earlier in the evening. Despite her annoyance with the other woman, Mattie couldn't allow her to go stumbling about the Club. She could hurt herself or someone else.

"Are you okay?" she asked, cautiously touching the woman's arm.

"Shick," Charlene mumbled, not even looking at her. "Baf-bafrum." Her arm came up and she motioned toward a door near the end of the hall.

Unfamiliar with the majority of the upstairs of the Club, other than the rooms Bryce had taken her to, Mattie nodded. "Okay, let me help you." Draping one arm over her shoulder, she helped the model weave her way down the hall to the narrow door. After reaching their destination, she propped the girl up and pulled open the door beside them. "Give me a sec—" she began, only to feel firm hands shove against her shoulders, pushing her into the dark confines of the room.

The abrupt collision with the wall had her head spinning, but she was aware the door was slammed shut behind her and the click of a lock had her cursing. Something tickled her scalp and she swung at it, thinking some spider had fallen from a web into her hair. Instead, the cool metal of a light pull slithered across her hand. Grasping at it, she tugged and breathed easy as the light clicked on.

Forcing herself not to panic, Mattie checked the door to confirm if she'd been locked in.

She had.

Pushing down the fear trying to take hold, Mattie rapped on the door. "Char, this isn't funny. Open the door."

A snicker sounded through the wood.

Rattling the knob, she pounded harder. "Damn it, Charlene, enough with the jokes. Open the damn door."

"From what I've heard, you like closets." Frieda Makepeace's laughter was as nasty as the tone of her voice.

"Frieda?" Mattie looked around her. There were no shelves or rods on the walls to indicate the room was being used as a closet. Four coat hooks were bolted to the walls and door, the dull brass gleaming against the deep crimson paint covering the walls. Another shiver snaked its way down Mattie's spine. "This isn't funny, Frieda. Let me out of here."

"Tell me, Mattilda, what wicked little games did you play to make your father lock you up? Hmmm?"

The slam of a fist against the door had Mattie recoiling. Memories clawed to be free, but she fought to push them back. "Let me out, Frieda."

"Did you tell Bryce what you did?" Frieda's sneer was evident in her voice. "Does he know all about how your daddy shot your whore mother?"

Feeling as if the bloodred walls were closing in on her, Mattie glared at the door. Angry, terrified at the images coming to mind, she attacked the door, hammering at it with her fists and bare feet. "You bitch! Let me out of here! Now!"

"Like father, like daughter, right?" Frieda snarled. "You should have been locked away. Caged up for what you did."

"When I get out of here—" Mattie snarled right back.

"Who says you'll get out?"

Pressing her ear to the door, Mattie could hear the thud of footsteps fading. Pounding on the door, she called out, "Let me out. Frieda. Charlene. Goddamn it, let me out of here!" Over and over she shouted, hoping someone would hear her, but nothing.

Shaking, exhausted from crying out, hands, feet, and shoulders hurting from trying to force the door open, Mattie drew a deep breath and then another. "Okay, okay," she whispered. Her throat sore from calling, she stepped back and examined her surroundings.

If she stretched out both arms, she could put her palms flat against the wall. Turning, she did it again, this time pressing against the back of the room and the door. "So, good news." She tried to reassure herself. "I can at least be comfortable if I have to sleep on the floor."

Trembling, she made herself sit down facing the door with her back against the wall. Stroking her hand over her lower abdomen, Mattie soothed herself as she spoke to the baby she carried. "Sorry, kiddo. Mommy has a thing about closets, you know. That old bitch is wrong. We're not gonna be stuck here for long. Daddy'll come get us; you'll see."

Nodding to herself, Mattie closed her eyes, shutting out the color surrounding her and the memories it evoked. "We're okay," she repeated. "Everything will be okay." If she kept talking, the voices from the past couldn't get through,

Mattie assured herself. "There's a light. And Bryce is here. He'll find us. It'll be okay."

Downstairs Bryce grew tired of Lionel's slobbering excuses. "Go home," he ordered, pushing the older man toward one of the heavily muscled security officers. "You're drunk, and you don't know what you're babbling about, Makepeace."

"Your father ru'n'd ev'r'thin'," Lionel slurred.

"Go. Home." Bryce nodded at the man supporting Lionel and shut the door.

"Jesus." Richard waved his hand in front of his face to dispel the stench of alcohol the older man had left behind. "Maybe you should have sent him to a detox center instead of home."

"That's not going to fix Lionel's problem." Bryce shook his head, turning toward the stairs and the room where Mattie waited for him.

"Sending him home isn't going to help either," Richard offered.

"Until he—"

The slam of another body stopped his words. Looking down in exasperation at the overdone makeup and tight, thigh-skimming dress Charlene wore, he cursed the impulse that had made him bed her two years ago. Setting her away from him, Bryce shook his head. "I think you need to take a cab back to your place, Char."

He guessed the pout on her lips was supposed to be sexy, but to him it only looked pathetic. "Only if you come with me, lover," she purred.

"No, thanks." Bryce turned away, again heading for the stairs.

"What you see in that little bitch is beyond me." She snickered.

"I would watch it, Char," Richard warned before Bryce could do the same. When he saw his friend move the model toward the door, Bryce nodded his thanks.

"Why? She's useless." The redhead chortled over her shoulder. "Can't even handle being locked in a closet without freakin' out."

Bryce had her facing him before she'd finished her sentence. "What the hell are you talking about?"

"See, you need a real—"

"What the fuck did you do?" Ignoring the wary faces watching him, Bryce demanded, "Tell me, Char."

"Frieda said she needed to learn a lesson. I thought you should see that Mattie wasn't what you needed, so I helped her."

The fear on her face only made him more determined. "What did you do, Charlene?"

* * *

The crackling sound had Mattie's eyes flying open. It seemed like hours had passed since Freida and Char had left her here. The light above her flickered, winking off, then burning bright. "No no no," she whispered, pleaded, as she scrambled to her feet. "Don't, no, don't go out. Please," Mattie begged, knowing the light was the only thing harnessing the memories, keeping them locked away. Again the bulb faded, flickered, burned bright before dimming.

Even as she reached up, her hands wet with cold sweat, the light winked out and remained dark. Sobbing, she grabbed for the bulb, crying out at the heat and then screaming as the hot glass shattered against her wet hand. Nothing made sense. The explosion from the burst bulb echoed off the walls around her. Terrified, she stumbled back, falling against the back wall and sliding down. Glass crunched under her knees, the pain barely registering as the memories broke free, flooding her mind with images of bloody walls, screams, and pain.

Pointing over his shoulder toward the stairs, a key dangling from her fingers, Char's eyes grew wide. "The closet. At the end of the east hall, we—"

She hadn't finished speaking when Bryce pushed her away, ripping the key from her grip, and sprinted up the stairs, taking two and three at a time. The pounding of feet behind him signaled Richard and at least one other Club member had followed him.

"Pirate," she whispered, sobbing, knowing that if Bryce heard their safe word he would be there. He would take care of her.

Again she said it, this time louder.

Then again, louder still.

And again and again and again, until the tiny walls surrounding her nearly vibrated with her screams.

Across the landing and up the second stairway, he'd almost reached the newel post when he heard her scream.

"Pirate!" echoed up the hall twice more before he'd reached the door, unlocked it, and pulled it open.

"Oh Christ."

"Holy shit."

The curses behind him were ignored as Bryce focused on getting his wife calmed down. "It's okay, baby," he assured her as he knelt in front of her. "It's all right."

"I'm sorry," she sobbed, reaching for him, blood smeared across her fingers and dripping from her right hand. "I didn't know what else to do."

Pulling her into his arms, Bryce forced away all thoughts but getting her calmed and settled in a room. The blood he'd worry about later, the crunch of glass beneath his shoes and the repercussions of Frieda and Char's actions would be dealt with. Right now, all his energy would be focused on getting Mattie taken care of. Over Richard's shoulder, he spotted Dayton and Mike. Near the end of the hall, Ben waited. "Get your bag."

Against his neck, Mattie sobbed, her words tumbling out, making no sense to anyone but Bryce. "I didn't know what else to do...he was hurting her...and there was so much blood... I promise I'll be good. I swear. I don't need a collar... I don't...not if you love me. I just... Can you tell me that?"

By the time he had Mattie stretched out on the bed, Ben had returned with the medical kit he carried with him for emergencies. Dayton and Mike had been sent back downstairs to help close up early and get the members out to their cars. Richard had told him Char had run out as soon as he'd headed up the stairs.

Mattie had stopped crying, her words stilled as she watched him beside her on the bed.

Ben cursed. "Shit, she's got pieces of glass—"

"The light blew up." Mattie looked down at the hand Bryce was stroking, his fingers moving over and around the rings he'd given her. "It sounded just like the rifle. It was hot..."

"Well, sweetheart, it doesn't look like you'll need stitches, but I'm going to give you an antibiotic and a sedative—"

"No!" Mattie yanked her hand away, shaking her head. "I can't... I mean..."

"She's worried about our baby." Bryce gripped her wrist. "Let him finish with your hand, Lawrence."

"But, how...?" She allowed him to return her injured hand to Ben's care, all the while watching Bryce with wary eyes.

"How many weeks?" Ben interrupted.

"Probably ten," Bryce responded, his gaze holding Mattie's, letting her know he'd been aware of the secret she'd kept from him.

With his stethoscope, Ben settled the chest piece on different sections of her abdomen. His expression focused, he listened carefully before moving to another location. Nodding, but not commenting, Ben removed the earpieces and tucked the tool back into his bag before preparing an injection. "It's only a mild sedative, Mattie. No harm will come to the baby, I promise."

"I want to go home." Mattie grimaced at the pinch of the needle in her arm.

Since she was already tired from her ordeal, Bryce didn't doubt the sedative would work quickly. "Okay, baby. I'll get you home." Smoothing her tangled curls, he leaned down and kissed her cheek. "Just rest now."

Following Ben, he moved into the hall, leaving the door ajar so he could watch her on the bed.

"I don't think there's anything serious, but I'd suggest you get her in to see her OB."

That drew his gaze to the younger man. "Why? Do you think…?"

Again, Ben shook his head. "I'm just a PA, Bryce. An OB can answer your questions better than I can. The sedative I gave her was mild. I got all the glass out of her hand and knees, but you need to have her keep the wounds clean."

"Okay."

***

In one part of her mind, Mattie was fully aware of what was happening around her. The first time she woke up, she recognized the floating sensation as Bryce carried her down the stairs and into the car. Her mind drifted, separate from the thoughts spinning through her head. The next time she came to the surface, she knew the flashing lights and cool air on her cheeks came from the streetlights and slightly opened windows as Bryce drove toward the Folly.

Rolling her head away from the window, she blinked into focus the man seated beside her. "I'm sorry."

Bryce took his eyes off the road for just a moment. "Sorry about what, baby?"

"I thought if I could earn your collar, you could love me." Sighing, she closed her eyes and leaned her head back. "I just want you to love me, Bryce."

"Shhh," Bryce coaxed, one hand leaving the wheel to stroke over her hair. Lowering it to her knee, he smoothed the hem of the robe over her thighs. "Just sleep, darlin'. Just sleep. We'll be home soon."

Opening her eyes, she gazed over at him one last time. "I can live without ever wearing your collar if you would say you love me. Just once."

Her only answer was the hum of the tires against the road and the soft wash of cool air against her cheeks. The warmth of Bryce's hand on her knee slipped away as he returned his grip to the steering wheel.

Chapter Eighteen

Mattie grimaced as she opened her eyes. Hopefully the images flashing across her eyes were the dregs of some nightmare that had chased her through her dreams. The second she tried to use her right hand to lever herself up in bed, she hissed in pain and realized that the dreams of closets and screaming hadn't been confined to her sleep. Even worse, as she rolled upward, she noticed Bryce seated next to the bed, dressed and ready for work, with a blue velvet jeweler's case on the arm of his chair. She realized the pathetic pleas she'd made for his affections had netted her the one thing she'd wanted and now couldn't accept.

"Good morning," Bryce greeted, rising from the chair and moving to sit beside her in the bed.

Holding the covers close to her naked breasts, Mattie offered a quiet "good morning" in response.

Placing the box in her lap, Bryce leaned down to kiss her.

Mattie turned away, surprising both herself and Bryce with her refusal.

"I'm sure you're still a little upset over last night," Bryce offered.

She simply shrugged, her bandaged hand reluctantly smoothing over the case in her lap. "I'll get over it." Her assurance was couched in as cool a tone as she could muster, considering the heat his nearness stirred within her. *Down, girl.*

"Well, I want you to stay home today. Rest up." Placing his hand over the one on the case, he continued, "I've made an appointment with your doctor for tomorrow morning."

"Why? If you know I'm pregnant, why bother with confirming it again?"

"To make sure you and the baby are okay. After last night—"

"I was scared, okay. I admit it. That's no reason to go running off to the doctor." Sliding away from him, she ignored the blue velvet box she left behind as she rose from the bed. Tugging on her robe, she watched as Bryce picked up the box and held it out to her.

"Aren't you at least curious?"

Hands gripping the belt of her robe tight, Mattie didn't dare drop her gaze to the case he eased open. "I don't want it."

Confusion mingled with frustration on Bryce's face as he watched her. She could tell he didn't understand why she'd suddenly change her tune after practically—hell, why not admit it?—groveling for his approval in the form of his collar last night.

"Explain."

That tone, the one of her master, tugged at her need to please him. After weeks of ensuring his pleasure, Mattie balked at refusing him. But she did it. "No. I've said I don't want it. That should be sufficient."

"Don't push me, Lawrence." Snapping the case closed, he tossed it back onto the bed. "Take a shower; get some rest. Dana knows you won't be in, and I've asked Henrietta to check in on you during the day."

"I don't need your housekeeper to babysit me, Bryce."

"Funny." Bryce tucked his hands into his trouser pockets, the sides of his suit coat open and pushed back. "Just two days ago she was 'our' housekeeper." Turning away, Bryce strode out of the room, the door closing softly behind him.

Through a shower, dressing, and breakfast, Mattie held off the temptation to open the case, though she carried it with her as she moved from room to room. Wanting to go in to work, but still feeling a bit shaky, Mattie headed into the study to use the computer, the blue case tucked under her arm.

"I'm going down to set lunch for my husband, Miss Mattie," Etta called from the hall.

Turning, Mattie smiled. "Thanks for everything. I'll be fine the rest of the day, I'm sure."

Giving her a decidedly motherly look, Henrietta shook her head. "I'll be back to check on you by two."

Chuckling, she gave in. "Okay, Mother Hen." Mattie waved her off before settling into the chair behind the desk.

The case taunted her from the corner of the desk blotter as she logged into the computer and connected to the company server. Through ten e-mails, she resisted until finally... "All right, all right." Taking a deep breath, she pulled the case in front of her and snapped it open. Then immediately closed it.

"Damn it." She sniffed, holding her hands, fingers spread wide, on the desktop on either side of the box. Even squeezing her eyes shut didn't dispel the memory of the gleaming platinum links he'd chosen for her.

Determined to keep from opening the box again, Mattie tugged open the drawer and started to tuck it inside. Her name on a file folder stopped her.

* * *

"Dana, can you get Henrietta on the phone?" Bryce didn't look up when he heard the door to his office open. Having just buzzed the receptionist, he assumed it was her entering the room. "I want to see how my wife is doing."

"I'm doing just fine, Bryce," she informed him, dropping a file onto the pile of papers in front of him. "But maybe you can explain what the hell this is for?"

Not bothering to open the folder, Bryce leaned back in his chair and shrugged. "Exactly what it looks like." His gaze drifted over her casual slacks and loose blouse, noting, with irritation, that the collar he'd given her this morning wasn't around her neck.

"It looks like you were investigating my sexual history," Mattie snapped, her brown eyes flashing as she crossed her arms over her breasts.

"I was."

"Why? Wanted a kinky little thrill or two? Or were you looking for the list of lovers so you could make sure I didn't break rule number one?"

"You were a virgin, Mattie."

"And did that make you feel like a big, strong man?"

"You know I don't fuck virgins, Lawrence." His laughter was derisive and cold. "They tend to put too much emotion into a situation that has nothing to do with emotion and everything to do with sensation."

"You sure as hell married one—"

The memory of their wedding night brought a grin to his lips. "Yes, I did."

"Then why me? If you knew…" Mattie snapped.

"Business." He shrugged, the lie rolling easily off his lips. Better to have her pissed at something small than know the truth. "A means to an end, Lawrence. Plus, I was tired of waiting."

"Waiting for what?"

"You to grow up. Get past the things that happened in your childhood and start acting like a grown woman."

"You mean stop panting after you like a bitch in heat." She glared at him, her heart in shreds. "Don't you?"

"If you want to put it like that." Bryce fought the need to reassure her that those motivations hadn't been it at all, but his pride refused to let him back down. She'd refused his collar when he offered it. "You're a born submissive, Lawrence, and a smart businesswoman."

"Don't try to placate me, Halsey." Mattie pushed back the tears building behind her eyes. That little voice inside her head had been right. He didn't love her, and no matter how long she waited or how hard she tried, his collar would never grace her throat, and he'd never say the three words she needed most to hear.

"We've worked too long together for you to pussyfoot around the subject," she told him. "You're tired of my attention and my refusing to see the forest for the trees."

"Lawrence..." he started, but her words ran over his.

Ignoring his attempts to speak, Mattie moved toward the door. "I understand now, Bryce."

"Where are you going?" Bryce demanded.

"My office for right now." She laughed, no humor in the sound, just as there was little amusement in her. "After that, we'll have to see."

"Don't do anything rash, Lawrence."

"Fuck you, Halsey." She gave in to the need to vent. Turning what she hoped was a cool, emotionless face toward him, she added, "You don't own me anymore, so don't bother giving me orders."

The door slid shut without a sound, despite her need to rattle the walls.

Chapter Nineteen

After a week of silence between them, finding the blue velvet case on her desk was the last thing she expected. She'd moved her things into the bedroom usually reserved for the mistress of the house. And despite the cool looks at the office, Bryce had remained friendly when they worked with the horses or prepared dinner at the Folly.

The papers she'd just printed could change all that. Giving in to temptation, she reached for the case. Opening the box took more effort than she thought it would. Actually seeing the delicate links of the platinum collar had her hands trembling. Not daring to touch it, Mattie stared at the final sign of Bryce's ownership and realized the offering had come too late. Much as she loved him, she'd realized in the last few days that she needed more than he was willing to offer.

She couldn't get past feeling numb. As if she were encased in ice, nothing seemed to penetrate the shell around her. She came to work, went home, talked to her sister, and carried on conversations with Bryce, but it was all a fog. Hell, she wasn't even angry about the file she'd found and the realization that her childhood wasn't as secret as she'd thought it was. Closing the case, she wondered if Lyssa wouldn't mind company for dinner. She needed to do something, anything, so she could start rebuilding her life. Without Bryce.

Absently, her hand drifted down to cover the curve of her belly. By now he had to have received the report from her doctor. Bryce was nothing if not thorough. He'd know she'd gone to the obstetrician her regular doctor had recommended, and following the blood test, an ultrasound had revealed she was not only pregnant, but carrying triplets. It was very likely Bryce would protest her transfer, especially with the babies, but she'd deal with that later.

Drawing a deep breath, she rose, collected the papers and the necklace, and stepped into her husband's office. He glanced up, a warm smile lifting his lips as she shut the door behind her. When he would have moved to stand up, she motioned him to stay seated, crossed the room, and placed the letters and case on the papers in front of him.

His eyes shot to her throat, then back to the case. "I thought we went over this—"

Mattie put her hand over the case. "We did. You weren't listening."

The crease in his brow evidenced his frustration. "No?"

"I don't want it," she clarified again. Ignoring the expression in his eyes, Mattie tapped one of the documents. "I wanted to get your approval on the necessary job description for my replacement."

"Replacement?"

"I would offer it to Dana, but the amount of travel involved would keep her away from home." She ignored his question.

"Wait." His firm tone stopped her practiced speech. "Why would you need replacing? The babies aren't due—"

"For six months," she finished. "I know, but it's going to take at least two months to get me moved, and I want to make sure whoever takes over for me—"

"Moved?"

"I want the marketing manager position at the Sydney office."

"No." This time, Bryce shot to his feet, fisted hands planted on the desk as he leaned toward her.

From the glint in his eye and the tension in his body, Mattie didn't doubt for one second he wouldn't hesitate to leap over the desk if she made a move to leave. She didn't. Standing her ground, as she had in the many discussions they'd had before and after they'd married, she raised her chin and fought back. "Yes. I'm more than qualified for the position, and I think I've earned it."

"You're my wife..."

"I'm your cover story."

"You're carrying my babies."

"No." She shook her head. This was definitely where their opinions were going to collide. "I'm carrying *my* babies. You just happen to be the biological contributor."

"What the hell do you mean by that?" This time he didn't stop himself from striding around the desk and closing in on her.

Mattie swallowed hard, forcing herself to remain where she stood. The urge to drop her gaze and beg his forgiveness pounded through her. Damn it, she loved him that much. It was killing her to know she had to leave, and the bastard was too blind to see it. It was that blindness, that wall of indifference, that made her realize she couldn't remain. She didn't know what it was, but something kept him from loving her, and no matter what she did, it would always be that way.

The warmth of his palm settled over their...*her* babies. "These are my babies." His other hand lifted her left hand to stroke his fingers over the platinum wedding band and engagement ring. "And you're my wife. You're not going anywhere."

"Tell me you love me." She held his gaze. "Say it, Bryce, and I'll stay."

"You love me." He avoided her demand by stating the obvious.

"Yes. I've loved you for years," she admitted. The heat of tears pressed against her eyelids. She couldn't blame the hormones zipping through her body. Even if she weren't pregnant, facing this uphill battle would have made her break down. "But you don't love me."

He didn't protest. There was no denial or argument in his clear green gaze.

"And if you can't love me, despite everything we've shared, how can I ever expect you to love our children?" Pulling free of his hold, she wiped at the tears wetting her cheeks. "Once you've approved the job description"—she forced her voice not to shake—"I'll have Brenda in HR post it internally. There are a few candidates I've checked out that I think can handle the position."

"No." He crossed his arms over his chest, the expression on his face resolute. "You can get this crazy scheme out of your head, Lawrence, because there's no damned way I'm letting you leave. No damned way you're traveling halfway around the world with my children."

"You don't own me, Bryce." Her finger shook as she pointed at the case on his desk. "Just because you've finally decided I'm worthy enough to wear your collar doesn't mean I'm interested anymore."

"You love me," he gritted out between clenched teeth.

"But I don't want to," she lied. "I'm done, Bryce. Finished. Tired. I may go to my grave loving you, but my babies and I deserve better than what you have to offer." Ignoring the need to go to him and soothe the stunned look from his face, Mattie turned, walked to the door, and paused. Eyes focused on the polished mahogany and knuckles growing white as she gripped the knob, she added, "I can have my things out of your home by the end of the week."

***

"Where the hell is your head, Halsey?" Richard demanded as he dropped into the chair facing Bryce's desk.

"What do you mean?" Bryce focused on his friend's disgruntled expression and forced his thoughts away from the path they'd been wandering since Mattie's departure an hour earlier.

"What do I mean?" Richard shook his head and leaned forward. "I've had Mark Conlin bitching at me about not being able to get Mattie on the phone. Your dad griping at me about how you're throwing away the board's support.

Dayton and David and Ben wondering why you and your wife haven't been back to the Club."

"We're working some things out," Bryce hedged. The blue velvet box mocked him from the center of his desk.

Richard noticed it. He shook his head and rubbed at his closed eyes. "You did something stupid, didn't you?"

"I have no idea what—"

"Damn it, Bryce, I just had Ian King on the phone demanding to know why your wife is contacting him about the marketing department in Sydney." His gray eyes reflected the frustration in his voice. "What reason would Mattie have to start looking at moving halfway around the world if you didn't go and pull some boneheaded stunt? Not that Ian wouldn't love to have Mattie working with him. He repeatedly assured me of that. But it would be like throwing a guppy in with a great white."

"What is it with you and Mike and the fucking shark analogies?" Bryce snapped. Shoving back his chair, he paced to the windows overlooking the warehouses. Farther toward the ocean, the hulls and skeletons of various ships in different stages of construction dotted the landscape, while others rocked on thick anchor chains in the bay.

"Probably because you've been circling around her like a shark around its prey for the last eight years," Richard offered. "If anyone even hinted at getting close, you'd run 'em off. And now that you finally have her, you're letting her go?"

"I'm not doing anything. She is. She's walking away, just like every damned woman walks away," Bryce growled. He forced himself to ignore the pain centered in his chest. It had nothing to do with Mattie leaving him.

"No, my friend, she isn't walking away. You're pushing her away."

Standing beside him at the window, Richard watched him. Bryce could feel his gaze on him, but he refused to turn. "I did everything I could think of to keep her, Rich. I married her. I showed her the pleasure in submission." He shook his head and chuckled mirthlessly. "I even poked fucking holes in the condoms and her diaphragm to make sure she got pregnant." Meeting Richard's gaze, he asked, "How is that pushing her away?"

"Did you tell her you love her?"

"I don't." The pain in his chest made a liar of him.

"She isn't your mom or Miss Helen, Bryce." Richard's hand gripped his shoulder tight. "They didn't choose to leave. They died. Mattie is still here. Don't fuck it up, my friend, or another Dom will be more than happy to take care of her."

* * *

It was all so familiar. The grave, his father in a dark suit, the dull thud of moist earth striking the coffin, but something was wrong. Gray threaded his father's hair as he stood beside him, while Michael was grown, no longer a little boy, and taking up a position at his right shoulder. The soft weight of a child filled his arms.

In his sleep, he twisted in the covers. *No, it wasn't right,* Bryce thought as the dream continued. *The mop of chocolate* curls and bewildered green eyes looking up at him didn't belong to his younger brother, but a little girl. His little girl.

And Mattie was gone.

His heart beat faster as he stared down into the grave, recognizing the white magnolias disappearing beneath the soil filling the pit. Lawrence loved magnolias, especially traditional white ones. But this wasn't right... Across from him, he spotted Lyssa and Richard both focused on him with sad eyes filled with sympathy.

Again he shook his head. No. It was Helen, not Lawrence.

"She's so pretty."

He heaved a sigh of relief. Her voice sounded beside him. It was all right. He knew she wouldn't have gone and left their little girl behind. "Damn it, Lawrence," he whispered, turning to glare at his wife.

His heart slammed against his ribs. She was there, but not there. Her image shimmered in the sunshine, hazy, indistinct. Her dark brown eyes were sad as she smiled at him before her pale hands eased his little girl from his arms.

"No." He tried to hold tight, but she slipped away. "Lawrence?"

"She's so pretty." Mattie smiled again, her gaze focused on the tiny replica of herself before tear-filled eyes met his. "It'll be all right, Bryce."

"No." He shook his head. "You're supposed to stay here. Damn it, Mattie, you can't do this."

"You'll be fine, Bryce. You have what you want." She nodded to his father and brother. "You have your family and the company."

"We had a deal, Mattie."

"She wasn't part of our deal, Bryce." Her fingers smoothed over the springy curls as the baby snuggled against her. "Love wasn't part of the deal."

"Stay." Her image shimmered, out of focus.

Shaking her head, Mattie stepped away. "Babies need love, Bryce. You don't want that. You never wanted it." Nodding, she smiled. "It's okay. She'll be with me."

"No, you need to stay here." His voice cracked. "Both of you need to stay here."

"Why?" She stepped closer, her breath whispering across his lips, her fingers reaching up to wipe the rain from his cheeks.

Rain? He glanced up; there were no clouds.

Her demand came again, quiet, curious, pulling his attention from the blue sky. "Why?"

"You love me." Leaning down, he brushed his lips over hers, stroked the pale pink cheek of his little girl. "You both love me," he repeated.

A single raindrop splashed onto Mattie's cheek as the hope faded from her eyes. Licking it away, the salty taste made him realize it wasn't rain, but a tear. And not from her. From him. Even as his fingertips found the evidence on his face, Mattie was fading, his little girl as well.

"We'll always love you, Bryce, but that's no reason for us to stay."

His eyes drifted to the headstone, not wanting to believe. The pain arrowing through his soul sent him to his knees. Her voice whispered through his mind as he finally took in the names carved into the gray marble.

"*We'll always love you, Bryce.*"

Beside him his father and brother watched him, their heads shaking in bewilderment. "*You have your company, Bryce. What else do you need?*"

"Mattie!" The words burst from his lips as he sat up in bed. His chest heaved, his heart pounded, the darkness swallowed his cry, but the dampness of his cheeks and the trembling of his hands as he buried his face in them terrified him. Beside him, the bed was empty, as it had been for the last week.

Throwing back the covers, Bryce stumbled to the connecting door and pushed it open. The wash of moonlight through the open curtains outlined the body beneath the mound of covers. The cold sweat coating his skin made him shiver, but the pounding of his heart began to settle. The knot twisting in his gut smoothed out, but not enough to send him back to his bed. Just seeing her there wasn't enough.

Crossing the floor in four long strides, Bryce eased beneath the blankets. She murmured a protest as the chill of his flesh came into contact with the warmth of hers. Curled on her side, she had one hand tucked beneath her pillow and the other cradling the curve of her stomach. The warmth of her body against his surprised him. In the week she'd refused his bed, he was sure she would have reverted to her habit of wearing an oversize T-shirt or pajamas to sleep. Tucking himself up against her back, he was careful to slide his left arm beneath her head while his right smoothed over her hip. Coasting along the soft flesh until he reached her hand, he took a moment to investigate the changes his babies had created.

The soft curve of her belly was firm beneath his fingers. He wondered how soon before the little ones inside started making their presences known with tiny kicks and jabs. Not for a moment did Bryce doubt that one, if not all, of the babies was a girl. "My Lawrence would never do anything as mundane as giving me a boy the first time out," he whispered into the darkness.

The scent of sleep, moist skin, and a hint of magnolia clung to Mattie. Even as he shifted against her, tucking himself in closer, she adjusted to his movements, allowing one of his long legs to settle between hers while the firm jut of his arousal pressed against her backside. A week of denial had him aching more than he'd expected. Even in his first days at university, when the women were just beginning to get to know him, Bryce had never felt this desperate for the touch of a single, specific woman.

The smooth feel of her skin against his palm stirred the need for more. Easing up from her rounded belly to the heavy fullness of her breasts, Bryce investigated the differences to be found. Her heightened sensitivity was evidenced in the speed with which her nipples firmed beneath the caress of his fingertips. Even asleep, Mattie responded to his touch. The cheeks of her ass wriggled against his cock even as the first telltale dampness pooled against the thigh pressed against the heart of her body.

Shifting again, Bryce moved her leg so it rested along his while he pressed his erection into the moist tunnel he'd been missing. With the first firm stroke, Mattie's eyes fluttered open, her body arched beneath him, deepening his penetration, before she appeared to become aware of his actions. Two more thrusts and tears filled her eyes.

"Don't do this to me, Bryce, please," she begged, even as her body gripped his, her arm curling beneath his to gain purchase on his shoulder and steady the rhythm of his body as it rocked forward and back within hers.

"Don't leave, Lawrence." Even as he spoke, he knew the words weren't going to work.

"Tell me you love me."

Her body flexed beneath him, the tensing of her thighs and the hardened peaks of her breasts signaling her building climax. "You don't want to leave me."

"Tell me you love me," she repeated, the tears falling freely now, even as her body moved in time with his.

"Our little girls need me. You need me," he countered, again avoiding answering. The tingle of his approaching orgasm matched beat for beat with the one he could sense building within Mattie. "Tell me you won't leave," he demanded.

"Tell me you love me," she responded.

"You love me."

"Tell me, please," she begged as she tensed beneath him, balanced on the edge of coming.

He challenged her. "Would you believe me if I said I do?"

It was there, just an instant, then hidden away, but still he saw the mistrust she'd been so careful to hide. "Yes."

He shook his head. "No, baby, you wouldn't." His lips smoothed away the tears on her cheeks. "I can say the words, but you still don't trust them."

And just as quickly as his climax teetered on the brink of exploding, he felt it dissipate with the light fading from Mattie's eyes. Her own arousal disappeared, and the quiet tone of her voice sent chills through his body.

"That isn't enough." Pulling away, she smoothed her hand over his cheek one last time. "I'll always love you, Bryce. Now let me go." Turning away, she settled close to the edge, leaving a wide space between them.

Something kept him from closing that gap. He could tell her what she wanted to hear, but then what? Controlling his needs, harnessing his emotions, kept him from making the same mistake his father had made all those years ago. But it was still gaining him the same pain. Even as the sobs grew silent and she eased back to sleep, Bryce realized acknowledging his love for his wife wouldn't be enough. In the same way that she had repeatedly rejected his offer of a collar this last week, his voicing his feelings would come too little too late.

Scooting across the expanse dividing them, Bryce tucked Mattie back into his arms and held fast. He may have fucked up tonight, but he had a plan. In the morning he'd discuss it with his father and Richard. They'd know what was necessary to convince her how sincere he was in his offer of a collar, and there was no damned way he was letting his woman run from him. "It's okay, baby." He smoothed her hair from her tear-stained cheeks. "I got the message. You need more than the words for proof." He pressed a kiss to her temple. "I'll give you the proof, Mattie. I swear."

Chapter Twenty

"Richard, what are you...?" Mattie watched Richard set a box on the bed.

"You need to get dressed, sweetheart." Richard gripped her hand and pulled her from the chair she'd curled up in by the balcony doors.

"For what, Richard? My plane doesn't leave until tomorrow."

"You're not getting on the plane, Mattie."

Pulling free, she shook her head. "Richard, it isn't going to work."

Leaning forward, Richard cupped her cheeks, his eyes holding hers. "Give me a chance, Mattie. Get dressed, come with me, and then decide."

"Come where, Richard? Do what?" Dropping onto the bed, she pulled the box into her lap but didn't open it. "I've made my decision. Bryce knows my reasons."

"There's more to our lifestyle than bondage, discipline, and sex."

"I'm aware—"

"No, Mattie, I don't think you are," Richard cut her off. "Bryce doesn't live the lifestyle twenty-four-seven, but it's not just a choice for him."

"I know about how his great-great-grandfather founded the Diablo Blanco Club when he first settled here. How he and his wife—" She tried to stop him, but again he silenced her before she could say more.

"Quiet."

The tone alone would have had Mattie demanding he leave, but when coupled with his expression and the way he held himself, she recognized it as the same one Bryce assumed when mastering her. Fighting the instinct to lower her head and drop her gaze from his, Mattie waited.

"Bryce isn't playing at being a Dominant, Mattie. He is one. His father, grandfather, great-grandfather, and great-great-grandfather raised their sons and daughters in the lifestyle. Some were Doms and Dommes, others were submissives, but every one of the Halseys passes his or her knowledge on to the next generation. The Diablo Blanco Club wasn't just some sex club a retired pirate and his wife dreamed up because they were bored."

"But, he said he didn't expect—" He was confusing her. If Bryce was a Dominant in the way Richard was describing, why would he only require her submission as it related to sex and not in all aspects?

"And he meant it," Richard assured her. "Bryce doesn't need to dominate in order to reaffirm what he is."

"It still doesn't resolve the problems between us, Richard. Can't you see that?" She pushed the box aside and paced back over to the French doors leading onto the balcony. "It doesn't change the fact that he won't let himself care."

"Who says he doesn't, Mattie? You?" Richard again turned her to face him. "You may have been beside him in the office for the last eight years, but you weren't there when he lost Miss Helen. You weren't there when he had to fight tooth and nail to get his father to accept that the future of the company was on the West, not the East Coast."

"And the only emotions he shows are related to the business." Mattie moved to settle on the bed again, her hand smoothing over the curve of her belly as if the babies inside needed soothing as much as she did. "Other than sex, Bryce has..."

"Loved you better than any man ever could."

Her head came up at the gritty tone of his voice. "Because he shared me with you?"

"And he will again when you're ready for it," Richard admitted. "Last time may have been a mistake, Mattie, but there were some moments when you were just as aroused, just as caught up in the experience as Bryce and I. Do you deny it?"

"I'm not denying—"

"Come with me."

Richard gripped her wrist and drew her off the bed and out of the room before Mattie could voice another protest.

Down the stairs she trailed behind him, finding it easy to keep up with his shortened strides. The study door swung open, and he tugged her into the room.

"I'm sure Bryce told you about his namesake and his wife."

Mattie nodded. Motioning to the two paintings facing one another from across the room, she assured Richard, "Yes, he told me about Collas Halsey's Margaretta."

"Did he explain about the jars?" Richard motioned to the various containers settled on the shelves around the room.

"No. I just assumed they were antiques." Glancing around, Mattie counted ten containers. Each one was filled with dried flower petals.

Opening one of the glass-fronted bookshelves, Richard drew out a crystal container, its contents barely recognizable. "These are the petals from Collas and Margaretta's ceremony."

"Their wedding?"

"No." Richard handed the jar to her. "Her Collaring Ceremony."

"Collaring..." Mattie marveled at the weight of the decanter until she realized that the delicate etchings on the sides weren't designs but actual words. Raising the glass closer, she read them aloud. "'I give unto you this body, this heart, and this soul, knowing that I can trust you never to bring them harm. To think only of what is truly the best for me, and that your every command is given as a means of encouraging my awareness of the strength within me. I submit willingly to your mastery, endeavoring only to please you.'" Even as she finished, a shiver tingled through her, and she lifted her gaze to the portrait of Margaretta Halsey. The fire in the woman's expression was there, but there was also devotion and love. A similar expression Mattie had often fought to keep from appearing on her own countenance for fear that it would be used against her.

Even as Richard lifted the container from her grip and returned it to its spot on the shelf and secured the cabinet door, he nodded toward the two paintings. Mattie's gaze moved to the one of Collas Halsey, again marveling at just how uncannily the man's likeness mirrored her own husband's wicked good looks. Only the neatly trimmed beard and mustache as well as the period clothing identified the man as being a relative rather than Bryce himself. Looking more closely, though, she realized the eyes were a darker shade of green, much like the color Bryce's took on while he made love to her, or when he coaxed her body to climax with his words. The amusement that softened the wry smile lifting his lips and the twinkle in the man's eyes assured any viewer that the man wasn't as hard as he attempted to appear.

"You'll notice that every one of the jars is only half-filled."

Mattie nodded. "I assumed the contents had settled."

Richard shook his head. "No. As part of the family tradition, when a Halsey finds his true Dominant or submissive, and they exchange their vows in a Collaring Ceremony, the roses used in another ritual performed during the ceremony are dried and the petals placed in the jars. Then, when they pass on, no matter how many years fall between the death of one and then the other, one fourth of the petals are sprinkled on the sub's grave and another fourth are sprinkled on the Dom's or Domme's grave."

"This is all very enlightening, Richard, but how does it relate to Bryce and I? He's never offered me a collar," Mattie started, then realized her statement wasn't quite truthful. "At least he never offered one without having been coerced or guilted into it."

"That's because he already considered you committed to the relationship, Mattie." Lifting her left hand, he gently tapped her engagement ring and the wide platinum wedding band as well. "Do you think he'd expect you to wear a collar when you've only just begun exploring our lifestyle? This ring carries just as much symbolism as a collar among the members of the Diablo Blanco Club, Mattie." Turning his gaze from her to the painting of Margaretta Halsey, he pointed toward the hand holding the cat-o'-nine on her lap. "Only the true submissive of the eldest Halsey male is given the Dragon Rose ring. Every member of the Club knows this."

"Oh." The tiny sound made Mattie feel small, but she didn't know what else to say, how else to express her dismay. All the weeks she'd felt as if Bryce was denying her devotion to him and the lifestyle their marriage had made available to her, the mark of his ownership was settled on her hand. "I feel like an idiot," Mattie muttered, pulling her hand from Richard's and fingering the rings she wore. Even her sister had figured it out before her.

"Do you love him, Mattie?" Richard asked, his gaze serious as he stood looking down at her, hands on his hips, the black silk shirt and black leather pants making him look even more threatening.

"Yes. More than I ever have."

"Then let's get your ass moving, or we're going to be late."

"You still haven't told me where or why, Rich."

"The Club. Bryce is waiting."

* * *

Bryce fought the need to look at his watch again. It wouldn't make his wife appear any faster, and Richard had already called to say they were on the way. All the preparations had been made and the central lounge of the Club held only those members he'd invited. Although similar in many ways to the formal wedding his father had helped plan just a few months earlier, this ceremony carried more weight and was of greater importance to the lifestyle his family had embraced for over seven centuries.

Drawing a deep breath, Bryce moved away from the window and settled into the desk chair.

"She'll be here, Bryce," Michael assured him. The comment was tossed over his shoulder as his younger brother focused his attention on the monitors displaying the entrance and lounge area of the Club.

The kit containing his camera equipment rested on one of the seat cushions of the battered sofa shoved up against the wall opposite the monitors. He'd checked both the film and digital cameras when he'd first arrived and hadn't touched it since.

"I wish I had your confidence, Mike," Jacob announced as he entered the room. Despite the gray threading through his hair and the lines radiating from the corners of his eyes and bracketing his mouth, Jacob could have easily been mistaken for a man twenty years his junior.

Bryce smiled at his father's nervousness. It was nice to know he wasn't the only one worried about his wife's attendance.

"Hey, her sister showed up ten minutes ago, so Mattie must not be far behind," Mike assured them.

Ah. Bryce fought the grin as he realized why Mike's attention had been glued to the screens. *Maybe I should warn Mattie her sister is on the endangered species list,* he thought, then dismissed voicing his warning. *Let her find out on her own.* He watched Mike's body tense as Ben approached Lyssa and began chatting with her. *In fact, maybe I should make sure he has plenty of opportunity to run into Lyssa...*

The discreet buzz of an intercom interrupted the silence just as Bryce noticed the front doors of the Club opened, and Richard entered with a cloaked figure. Rising from his desk, Bryce exited the office behind his father while Mike gathered his cameras and followed.

In the hall, they separated. Bryce moved to the stairway leading to the rooms on the second floor, while his father and brother turned to the door that opened to the left of one of the staircases. Based on the plans he'd made with his family and Richard, Bryce knew his father would enter the lounge and stand before the bar, the polished teak covered with a length of crimson silk, the intertwined blue, green, and red of the letters *D*, *B*, and *C* edging the ends of the cloth.

From upstairs, the single peal of a bell had Bryce moving. Descending the steps, he noted the presence of his friends and fellow Doms and Dommes, each clothed in black, some in formal wear, while others dressed as he, Richard, his father, and Michael had chosen, in black leather and silk. Lined up along a length of golden cloth stretched across the floor from the doors to just in front of Jacob, they waited. Submissives were behind their masters or mistresses, some kneeling, others standing, legs shoulder-width apart, hands clasped behind their backs, and heads bowed.

On the landing above the bar, Bryce watched as Michael entered from another side door; in his hands was the black leather case carrying the gift for his wife. As his brother moved past Lyssa, Bryce was surprised at the way she paled and turned her gaze away from Michael. Even Ben, who stood beside her, was taken aback at her attempt to slip away, but stilled Lyssa by settling an arm around her waist and whispering something in her ear. Once his brother took his place to their father's left, the case held in his hands, Bryce moved to the stairway closest to the entrance.

He paused at the foot of the stairs, his gaze on the doors leading to the foyer. As he waited, they swung open, revealing Richard standing beside Mattie, the crimson cloak shrouding her from head to toe held closed with a single frog at her throat. From just beneath the hem of her covering, her bare toes peaked out. Taking four steps forward so he stood on the golden fabric just as Richard led Mattie to him. He waited.

When Richard moved aside, Bryce watched her lift her gaze to his and smile. The hood shadowed her features, but in her eyes wicked humor glinted up at him. He didn't doubt she'd done something to draw a punishment—his Lawrence loved her spankings—but Bryce fought the urge to grin. Instead he stepped closer and lifted the hood, careful not to tangle his fingers in the coiled curls secured on top of her head. As his fingers eased around to the front of her covering to slip the fastening at her throat free, Mattie's lips twitched in a grin, but she made no move to stay his hand.

Once the cape was released, Richard lifted it from Mattie's shoulders and handed it to an attendant before stepping away, his amusement evident in the grin he gave Bryce before moving to join Jacob and Michael at the center of the room. Bryce couldn't stifle his grin as the guests got their first clear view of Mattie. The muttered compliments, sighs, and groans from the men and women watching merely increased his admiration and pride in his wife.

Not many women would put themselves on display as she was, in order to please their husbands. Cupping her face, he leaned down to press a kiss to her lips. In a voice only she could hear, he whispered, "That's one, Lawrence."

When he turned to lead her toward Jacob, the quiet sighs and stifled groans only made him more amused. Clothed in the waist and nipple chains he'd sent her, the triple strands of platinum chains emphasized the sexy shape of her body, her rounded hips, and full breasts. The white length of silk he'd sent along with the body jewelry swathed her lower body, tucked beneath the chains on each hip and leaving her naked from the waist up. Beneath the delicate fabric, her bare pussy was shadowed, but visible to everyone.

Threading the fingers of his left hand through her right, Bryce walked her to stand before Jacob, making sure she never fell behind him, but remained at his side.

Jacob's eyes twinkled with amusement, but he didn't allow the humor to show on his face as the room fell silent, and he began to speak. "Brothers and sisters, it has been nearly a century since one of us has conducted a ceremony as sacred as this. In all that relates to our lifestyle, the giving of a collar can signify more than a coming together of needs.

"In the case of this pair, it is the sealing of a bond already made legitimate in the eyes of the law.

"The giving of a collar symbolizes the strength of commitment a master has for his submissive. It is not a responsibility taken lightly, nor without careful and deep consideration. In the same manner, the accepting of a collar reveals the trust a submissive places in her master. It reflects the power she cedes over to him to guide her in her journey to enlightenment and opens the door to exploring the self in a more profound way than ever before.

"As you have determined to join your lives in a method recognized by the leaders of this country and within this state, do you now both confirm that you stand before this assemblage to enact a ritual that will identify you to your family as forever bound to one another?"

This was the moment of truth, Bryce decided as he held his wife's gaze and replied in a firm, clear tone. "Yes."

Though she nodded, Mattie had to clear her throat twice, tears streaking her cheeks and clogging her voice, making it hard to hear her. "Yes."

"Take your places before your family." Jacob directed, motioning to the people in attendance.

Turning so he faced Mattie and they stood in profile to both Jacob and the guests, Bryce was disturbed when Mattie pulled her hand from his. Though his expression never betrayed him, surprise slid into stunned disbelief as he watched her adjust the folds of silk and gracefully lower herself to kneel before him. In the time they'd been together, he'd never asked her to assume the position of a slave. The only times she'd ever knelt were when she'd pleasured him with her mouth. His heart hammered against his ribs and pride swelled his chest. He felt as if he stood taller than before, strong in the knowledge of what his woman was offering with this simple act of faith.

"You have selected your Formal Collar?" Jacob prompted.

Bryce nodded. "I have." Looking to Mike, he watched as his brother moved forward.

Mattie knew she'd surprised Bryce with her gesture. He may not have shown his dismay outwardly, but his eyes had given him away. Kneeling before him had seemed the right thing to do. Only her inner voice had prompted her to do such a thing, and she was glad she'd listened. Her thoughts scattered as the aged leather box in Mike's hands was opened.

Tears filled Mattie's eyes as she gazed at the necklace Bryce had selected. She'd wondered about it for a while after seeing it adorning the neck of his great-great-grandmother in the portrait on the study wall.

The fine detailing in the piece was breathtaking. In the same style as her engagement ring, the platinum collar was designed similar to a choker with the rose-and-dragon's-claw-style of her ring repeated in the front-facing clasp. The half-inch-wide chain was made of such finely woven links, it resembled the scales of a dragon. Even the black fire opal clutched in the center of the claw was a near-perfect match for the stone in her ring.

"In honor of her strength and fortitude, I offer this collar as a symbol of my commitment to this partnership."

The very stillness of the observers and the manner in which Bryce removed the collar from its velvet bed confused Mattie. Until he passed it to Jacob and her father-in-law began to speak.

"Since the fourteenth century, the Dragon Rose has only been offered to two other women. Crafted by a knight and gifted to his chosen submissive, the very metal it was wrought from symbolizes true love and eternal loyalty.

"The stone has survived when others similar to it crumbled to dust, identifying the longevity and fortunate nature of giver and recipient in its very presence after nearly seven hundred years.

"Last, and most important, the design itself denotes the synergistic nature of master and submissive. For within the delicate body of a sub is the strength and fire of an elemental creature. It is the duty of the master to harness this strength, to focus the energies of the submissive into passion and then test the boundaries again.

"Understanding the duties entrusted to you and the responsibility you are acquiring, do you offer this collar to your submissive?"

"Yes." Bryce showed no hesitation in his response even as Mattie's mind went numb, realizing that in all the weeks they'd been together, Bryce had never hesitated or wavered in his treatment when mastering her.

Her mind still spinning with the knowledge that her doubts were the reason for this ceremony, not his, Mattie turned to face Jacob as he held the collar out for her to see clearly.

In the same solemn tone, he asked, "Understanding the duties and responsibilities you acquire upon taking his collar, do you accept?"

Mattie nodded. "Yes, Sir."

Passing the collar to Bryce, Jacob directed. "Speak your vows as you set this upon your submissive's neck, but do not fasten it until she has spoken her vows to you."

Signaling his understanding, Bryce accepted the collar, pressed the two petals directly over the links to release the catch, and eased one end of the chain free.

The cool metal caressed her throat as he put it in place. Lifting her gaze to his, Mattie listened to every word, committing them to memory while trying to stem the tears filling her eyes and slipping down her cheeks.

"With your acceptance of my collar, I vow to be worthy of your trust. I will hold you safe and most prized of all my possessions.

"You will never have cause to doubt the respect, honor, and love I hold for you. Your submission is a gift that I will never give you cause to regret. In all aspects of your training, I swear to keep your needs in mind while striving to test your limits.

"Our children"—Bryce paused to use the fingers of one hand to smooth away her tears—"our children will be cherished as symbols of our love and evidence of our unity, as well as for themselves. They are the best of both of us and should know their full potential as individuals as well as being our sons and daughters.

"All this I pledge to you for the rest of our lives and beyond."

Eyes swimming, Mattie could barely make out Bryce's features as she stared up at him. She could hear the sincerity in his voice but needed to see his face as well. Reaching up, she tried scrubbing the tears away, but they fell too quickly. The creak of leather and the warm clasp of Bryce's arms registered before she realized he'd squatted down and pulled her close.

"It's okay, love; take your time," he soothed, his fingers wiping away her tears and his lips warm against her brow. The slide of his hands along her back and shoulders had the sobs easing and her breathing slowing to a more manageable level.

Mattie hadn't even realized she clutched his shirt until she tried easing away from him. Meeting his gaze, she sniffed and offered a shaky smile. He cupped her cheeks and took her mouth with a slow, breath-stealing kiss, his tongue sliding inside to caress and seduce before slipping away. Holding her gaze, he rose to stand over her again.

Her already-clamped nipples throbbed in time with the heat filling her belly. The damned man loved turning her on—almost as much as she did. Steadying herself, she rose up on her knees, her spine straight, eyes on his, and began to speak. The words had circled her mind from the first time she'd read about bondage and submission. Once she'd recognized the attraction she felt for Bryce also involved the fantasy of submitting to his control, the ways to tell him had hovered in the back of her mind. After reading the vows etched into the jar holding Margaretta and Cole Halsey's rose petals, it made sense to repeat them as well. At first the words were shaky, but as she continued, her voice grew stronger.

"I accept your collar as a symbol of our union. I entrust to you my body, heart, and soul, knowing that what you expect of me is not beyond my means to give.

"I promise you that no safe word need ever be between us, for your every action is made with my utmost care and protection in mind. Never will I deny your request. Your pleasure is my pleasure; your need is my need; your want is my want.

"As you are gifting me with your collar, you have already given to me, in trust and love, your children to bear, nurture, and love." Even as she spoke, her hands smoothed over the soft curve of her belly, including them in this pivotal event, just as Bryce's words had earlier. "With your guidance, I will learn the strengths within me, as well as the passion, so that should challenges arise, I can draw on your teachings and know I will prevail.

"Just as your collar signifies eternal love and loyalty, so does my acceptance of it solidify my commitment to you and our union. My *complete* trust in you. Only your commands will I follow, and only you can remove the collar that binds me to you."

Reaching up, Mattie placed her hands over Bryce's. Holding his gaze, she worked with him to slide the clasp together until first one and then the second petal on the rose snapped back into place.

The sound of sobs whispered through the room, but the double click of the collar fastening around her throat stilled her tears. Heat filled Mattie's belly and spread outward, causing her eyes to widen in amazement. Only with Bryce's touch had she ever felt such arousal, but even as she worked to comprehend the feelings, her husband was directing her hands away from her throat so they rested at her sides. The caress of warm metal along her skin had her glancing down to see him lift the chain dangling from the clamp on her right nipple. Although she couldn't see what he did, Mattie was sure the tiny hook at the end of the chain was being slipped through a loop on one of the rose petals. A tug on the clamp along with a simultaneous pull on the collar only reinforced her suspicions.

"Loyalty," Bryce declared as the chain was put in place. His lips pressed against hers before he moved back to gather the other chain dangling from the clamp on her left peak.

Again the tugs just as her husband spoke. "Honor." Another kiss.

Then he held her gaze as his hand smoothed down her body and settled on her abdomen, his fingers stroking her flesh as if touching the fragile infants within. Moving farther down, he gathered up the only length of bejeweled chain. Interspersed between the platinum links, a yellow topaz, an emerald, a ruby, a sapphire, a black fire opal, a milk opal, and a black diamond winked in the Club's subdued lighting. Lifting the last link, Bryce set it in place and announced, "Fealty. These three things I swear to you and claim you as my own, my love, for all eternity."

"For all eternity and beyond," Mattie whispered.

THE END

Qwillia Rain

Qwillia Rain grew up loving books. From an early age she was creating stories to go with the pictures. By high school she was penning romances for her friends and shocking them with the graphic nature of the love scenes. After leaving her home in Las Vegas, Nevada for Anchorage, Alaska, Qwillia discovered there were other authors who enjoyed throwing open the bedroom doors and exploring the darker side of human nature. She left Alaska for Billings, Montana, but the travel bug struck again. Currently, Qwillia resides in Raleigh, North Carolina, drawing inspiration from the history, scenery, and rich diversity of the South.